PENGUIN BOOKS

THE OTHER GIRL

Emily Barr worked as a journalist in London but always hankered after a quiet room and a book to write. She went travelling for a year, which gave her an idea for a novel set in the world of backpackers in Asia. This became *Backpack*, a thriller that won the WHSmith New Talent Award. Her first YA thriller, *The One Memory of Flora Banks*, has been published in twenty-seven countries and was shortlisted for the YA Book Prize. *The Other Girl* is Emily's eighth YA novel. She lives in Cornwall with her husband and their children.

Follow Emily Barr on Instagram @Emilybarrauthor.

Books by Emily Barr

THE ONE MEMORY OF FLORA BANKS
THE TRUTH AND LIES OF ELLA BLACK
THE GIRL WHO CAME OUT OF THE WOODS
THINGS TO DO BEFORE THE END
OF THE WORLD
GHOSTED
THIS SUMMER'S SECRETS
A GIRL CAN DREAM

THE OTHER GIRL

EMILY BARR

PENGUIN BOOKS

PENGUIN BOOKS

UK | USA | Canada | Ireland | Australia
India | New Zealand | South Africa

Penguin Books is part of the Penguin Random House group of companies
whose addresses can be found at global.penguinrandomhouse.com

www.penguin.co.uk
www.puffin.co.uk
www.ladybird.co.uk

First published 2025
004

Text copyright © Emily Barr, 2025
Cover illustration copyright © Sophie Donaj, 2025

The moral right of the author and illustrator has been asserted

Penguin Random House values and supports copyright.
Copyright fuels creativity, encourages diverse voices, promotes freedom
of expression and supports a vibrant culture. Thank you for purchasing
an authorized edition of this book and for respecting intellectual property
laws by not reproducing, scanning or distributing any part of it by any
means without permission. You are supporting authors and enabling
Penguin Random House to continue to publish books for everyone.
No part of this book may be used or reproduced in any manner for the
purpose of training artificial intelligence technologies or systems. In accordance
with Article 4(3) of the DSM Directive 2019/790, Penguin Random House
expressly reserves this work from the text and data mining exception.

Set in 10.5/15.5pt Sabon LT Std
Typeset by Jouve (UK), Milton Keynes
Printed and bound in Great Britain by Clays Ltd, Elcograf S.p.A.

The authorized representative in the EEA is Penguin Random House Ireland,
Morrison Chambers, 32 Nassau Street, Dublin D02 YH68

A CIP catalogue record for this book is available from the British Library

ISBN: 978-0-241-64344-0

All correspondence to:
Penguin Books
Penguin Random House Children's
One Embassy Gardens, 8 Viaduct Gardens, London SW11 7BW

Penguin Random House is committed to a
sustainable future for our business, our readers
and our planet. This book is made from Forest
Stewardship Council® certified paper.

For Lottie.

Have lots of adventures, but don't do this.

PART ONE
Tabbi

1

I'm sitting next to a stranger, using her as a shield. The train is speeding onwards, fast but smooth, and all I need to do is get to the next station, so I can get off and melt away. That's my one impossible job: stay right where I am until I can escape. I stare out of the window. The fields turn to buildings and then back to fields again, so fast it's almost a blur.

It's busy in this carriage. That's why I chose it. I'm in the one spare seat in the middle of a group of Japanese tourists, and they're all talking, and I understand a bit because I learned some Japanese at school, because that's what my school was like. Everyone in the group is older than me but still young. I want them to talk about me so I could surprise them by joining in, but they're just discussing a Netflix show. Before I can even work out what it is –

'There you are.'

I close my eyes and will myself away from here. Like a naughty toddler, I have been found.

'Come back.'

I screw my eyes tighter shut. If I can't see her, maybe she

won't see me. The world goes strange. My head is buzzing and I feel dizzy. I clutch my necklace.

Then the passenger next to me taps my shoulder, helpfully passing on the fact that someone is trying to get my attention, and I can't ignore her too. I'm busted. I sigh and open my eyes.

Jana, my chaperone, is looking at me with a pissed-off expression (though that is also her resting face, so who knows?).

'Don't be so *stupid*,' she says, so loudly that everyone up and down the train turns to look at me. I stand up and follow her. Back through the cafe carriage, down another one, past the smell of oranges, through the sound of excitable YouTubers, and up the stairs to our first-class seats.

I go back to my table. She sits in her seat, a little way down from me, across the aisle. I look at her. She gazes back and I can see how much she hates me. I put my arms on the table and my head on my arms and try not to cry.

It's happening. I can't do this. I tried to run away in Paris but it didn't work. I've tried to hide on this train but no joy. Maybe I can try again in Zurich, but let's face it: that won't work out for me either. They might as well have handcuffed me. I am on my way to Switzerland to face up to what I've done. I can't face it, but I'm out of options.

I lift my head up.

And there's a girl coming towards me.

She looks relaxed, happy, non-messed-up. Like the worst thing she's ever done is let someone copy her homework.

Swinging down the aisle of the train, checking out the empty seats in first class, deciding not to sit in them, a big backpack with lots of badges sewn on to it on her back. She looks as if she wants a space of her own, but here I am, at a table, and when I see her I plaster on my most charming smile, put my bottle down and motion for her to sit opposite me.

I know she speaks English. She just has that Anglo look about her: I can always tell. She's wearing a bad purple wig. Her nails are home-manicured with peeling lilac, her eyebrows are shaggy and wolfy, and she is properly scruffy in cut-off shorts and a baggy yellow T-shirt. Her eye make-up is great, even with those wild brows. In fact, I almost like the wild brows, on her.

I look down at myself. I'm in a silky black dress, close-fitting and mid-calf length. We're both wearing flip-flops, though mine are silver and sequinned and hers are those plastic green ones that hotel porters wear in Thailand. We are, I think, both signalling who we are through clothes, and that is very helpful right now. Her wig, in particular, is the best thing that could possibly exist; the biggest sign of them all. When you've got purple hair, no one is really going to see anything else.

Are they? Let's find out.

Even as the plan starts to form in my head, I know there's not much chance that she'll actually do it. But she might. She might be exactly what I need: a potential dupe. Innocent enough. Straightforward enough. Up for some fun.

We must be about the same height. We're both white

girls with tans. Hers is more sun-based, less chemical, than mine, but whatever.

'Hey,' I say as she walks past. She carries on walking. I have to stop her. In the couple of seconds since I saw her, I've leaped into the future, but in fact she could just keep walking and it would all be over.

She pauses, and looks back, wary. I indicate the seat opposite me, again.

Time stands still. *Sit down sit down sit down.*

After an eternity, she shrugs and throws herself into the seat, drops her bag beside her and looks out of the window.

'*Bonjour*,' she says. Bonn. Jour. Definitely English, or thereabouts.

I say, '*Enchantée*,' and instantly wish I hadn't.

She gets her phone out, and some headphones. I can't have her disappearing into music or podcasts or whatever, so I need to speak *now*.

This is the moment. Everything hinges on it. I need to hook her interest.

'Off to Switzerland?'

I manage to say it just as she's putting an earphone in. She has the cheap wired ones. I sound like one of those grown-ups who state the obvious to fill a silence. *Off to Switzerland*. For fuck's sake, Tabbi. That's not interesting. Still, it halts the earphone momentum.

'Interrailing,' she says, putting it down. She sounds a bit dreamy. Away with the fairies. Maybe too scatty for this.

'Oh my God,' I say. 'That's immense! How cool. On your own?'

She sighs. Looks out of the window for a moment.

'I mean, yeah,' she says. 'Guess so. Now.'

I decide not to ask. Instead I find the Haribo in my bag. I bought a massive pack at the Gare de Lyon because I knew there was a sugar crash incoming. Breaking them out is an act of faith: they were part of my survival kit for later, but now I'm gambling that I might not need them. I open the bag and put it on the table. She takes one, and another and another, filling her mouth before she starts chewing them all at once.

'I mean,' I say, 'Switzerland doesn't feel like a very Interraily sort of place. Isn't it super expensive?'

I'm playing this straightforward. No swearing. Keep going with the sort of things a random adult might say while I feel my way to a rapport.

She nods and carries on chewing. She's about my age. Maybe a tiny bit younger. I'm humiliated that I'm being escorted across Europe by some bored woman who hates me, and this dreamy girl is just jumping on trains with her backpack. She's also incredibly pretty, much more so than me. She has a little bump in her nose that makes her, somehow, look even better. It makes her real. She's prettier than me and she's free, but I bet I have more money.

'I just wanna see the mountains,' she says when she's swallowed all the sugar. 'I don't really have a big plan. I, like, really love mountains? And I have a rail pass, so I can just travel around whenever I feel like it? Probably sleep on trains a bit. I'm good at sleeping.'

She takes a fried-egg sweet and then a gummy bear. I find the baguette sandwich I bought earlier and push it across the table.

'Want that? It's spare.'

She looks at it. It's cheese salad, wrapped in plastic. Honestly, *nothing* to get excited about, but you wouldn't know it from the way she goes at it. I wonder when she last ate. If she's poor and hungry, then we are ON.

I'm a bit worried she's not focused enough, but all I have to do is get away from Zurich station and after that, if she tries telling them she's not me, I'm pretty sure they won't believe her.

'Thanks,' she says, looking up after finishing half of it. 'Want the rest?'

'Nope. Go for it.' I pause. 'I'm Tabbi.'

'Short for Tabitha?'

'Yeah, but no one calls me that. It's either a witch or a cat, right? I mean, I know Tabbi is a cat too, but what can you do? I spell it with an i at the end.'

She grins. She has a magical smile, wide like Julia Roberts. I wish I looked like that. 'I think it's cute.' Her voice is soft and lovely. A bit Essex, maybe.

'My whole family is obsessed with the idea that their kids have to have stupid names. They could never be the sort of people who call their kid normal things like –' *Eek*. What might her name be? I hope I'm not about to say it. What's a normal name? I have to finish the sentence, so I just hope for the best. 'Sophie? But, once I started spelling it with an i, I liked it a bit more.'

I can't believe I just said 'my whole family'. As if that was a thing. As if I even had a family any more.

'I'm Ruby,' she says. 'Is that a normal name? I guess it is. And you want to know something? This isn't my real hair.'

I reset myself. Smile. 'No way.'

She pulls the wig off. Underneath, her hair is very short and dark. Mine is long and blonde. I run through the options fast. There is only one. I take a moment to mourn my lovely, expensive hair.

I glance over at Jana, who is still reading her book, and take my water bottle out again.

'Want some water?' I say. I lower my voice. 'It's vodka.'

For a moment, she doesn't react. Then she looks as if she's going to say no. She looks like someone who doesn't trust the stranger offering her vodka on the train. Something passes across her face. A sensible moment when she seems older. Then I see her dismiss the sensible self.

She takes the bottle from my hand, lifts it and takes a big gulp. I watch her throat to be sure she's swallowing. She is.

A bit later, Ruby goes to the bar carriage to get a couple of paper cups, and some more food, with my current-account card. I know! But she can hardly run off with it, because we're on the train, and the next stop is nearly an hour away. Also, I'm not sure it would even occur to her: she's exactly the kind of clueless innocent I need. By the time she comes back, I've put all the food I have with me on the table, and we are ready to go.

I cannot get to the destination. I can't face the next six weeks. This is my last chance.

She passes me the cups. I check Jana again, and half fill them with neat vodka. Ruby tops both up with the Diet Coke she just bought, and there we are, two teenage girls drinking soda on the train.

'So,' I say, 'I want to know everything about you.'

She laughs. 'Really? Do you? Why?'

I have less than four hours to make this work. By the time we stop at Dijon, we are semi-drunk, and she looks happy. A ticket inspector has been round, and I've told him she's my friend, and paid for a first-class upgrade for her. By some place called Mulhouse, we have finished the vodka and Ruby is glassy-eyed and giggly. I wish we could get more, but I know they won't sell either of us booze on this train because she is, as I suspected, sixteen, and I am seventeen, and we both have our passports with us. I check Jana from time to time: she's mainly chatting in German to some old guy across the aisle. Flirting. Gross.

After Mulhouse, a customs officer walks down the train. I feel guilty, though I'm not sure why.

I break my precious last oxy in half. No idea what I'm going to do without these.

'Here you go.' I hand half to her and fake swallow mine. Put it back into my pocket with a sleight of hand that, after half a reasonable amount of vodka, I think is pretty impressive. I watch her take hers. I see her swallow. Excellent. The vodka is sharpening me up, making me focus.

These are the things I find out about Ruby before I feel ready to drop my precision bomb: her family is Irish, but she has always lived in Norwich. Her mum had her very young and she was brought up by her grandparents until they died when she was nine. Then she had to go and live with her Uncle Matthew and Aunt Claire, who didn't want her. She's not in any rush to go home.

'I'm going to drift around and see what happens. Might never go back because it didn't really ever feel like home, you know?'

Poor Ruby and all that, but this is *perfect*. She definitely (this is the big one, the *thank-you-God* one) won't have any contact with family over the rest of the summer. She was travelling with someone she'd hooked up with in Amsterdam, a French guy called Nathan, but now she's on her own because he didn't want to go to Switzerland.

'I really did want to see the mountains,' she says with a shrug. 'So I was like, OK, I'll go on my own then, and maybe we can meet up again later if the stars align. Everything happens for a reason.'

Did she just say *everything happens for a reason*? Christ. Still, it works for me. I look at her with a *carry on talking* expression. She does.

'If I need to, I'll get a job. I've done some waitressing before, and I'm sure I can pick up something. I mean, I'll run out of money, but I guess I'll be OK. I just need to see the mountains first. When you grow up in Norfolk, mountains are just, like, magical. So I'll let them guide me and just go where the spirit takes me.'

'That sounds brilliant.' It actually does, and I want it.

While she talks, I look at Ruby's eyes. They're bigger than mine. Her eyes are, in the nicest possible way, cow eyes. She has huge long lashes and they're not even fake, because she wouldn't be able to afford fakes that good. I have some in my case that would be close enough. Her actual eyes are brown, like mine. That's good: important. Her brows are all over the place, but I should be able to tame them, and I can mess mine up a bit with a pencil.

She's so beautiful that I wouldn't pass for her for a moment to anyone who knew us.

But no one in Switzerland knows us. No one knows me apart from Jana, and we met last night so it's not like her heart's in it. She has one job and, as far as she's concerned, it ends in a couple of hours.

'Go on then,' she says. 'You'd better tell me about you.'

I lean back. Pick up a Haribo ring and put it on my finger. This is my moment. Don't say it.

'I'm a messed-up rich girl,' I say. 'I mean, I guess you can see that. But I am the full walking, talking cliché. Plenty of money, boarding school, horses, all that shit. But no love.'

I make an exaggerated sad face, then feel tears pricking at the back of my eyes. *What the hell?* I blink them right back.

'I mean really. I haven't seen my dad since I was three, and I don't remember him, though I've spoken to him on the phone once, to arrange this trip. Never again. I don't speak to my mum.' She doesn't speak to me, more like. Still, same outcome.

'You don't have a relationship with either of your parents?'
'That's right.'

I take a deep breath. I wait. Is she going to ask? What am I going to tell her?

She does ask.

'Why don't you talk to your mum?'

It hangs in the air. Then I shrug.

'There's only so many stepdads one girl can have.'

Apparently I am not going to tell her. Of course I'm not. Deflect with stepdads instead.

'Right,' she says. 'Fair enough. It's just – I don't often meet someone else without the usual family stuff. Most people are all like, oh, this is my mum. This is my dad. They love me and that's all normal.'

I nod. I get that.

'Have you seen *Succession*?' I am addressing some cows in a field outside the window. 'All the money, none of the love? My life is like that.'

'What would you do if your mum wanted to talk to you?'

'She wouldn't.' The most truthful thing I've said all day.

The silence hangs between us. Ruby wants to know the full story. I am not going to tell it. I do, irritatingly, feel my eyes starting to prickle again. *Fuck it*. This time they're brimming. I blink hard, but of course she sees.

'Wait there,' she says, as if I could possibly do anything else. She sets off down the carriage, and I think she's just going to bring me tissue from the loo, but she takes ages and then comes back with two of those little bottles of red wine they give you on flights stuck into her waistband.

I grab one from her and snap the screw top off. I drink straight from the bottle. I want to blot this out.

'How did you do that?'

She smiles. 'Went back to the bar. I figured you'd like a drink and I knew the universe would provide. There was a guy there, so I just asked him to get them for me.'

I glug the rest of the wine into my cup. Quick check of Jana: still flirting in German.

'I love you.'

'Thank you.'

We have a moment. We smile at each other. This is my chance.

Then, just as I'm about to speak, she does. I miss my moment.

'Do you have a boyfriend or girlfriend or anything? Sorry – I'm not normally this nosy with people I've just met! I just feel, like, a connection with you. Like we've skipped a few levels. Like the forces of the universe want to bring us together.'

I shake my head. 'Right? No. I had a boyfriend, Barney. For a couple of years. We broke up. It was his idea, I guess.'

Do not think about Barney. Do not. Don't go there.

I remember that I'm on a deadline.

'So do you have brothers or sisters?'

'Nope,' she says. 'I'm literally the only person in my generation of the family. No cousins, nothing. You?'

'Big sister,' I say. 'Leonora. Half-sister, and again I haven't seen her for ages. I like her – I loved her when we were kids – but she lives in Dubai. We used to be really close, but I . . . Well, we drifted apart. I have two cousins I used to babysit for. Boys. They, like, go to prep school and have stupid names. Packed off to board while they're super young to make sure they get damaged enough to fit in with the rest of the family.'

'I *have* to know the stupid names.'

I grin. 'Ptolomy and Pericles.' I look her in the eye and give a little nod. 'Not even joking.'

There's a moment, and then we burst out laughing. 'Known as Tolly and Perry,' I say. 'But still. Poor arseholes.'

'It's weird, isn't it? That we're both alone on this train when, like, everyone else is bumming around with friends and watching Disney Plus. Or working summer jobs or whatever. So what are *you* doing when you get to Switzerland?'

This is it. This is the moment, right here.

'Heading up into the mountains too.' I keep my voice as casual as I can. I know it's shaking, but I don't think she can hear that. It's an internal shake. 'I'm staying at a fancy hotel for the rest of the summer really. I'm meant to be chilling out, you know? Getting away from it all. Going for long walks. Breathing fresh air. I became . . . very stressed at school this year.'

She nods. A *keep talking* nod. The same nod I gave to her, a while ago.

'I fucked all my exams, and they said I have to leave unless I get it together because I was going to mess with their stats.'

'Rude,' she says.

I'm trying to stay as close to the truth as I can. That's the way you make things work.

'They sent me to some doctor who said I was actually OK, but that I should spend the summer properly relaxing. My dad sorted it out, even though I haven't seen him since forever. He never wants to see me, but he agreed to pay for this. You can imagine it's a lot – a five-star hotel for six weeks, with staff keeping an eye on me throughout. He decided he'd rather shell out for that than actually see me. So here I am. Going to breathe some Swiss air at a fancy hotel, like the Von Trapp family, except that I'm tragically alone apart from twatting Jana, and she's only there to make sure I get in the car to the hotel. That I don't run away and spend six weeks drinking and shooting up.'

I incline my head to indicate Jana. Ruby leans round to look. She turns back and squints at me.

'You're with her? What?'

I sigh. I hate having to admit it.

'She's my chaperone. Yes, I'm seventeen. Yes, apparently I have to be chaperoned. Someone from the hotel is meeting me at the station, and Jana's job is just to hand me over. She's literally bringing me to Switzerland like a parcel, dropping me off and then ... God knows what she does after that. Don't care. She despises me.'

I glance over again. Jana is in her forties or maybe fifties. She's German or maybe Swiss, but she's that kind of European person who speaks every language, so it doesn't really matter where they're actually from. She has short hair and a trouser suit – a Euro Theresa May.

She senses me staring and our eyes meet. She gives me a look of total disdain. A look that says, *You are a brat and I hold you in contempt. I am doing this for the money and I resent the fact that I need to.* I give her a huge fake smile in return.

She turns back to her new friend, the old guy with a bald head. I'm all in favour of him. Distraction Man.

'They don't trust me not to run away and do what you're doing,' I say.

'God,' says Ruby. 'Why would you, though? I'd just, like, stay in the luxury hotel? That sounds like plan A.'

She is perfect. I could kiss her.

'Oh God! You know what?' I say it as if I haven't been thinking about it non-stop since the moment I set eyes on her. 'Let's swap places!'

I look at her face. She laughs, and then something changes in her eyes as she realizes that I mean it. She leans forward.

'Are you serious?'

'You love mountains. I hate them. Too uphill. You're off having adventures on trains for the rest of the summer. I'm going to stay at a luxury hotel in the actual Alps for six weeks. Charging everything to room service, not allowed to do anything except chill out. You want the hotel in the Alps. I want the adventures on the road. Rail.' I give a little shrug. 'And,' I say, 'the only person we have to fool is her.' I indicate Jana with my thumb. 'Trust me: if we do it right, she's not gonna notice.'

Ruby looks at me for a long time. I can hardly breathe. *Say yes say yes say yes.*

The corners of her mouth start to lift. Her face changes.

She laughs. Then pulls herself back under control and feigns nonchalance.

'Seriously?' she says. 'You'd do that?' She looks me in the eye. I give a little nod.

She leans forward, elbows on the table. 'If you actually mean it? Then yeah. I'm in. This is the best idea I've ever heard. The biggest adventure. Swap lives for . . . did you say six weeks?' She gets her phone out and looks at the calendar. 'So until late August? Then we can meet back at Zurich station and swap back?' She pauses. 'You're seriously offering me six weeks at a five-star hotel in the mountains? Are you?'

I check my phone calendar too.

'Meet you back at Zurich station on August the twenty-third? At midday?'

She nods. She starts to laugh. I do too. We both try to do it quietly to avoid attention, but we're soon crying with laughter at the brilliance of a thing we haven't attempted yet. I know I have panda eyes. Ruby's eyeliner flicks have semi-dissolved and are seeping into her skin. My stomach hurts from laughing. Every time we stop, one of us starts up again. Eventually, though, we pull ourselves together.

'Right,' says Ruby. Her tone has changed. She's businesslike now. She checks the time on her phone. 'We have a lot of work to do. And we've got less than two hours to do it.'

2

We work out what we need to do, and then get to it. We consider swapping phones, but decide that it'll be more straightforward to keep the ones we've got so we can deal with any messages that come in. We're both going to sign off and delete our socials right now. No Apple Pay or anything like that. We turn off the location services we've got on. We'll both stay dark for six weeks. The idea of having an Interrail Pass and no Insta, Snap or contactless for six weeks is wild. I can't wait to get going.

'Let's get a photo together?' I say.

I know myself, and I know that if we pull this off, I'll need some form of proof, to convince myself that it really happened, that there really is a version of me up in the mountains. And if we don't, I'll need to look back on what could have been.

Ruby isn't sure. She refuses several times, for some reason, but eventually I convince her by promising that I won't ever do anything with the picture.

'I swear,' I say. 'Just to commemorate the moment. We

can take a matching one in August. No one else will ever see them.'

We lean together, Ruby still in her wig. I arrange my expensive hair over my shoulder while I still have it. She looks away at the last moment, so it's basically a photo of me and a girl in a purple wig, but it'll do.

'We need a contingency,' she says. 'To get in touch with each other if we have to. Do we just message each other?'

That makes me pause. Considering this is my idea, she's doing a lot of the heavy lifting. We *do* need a contingency, and it shouldn't involve phones. For one thing, she won't have access to hers for ages – she just doesn't know it yet.

'Let's set up a Gmail,' I say. 'If we both know the password, we can check in there if we need to. Just keep an eye on it.'

She nods. 'Good plan.'

It takes us a while. The account name traingirls is taken, and so are various others we try. In the end, we have an account called the2traingirls@gmail.com and its password is yeahwedidit! Display name: Train Girls. We both add it to our phones. No one in my life likes me enough to rock up and visit me in the mountains, stare into my eyes and declare that I am too pretty to be my real self, but I guess, if they do, at least Ruby can call on me for help.

Literally, though, our only issue is Jana, and once we've dealt with that I'll be free.

'Maybe use a different name?' she says out of nowhere. 'I mean, not necessarily Ruby Robinson. Call yourself something else.' That hooks my attention.

'Why?'

'Just in case my aunt and uncle notice that they've lost the kid they were meant to look after and decide they'd better find me. They won't, but just in case. Keep your head down.'

I nod. Makes sense. I don't want to be tracked down by anyone at all. I'll keep the *Ruby* because I like it, but maybe I'll use a different surname. How often do you use your surname anyway, while you're bumming around on trains? I file that away to think about later.

Appearance-wise, our hair is the biggest issue. It's time to take action.

'Do you have any scissors?'

She actually does: a pair of nail scissors she pulls from a make-up bag. Better still, she has a razor. I take them both to the loo, making sure Jana sees me. In fact, I pause in front of her and hold up the scissors (keeping the razor out of sight: even a chaperone as crap as her might hear distant alarm bells at the sight of her charge locking herself away with that).

'Gonna cut my hair ALL OFF.'

I use the maddest, druggiest voice I can manage. It actually isn't hard to talk like that because there is suddenly a thing inside me. A thing that is yelling, *This is going to work.* And, *This is going to be the maddest heist I've pulled so far.* And, *I get to stop being myself and all my problems are about to go away.* So, yeah, I am legitimately jittery. There's a lot at stake here: freedom is within reach. They don't get to tame me.

Jana huffs and rolls her eyes, and as soon as she thinks

I've gone she leans across the aisle to say something to her new boyfriend. I can just imagine it. *That girl. Too much money. I could tell you stories about her.* I shudder at the idea of the stories. Does she know? Of course she does.

The train loo is a lot nicer than the ones on British trains, but then so is everything. It's a bit bigger and a lot less grimy. I stand in front of the mirror and stare at my hair.

It cost me £200 to get it cut and coloured five days ago, so destroying it with nail scissors feels like setting fire to a pile of money. I start cutting, and instantly I love it. I am literally throwing money into the bin. And around the bin. And, basically, all over the whole cubicle, though I don't mean to. It's difficult to cut hair without it going everywhere: that's why there's always some poor teenager sweeping the floor at the salon.

I hack off everything I can. Then I lean over the basin, attempt to get a lather with weird train soap, and shave the rest as best I can with a razor that's intended for delicate armpits rather than skulls. It takes me ages to get it looking approximately like Ruby's, but I think I almost manage.

By the time I leave, the train loo is about as shit as the one on that CrossCountry train to Edinburgh I had to get last year, though at least in this case there's no actual shit involved. My roots are dark anyway (by design) and, when I am done, the match to Ruby's isn't perfect, but it's pretty damn close.

I try to look at my face, but my eyes keep darting away. I hate what I'm seeing.

An expensive haircut can hide the fact that your face is

weird, to a massive degree. Now I *really* look like a drug addict. My eyes are small and there's no getting away from that. There are dark bags under them. I always have dark bags, but I'd thought concealer sorted them out, and now I know that it doesn't. It was just my hair being a 200-quid distraction.

My face is pinched and strange-looking. Like a bird's. I cannot let Jana see it because Ruby looks nothing like this. Ruby is gorgeous, and I am now exposed as an ugly baby bird. One of those featherless ones that sits in the nest and shrieks for worms.

Maybe I do need that stay in the mountains. Now that I see myself without armour, I feel small, like a child. Perhaps I need someone to take me in hand and show me how to get on as a normal person.

Leonora lives thousands of miles away and hates me. My dad doesn't even send birthday cards, though he did manage to sort out my fuck-up, and banish me to Switzerland, from afar.

Perhaps I should go along with the plan. Maybe it's actually what I need. I know it took a lot of work from him to make it happen.

No.

I am going to become Ruby. Ruby doesn't know it, but she is absolute goals to me. She is normal, carefree, beautiful. Innocent, a bit ditsy. I want to be that girl and this is my moment.

Jana might not really have looked at me. I know we only have to trick her for a matter of minutes, but all the same you'd have to be quite shit at your job to get on a train with one person and off it with another without noticing. Luckily, I think she is quite shit at her job.

I walk back to our table, turning my face away from Jana. I pretend to be confident and saunter past, posing for the girl in the purple wig who is sitting at the table, not acknowledging Jana at all.

'Oh my GOD,' says Ruby. 'That's – you look so different!'

'I look shit.'

'Just different.' I can see it in her eyes, though: I look worse than she'd thought I would, with no hair.

I slide into the seat next to her to keep my back to Jana, and pick up my phone. I hate this, but we've agreed that this one has to be done for practical purposes, and then we'll delete them. She takes off her wig and we lean in together for a selfie. We use her phone this time, and she looks at the camera. I copy her grin and we fire off a series of pictures. Then she puts the wig back on and we lean our heads together and look at them. A message appears at the top of the screen, but I only catch the words Ruby - you before she swipes it away.

We talk about make-up and eyebrows. It's excruciating, but necessary. And then it's time for the big one.

We go to the opposite end of the carriage this time, to avoid passing Jana, and squeeze into the first toilet cubicle we find. Ruby takes off her T-shirt and shorts and stands in her underwear. She looks hot. I try to draw my eyes away from her, but there's no escaping the fact that this girl is sizzling and I am not. She's smooth and curvy and gorgeous. She's wearing a necklace, a red stone on a cheap chain. Not a ruby for sure, but maybe symbolic of one. I'm wearing a necklace too, but mine is a silver chain with a little star on it. Tragically, I bought it for myself last Christmas, and it was my best present. I spent over £300 – on myself. The only person I spent more on was Barney, whereas he got me a framed photo of us both, which I've since thrown into the Thames where it belongs.

I cringe as I pull my dress over my head. I'm much skinnier than she is. I look horrible. With my badly shaved head, I actually look ill. As soon as the dress is off, I reach for her clothes.

I pull on her shorts and loose yellow T-shirt and am instantly someone new. Something in me relaxes. She puts on my black dress, and of course it looks smoking on her. We are close enough to the same size to get away with it, for five minutes. I doubt Jana will notice, during the crucial few minutes at Zurich, that she's with the upgrade.

I touch my necklace. That's my tic. My safety move.

'Do we switch necklaces too?'

We look at each other. Ruby shrugs.

'It's not as if they've got our names on them. Mine was from Norwich market. My – someone gave it to me.'

'Mine was a present too,' I say, without mentioning that it was from me, to me.

We take off our own make-up and make each other up as ourselves. This involves me having dramatic eyeliner swooshes, which I love. I put on my fake lashes and immediately look a hell of a lot better.

I once had one of those plastic heads you can do make-up and hair on, until I destroyed it. I knew the hair wouldn't grow back. I knew permanent marker wouldn't come off. Yet I couldn't help myself. Anyway, turning Ruby into me feels like that, except that this one *is* reversible: this is a one-summer transformation.

Or maybe I won't go back. I can't live the rest of my life as Ruby, but there will be a way to sidestep going back to being the famous fuck-up Tabbi Courtenay. This could be my first step towards melting away and starting again, away . . .

Away from people who know I'm the worst person in the world.

There is barely space to look at each other, but still I can see that this is working. With the purple wig, and Ruby's clothes and eyeliner flicks, I'm almost fooling myself. I cover my eyebags in concealer, see the purple pulling the focus away from my horrible face. Thank God. I mess my eyebrows as much as I can.

The bit that takes ages is doing Ruby's eyebrows. It's much harder than I thought it would be. I take off too much, and have to draw a lot back on with pencil. I know it looks a bit shonky, and I mutter, 'Sorry.'

She says it's chill. But is it? Will this be the thing that gets us caught? I've never plucked more than a stray hair: I've always had mine waxed at the salon. It's harder than it looks. She scrapes the old bits of varnish off her nails, and I paint all twenty of our fingernails with a hot pink. We look in the mirror while we wait for it to dry.

The fact is what I look like doesn't matter because no

one is in charge of me any more. And Ruby only has to style it out for a few minutes. I stress a bit about using her passport until Ruby explains the Schengen Area. How did I not know about that? It turns out that even though Switzerland isn't in the EU it is in Schengen, which means there are no passport checks between here and *any* neighbouring countries.

'Seriously?' I say as she spritzes herself with my Chanel, holding the bottle carefully to avoid smudging her nails.

'Look it up, but I promise. That's why the train doesn't stop for border controls.'

She is different now too, in my clothes and make-up. Smelling like me. Not ditsy at all.

I check the map of the Schengen Area and see that she's right. I have an enormous amount of freedom. The only places I can't go to in the next six weeks are Bosnia, Serbia, Albania. Those kinds of places. I can live with that.

I do feel a tiny bit guilty. Of course I do: I'm not a monster (not that sort anyway). Ruby'll be fine. She really will be up in the mountains, looking at lovely views. It will be luxurious in its way.

I push it out of my head. I am on the brink of escape.

We walk down the train aisle. Jana doesn't look up. I give Ruby my current-account card, but I keep my other one in case of emergencies. I'll get some cash out with it at the station and make that last.

'My passport's in my bag,' I say, keeping my voice low, once we're sitting down again. 'So you just need to give me yours, and your ticket, and we're done.'

Ruby's ticket is electronic. I download an app called Rail Planner and sign in to her account. She shows me how to use it. And that's how I find myself in possession of an Irish passport and a two-month Interrail Pass.

Thirteen minutes later, we pull into Zurich HB and, however hard I'm trying to play this cool, my heart is pounding. I've broken all the rules in my time, but I've never tried to pull off a thing like this. It's not identity theft because it's mutual. Is there a name for it? Identity swap? If we get caught, how much shit will I be in? I know how much. If we get caught doing this, they will stop protecting me. That's a lot of shit.

I need a drink. I don't know if Switzerland is an easy place to buy booze underage, but I'll find a way.

If we do it.

If we pull this off, I am looking at freedom for an entire summer. I am sticking my middle fingers up to the whole world and specifically to my parents.

'Where are you going to go?' says Ruby. *Tabbi*.

I shrug, trying to pretend that I haven't been thinking about it obsessively.

'I think I'll get some cash out in Zurich,' I say. 'And then catch a train somewhere. Maybe Italy. I've always fancied Naples.' No idea where that came from. Random.

She grins. 'Good luck.'

'You too.'

We hug.

Yeah. A tiny bit guilty, but that's all.

Zurich HB is one of those massive stations. It will be easy to disappear. We look at each other.

'Ready?' she says. She says it like me. She has been working on my voice. It's a bit lower than hers, and when she talks like me she sounds more drawly. She's good at it. It makes me feel weird, like when you hear yourself on a voice note.

As for me, it doesn't matter how I speak. I'll go before they do, leaping off the train with Ruby's backpack the moment the doors open.

The train stops. We hug again.

'Keep in touch on the Gmail,' she says. 'August twenty-third, at midday. Right back here. Under the station clock. There's sure to be one.'

Escape is in sight. I have beaten everyone who wants to lock me up. Survival of the fittest. For the first time in a long, long time, I feel like the fittest.

I pick up her backpack, loving how battered it is. I wonder, for a moment, where else it's been. I shout goodbye in what I think is Ruby's voice. I see Jana look up, but her eyes skate over the girl at the end of the carriage in the itchy purple wig.

The train stops. I am first off, and I walk away without looking back. I walk into six weeks of freedom. I feel the smile spreading across my face as I go. I start to run. I start to hum. This is everything. I have done it.

I'm not even sorry.

3

The train has arrived at an underground platform. I walk into the middle of a crowd of people and feel myself vanishing. Up an escalator, walking on the left, hurrying away. Huffing at people who are walking too slowly.

Then I'm in daylight, on the main station concourse, and it's busy and bright. It's one of those hefty stone places with a high ceiling and lots of space. Loads of people walking, waiting, milling around. A meeting-point clock. A sculpture on the ceiling. I don't look at anyone. I'm pretty sure one of these people is here to meet me and I'm speed-walking away as fast as I can.

I can see the outside world right there, and I walk across the concourse and step into it. By the time I reach the street, I'm running. I burst out into the sunshine and stop.

The sun beats on my bare arms. I'm sweating. The pavement is wide. The road is massive. There's a tram, cars, a long rack of bikes, a distant church spire, a nearby hotel. The sunshine here smells different. It smells like warm stone, like distant lake. Exhaust fumes and different rules and different life and adventure and new things and being foreign and on the move. Ruby's backpack pulls on my shoulders.

No one looks at me. Plenty of people are going in and out of the station. No one has time for a cheaply dressed backpacker in an itchy wig.

Anyone who says running away doesn't work hasn't tried it.

I stand in the middle of the pavement and turn my face up to the sun, and apart from a well-dressed couple (shorts with creases down the front, Ralph Lauren polos) who look like they'd be friends of my mum's, but who now make a point of giving me a very wide berth, everyone acts as if I'm not there. I say a little hello to urban Switzerland in my head, hoping that I won't be here long, and then I walk away from the doorway and wait.

It takes longer than I expected, but eventually I see Ruby, dressed as me but with no hair, walking out. My heart is pounding as I stare at the new Tabitha Courtenay. I walk away, pretend to be trying to unlock a bike, hoping its owner won't come back. She's with some guy, an older one. I see the way he's watching her, ready for her to bolt. I wonder whether she's realized yet.

Then she looks around. Our eyes meet for a second before we both look away. I wait for Jana, but I don't see her, and I know there are other exits so, after loitering for another twenty minutes to be totally sure, I take another deep breath of Zurich air and head to the ATM. I withdraw as much cash as I can and then I snap my bank card in half and drop it into a bin. Now I'm on the run.

I need to make this rail pass work. It has to get me the hell away from here, fast.

The destinations swim before my eyes. Lausanne. Geneva airport. Bern. I don't want those places. Where do I need to go? How do I work out how to do it?

The word 'Milano' catches my eye. That could be fun? I don't know anything about Milan except that it's the fashion capital. What would I do there? I know what Tabbi would do, but what about Ruby? The word 'Rorschach' catches my eye, and I thought that was blobs that you see shapes in, not a place. I feel my head spinning. How am I going to manage on my own? Six weeks is a hell of a long time. People walk past. Hundreds of them. Everyone has a place to go except me.

I feel myself spiralling. Total freedom is confusing. I'm not meant to be here. I'm meant to be shut away, controlled. Now I can do anything. I despise Jana for letting us do this under her nose. She shouldn't have been so crap. I despise Ruby for walking into my trap so happily, for believing that anyone would actually offer six weeks in the mountains with no strings, as if that was a thing that happened. Maybe I will just go to Naples, like I said. I mean, *Naples*? Why did I say that? I've never given the place a moment's thought. I just pulled out a place that I thought made me sound cool. What do I know about it? Pizza, Pompeii, crime, football. Maybe that'll do.

I get on the Rail Planner app and, following Ruby's instructions, I type in the journey. It says I need a reservation.

I don't want to link my bank card to Ruby's app, so I walk into the ticket office and join a queue. Nine minutes later, I'm at the front. I don't enjoy those nine minutes: at first I do, and then I realize that Jana could still be in the station, and if she is she could easily be coming in here. She could join this queue at any time. Shouldn't I be lying low in Zurich for a couple of hours? Why am I not hiding in a random bar until evening?

I don't notice when it's my turn at the counter. The man behind me coughs and points.

'Oh sorry,' I say.

Might as well speak English since I don't speak German. Or should I have spoken French? Don't panic. Don't overthink. You are Ruby, and Ruby's passport is Irish. This is a big transport hub. Of course you can speak English.

I check over my shoulder again. No Jana.

I pass my phone to the ticket woman, who is surprisingly friendly. She gives me a big smile.

'I'd like to use this pass to go to Italy,' I say. She nods and taps on her screen. This is all totally normal to her. It's literally her job.

'Where would you like to go?' she says in perfect English.

She makes me some reservations and passes me a printout. I pay in cash. My first train, the Milan one, leaves in half an hour.

I walk away from the ticket office singing inside. I'm so happy that I forget to look for Jana, and so of course I walk straight into her.

She stops in front of me, annoyed that someone is in her way. Then she looks at me.

Our eyes meet, and I see her confusion. She looks at my wig, and then down at my clothes. She opens her mouth, but doesn't say anything.

I turn away. My breathing has gone weird. I focus entirely on getting away from her. *Walk!* I make my legs move. I head as fast as I can towards the platforms. There's a big group standing there, looking at a board, and I walk into the middle of them. On the other side, I see a train, and I see that it's about to leave, and I don't care where it's going. I'm going to get on it. This part of the station is bright and exposed. I'm easily spotted, with my purple hair.

I hear a voice behind me, but it's not Jana. It's a man and he's saying, 'Excuse me?' I walk faster and then I run towards that train, but he runs too, and he grabs my arm and spins me round. I pull away. I'm ready to fight.

He put his hands on me. One on each shoulder, the assaulting bastard.

It's the guy Jana was chatting to on the train. He's taller than he looked when he was sitting down, one of those white guys who thinks everyone has to do what he says, and if anyone else speaks out it's woke nonsense.

'You're the other girl,' he says. His accent is German or Swiss. 'Aren't you?'

'What are you talking about?' I shout it in his face, kick him in the shins to make him let go of me and run. I hear him shouting behind me, but I don't look back.

I hear a whistle, the kind that platform guards blow. I sprint towards the train that's about to leave. A train guy indicates to me to jump on at the door at the front.

I leap on board. The door beeps and closes, and the train starts to move. I hope Jana and her boyfriend sleuth along to the ticket office and find out that I had a reservation to Milan. I hope they go there, looking for me. I hope it's lovely and romantic for them. Gross.

I drop my rucksack and lean back, breathing heavily. I have no idea where I'm going (Bern, Rorschach, Geneva?) but the fact is that guy busted me, and I got away. I am on this train and I'm almost a hundred per cent certain that he's not.

The ticket inspector is in front of me. He's about forty maybe, wearing an impeccable uniform.

'Do you have a ticket?' he says, speaking English to me by default. I fumble around and show him my Interrail Pass. He takes it.

'Oh,' he says. 'Your reservation is to Naples! You have the wrong train.'

I shrug. 'That's OK. Where's this one going?'

He smiles at me. A genuine smile. For a few seconds, I want to kiss him, but I manage not to.

'Geneva,' he says.

So I'm off to Geneva. I don't even need a reservation.

I find a seat. I lean my face on the window and stare out.

It's so green and steep out there. I look at the little houses and the mountains on the horizon. As the distance between me and the threat of the busybody man who grabbed my arm grows, I feel myself relaxing, and then my eyes begin to close.

As I drift off, I let myself think about Ruby for a moment. Just a little flash of hoping she's OK. She doesn't need that sort of treatment so she'll sail through, but because I gave her vodka and oxy on the train they won't believe her when she says she's clean, and they certainly won't believe her if she says she's not Tabitha Courtenay. I remember the half-oxy in my dress pocket and curse myself. I wanted that. Still, I guess they'll find it on her, and it'll all stack up.

And then I am asleep.

4

The next morning I'm sitting on a top bunk in Avignon, leaning on the wall, panicking. My breathing is all over the place. I try to regulate it, but this is madness. I look at all my stuff. It's not even mine. Nothing is mine except my necklace. We didn't even keep our own toothbrushes. I have no hair and weird, drawn-on eyebrows. I'm a different person. I got what I wanted but . . . now what?

First of all, money. I was lucky to get a bed in this hostel when I arrived last night, but it was thirty-five euros. Seventy, because I paid for two nights. I turn my back on the rest of the room and put my cash on to my lap, facing the wall.

How can this possibly work? Six weeks without a bank card. It feels like real-life Monopoly: I only have the notes I'm looking at now to get me through, and although I'm not planning to buy a hotel and put it on Mayfair, I am going to need to buy myself a place to sleep every night. If it's thirty-five euros a go, the maths doesn't work.

I check the notes. I have the 500 euros the cashpoint gave me in Zurich, plus two of the 300 I was carrying before as a contingency. I've spent 100 already on train reservations, this place, and a sandwich. I screw up my face and try not to let the scream out.

I may not be clever, but I can do enough maths to see that I'm fucked. I remember Ruby talking about sleeping on trains, but I don't want to do that. If I had to spend two months travelling up and down the rail network, spending every night asleep in a train seat, I'd crack.

Would I? Maybe I should do it. Just spend six weeks eating crisps and chocolates, looking out of windows and sleeping upright. Then I remember paying for my reservations to Naples: that wouldn't work either. And I don't want to see the whole of Europe. I can't say this out loud, can barely articulate the thought, but here goes: *I'm scared*. I want to stick with places I know. I'm glad I didn't go to Italy.

I turn to the rest of Ruby's stuff. These clothes are awful. Her bag is almost empty, but what it does contain is by Shein and Boohoo. A garish short dress. A pair of blue shorts. Three cropped T-shirts. A battered pair of Converse that won't fit me. One single jumper and a horrible raincoat from Mountain Warehouse.

I think of the lovely stuff in my own suitcase. I gave it all away, to a stranger. What was I –

'Hey there!'

I look up. There's a woman sitting on a top bunk on the other side of the room and she's looking at me. She has frizzy blonde hair, broken veins on her nose and the friendliest face I've ever seen. Because she's the first person who's spoken to me spontaneously, I love her. All the same, I shove my money back into Ruby's tourist-style money belt and push it under the sheet.

'Hi.' She's older than me. Maybe late twenties?

'Love your hair.'

I shake my head, and the wig whips me in the face. 'You really don't.'

'I do! So cool. The purple.'

She's Australian, I think. All the backpackers here seem to use English as a universal language. The Japanese ones. The Dutch ones. Everyone. That's surprised me. I speak great French (au pairs, that's why), but I've hardly needed to.

Oh my God, I am so tired.

'Yeah,' I say. 'Purple's cool. It's not my hair, though. You wouldn't actually like my hair.' I pull the wig off, wincing.

Why did I do that? Why? Because I wanted to shock her, because that's what I do. Stupid, impulsive things that lead to trouble. I should have let her continue to act as if this nylon monstrosity was growing out of my head.

Could I buy a better wig? No. I have no money now. I look round the room. The walls are white, the floors are fake wood, and there are four sets of bunks. It's nice for what it is, I guess, but still.

I wonder what Ruby is doing, where she slept last night. She will most definitely hate me this morning. I'm pretty sure they'll have taken her phone off her, and she won't get it back for weeks. I can send an email on our joint account, but she won't be able to see that either unless she hunts down a computer terminal. Which maybe she will ...

Focus focus focus. There's an Australian woman looking at me, her hands to her mouth. I pull myself back to the moment.

'Oh my God! I see what you mean. Are you – I mean, have you been ... sick?'

That's almost funny. I look so bad with my train-loo haircut that she thinks I've had chemo. No one would have asked Ruby that.

'Yeah.' Easier than the truth. More plausible than saying I hacked my hair off in a train toilet to swap lives with a stranger. 'I'm OK now, though.' I look her in the eyes with a sad, brave little smile and put my wig back on. Subject. Closed.

'Oh, that sucks. You poor thing.'

She jumps down, encouraged by my admission. She walks towards me. *No!*

'I really am fine now.' I speak quickly because I can see she's gearing up to share something.

'My cousin had cancer. It was so brutal. Can I ask what type you had?'

She climbs my ladder and sits next to me. *Fuck.*

I shake my head. 'Can't really talk about it. I'm trying to look forward, not back.'

She nods. 'Bucket list?' I nod too, and she finally realizes that she needs to back off. 'Great! Hope you have a fabulous time. I'm Michaela. If you want to talk any time – well, you know where I live.' She points to her own bunk.

I give another little nod. 'Thanks. I'm Ruby.'

It's the first time I've said that. I signed in as Ruby last night, but that was just scary. Handing someone Ruby's passport, hoping they wouldn't look at it closely (they didn't). Saying it now feels good.

'Lovely to meet you, Ruby. How long have you been in France?'

She doesn't look as if she's planning to shift off my bunk, so I tell her about my Interrail adventures, sticking to Ruby's story as best I can, granting myself a boyfriend in Amsterdam called Nathan and substituting the French Riviera for Ruby's mountains. As soon as I can, I throw it all back at her.

Michaela and her boyfriend, Jack, have been travelling the world for more than six months. She tells me stories of Thailand and India, of bumpy bus rides up mountains and overcrowded ferries. It's a world I never imagined, the world of the international budget traveller. This is what I need. Michaela knows the stuff that I don't. She knows how you get things done.

'Can I ask a really crass question?'

'Your accent is adorable,' she answers, which I take to mean *yes*. I also take it to mean I've defaulted to boarding-school English, rather than Ruby's voice. *Try harder.*

'What about money? I don't have loads of cash. I guess I didn't think this through. I have a train pass, but what do you do?'

Michaela loves this. She gets straight down to business.

'OK,' she says. 'Where do you want to go? Riviera, you said?'

I think of the whole of Europe, at my feet. This ticket will take me everywhere. I could go to Spain, Portugal, Italy, Greece. Germany, Sweden, Norway, Poland ... It looms over me, the threat of adventure. I picture the countries on the map pointing at me, laughing in my face. They know I'm not brave.

She sees something in my reaction and shifts closer, putting an arm round my shoulders. She smells of sunscreen and onions. I shuffle away from her.

I think about it. 'Yep,' I say. 'I know I could go anywhere, but I think I just want to go south from here and bum around on beaches for a bit. I didn't realize how expensive it would be, just to sleep for a night.'

'Got a tent?'

I shake my head. *Tents! How had I forgotten about tents?*

'I mean, a tent isn't essential for wild sleeping, but it's safer if you're on your own. Rather than just sleeping outside. You are on your own, right? Now that Nathan's not with you?'

I nod. I start to say that I'm always on my own, but remember that I'm Ruby now, and I get to stop being Tabbi Courtenay, famous loser. Also, I just faked a serious illness. I should keep my mouth shut.

'What about you?' I say. *That's good. That works.*

'Oh, never,' says Michaela. 'I mean, Jack and I? We're always together. In each other's pockets. At times I crave a bit of my own company, but honestly? When that happens, I just go off by myself for a few days, until I miss him.'

'He doesn't mind?'

She grins. 'Nah. He does the same. So, yeah – you need a tent. There's always someone selling one, don't worry. You don't need to go to, like, Camping World or whatever the Euro equivalent is.'

I think about that for a second. I remember Ruby's raincoat. 'Mountain Warehouse?' But she wasn't actually asking. She's looking at me with a speculative expression.

'So, you heading to the beach, Ruby?'

'I mean, I've been to those beaches before.' Lots of times. 'And I like them.'

She's still looking at me. It's disconcerting.

'OK.' She gives a little nod. 'Maybe we can go together. Hook up. I could do camping on a beach on the Med. I feel like you need someone to take care of you for a while. I'd be happy to help, Ruby.'

I want to stand up and run away. I'm also wary about what she might have meant by *hook up*. I bite back everything I want to say and give the most non-committal nod I can manage.

'You're nice,' I say. 'Anyway, I'm off to look round town. There's a bridge, right? I remember a song about it from . . . school.' *Nearly said 'prep school' there.*

She nods slowly.

'You take care, Ruby.'

I can't get out of the door quick enough. What's wrong with me? Why am I pretending to be ill? I touch my necklace, the last remnant of my old life. That little star should ground me, but it doesn't.

I need to shake off this annoying woman. Also, I need a drink.

I straighten my wig and walk down the street. At least Avignon feels like a place I kind of know. I may be a different person now, but I've still spent a lot of summers in the South of France. That's why, with twenty-nine countries at my fingertips, I ended up taking a train here from Geneva because I could, and I'm pretty sure that if I'd caught the Naples train I'd have ended up turning round and coming here anyway. I may not have much money, but I know my way about. Not in this specific city, but it's the same. It smells of dusty ground and sunshine. It smells of holiday and relaxation and everything being exactly the way I want it to be. Of different plants growing madly under a hot sun. It smells of no one holding me accountable.

This is a place to sit with a drink in your hand, to contemplate the fact that you've just pulled off the most incredible heist and it's worked. It was a close call in Zurich, but here I am. That guy must have reported back to Jana. I wonder if she's told my dad by now? Maybe not, because she had one job, and he wouldn't pay her if she fessed up. Yesterday spins around my head. I'd expected to be waking up today locked in a tiny room without anything nice, and instead I'm here, and I still get to sit in the sunshine and drink, and that's what I am going to do.

I walk around aimlessly at first, knowing that I'd likely be ID'd in the supermarkets, wondering how to buy alcohol. Taking random streets until I find myself out of the pretty parts of town and into a bit that feels a lot seedier.

My flip-flops are hurting. I thought I had fairly dainty feet at size five, but Ruby's are smaller, and although it doesn't make much difference since they're flip-flops, they are rubbing between my toes like hell, and I keep half slipping off the backs. I guess my budget might extend to some new ones if I can find a tent and sleep on beaches for free. If you really can do that without being murdered, maybe I have enough money after all.

'*Bonjour!*'

I look round. A man has fallen into step with me. I keep walking. He keeps walking too. There you go. I start to worry about safety and some random guy attaches himself.

'*Comment vas-tu?*' he says. Straight into the informal 'you'.

'*Ça va,*' I say. I shoot him a sideways look. He's the kind of twat who walks up to strange women in the street, but he's also someone who would get served alcohol.

'Can you buy me some alcohol?' I say in French. Why not? Straight to the chase.

He laughs. 'Sure, if you give me money.'

'We'll go together.'

'You're not French?'

I consider pretending to be more interesting than I am. Then I remember my passport. 'Irish,' I say. So much cooler than being English.

He asks me about Ireland. I say it's very green, and the music is great, because those feel like safe and plausible things to say. He says his name is Yannick. I say mine is Ruby. He asks if I want to be his girlfriend. I say I do not. I add that I'm a lesbian to make it extra clear (I'm not), but he just looks more interested. We go to the shop.

Half an hour later, Yannick and I are sitting by the river, passing a bottle of rosé between us. He's stopped trying to be a pick-up artist, or whatever that was, and I don't mind him now. He's lived in Avignon for nearly a year. His mother is Algerian, his father French. He's twenty-two, and he's nice company, once you get past the bit where he approaches strange women in the street and asks if they want to be his girlfriend. The sun is hot on my head. I really want to take off the stupid wig, but I'm resisting for the moment.

'Why did you do that?' I say after a while.

'What?'

'Why did you start walking with me and talking to me? Were you trying to hook up?'

He gives me a sleazy grin. 'Wanna?'

'Nope.'

'Sometimes it works.'

'I don't believe you.'

I'm relaxing. The wine is hitting the spot. I'm sitting on a warm flagstone near the river, talking random shit to a guy I just met. I'm going to buy a tent and that will make my money worries melt away. I breathe deeply. In and out.

Yannick hasn't replied. He's not meeting my eye.

'Seriously?' I say. 'It's never worked, has it?'

He shakes his head, looking down.

'Do you know why that is?'

Another shake. A little shrug.

'It's because women *hate* that. It's really scary, Yannick. Walking next to a girl and talking to her is incredibly intimidating. I mean, I guess you know that already, but I'm just saying, from the other side of things, that it really, really is. The only feeling any girl is going to have when you do that is, *Is this a busy street? Who else is around? How can I get away from this man? Can I go into that shop? Can I run? Could I ask that woman for help?* Those are the thoughts we'll have. Not, *Oh, he seems like a nice guy*. It won't ever work for you, my friend.' I pause. 'Not consensually.'

'My friend! You just said that. And you're here with me, drinking.'

'I wanted something from you too.' I hold up the wine bottle, pass it over to him. 'I didn't want to hook up. Still don't. Never will.'

He shrugs. 'How long you in town?'

'Until tomorrow. Then I'm heading south. You don't happen to have a tent you could lend me, do you? I'll give it back in . . . about forty-one days.'

'A tent?' Yannick laughs. 'No, I don't have a tent.' He pauses. 'My friend might. He'd lend you one for forty-one days.'

We finish the wine and go back for another bottle. The first one slipped down so easily it hardly touched the sides. I'm feeling like myself again now, though not really. I feel like my new self, like Ruby Robinson, free spirit. Because that's who I am.

*

It's dark. I'm laughing and clinging on to Yannick. I can't quite walk. Even through the drunkenness, I know that I've done something spectacularly stupid. I've got leglessly drunk in the street with a man who walks up to girls and starts talking to them just in case they might be the one who doesn't run away.

I've become the one who didn't run away.

We've spent the entire evening and half the night drinking wine and vodka beside the river. I think Yannick messaged his friend and found me a tent. At one point he left and came back with a cardboard box of chips. Now he has an arm round my waist. I push his hand away.

This is why they sent me to the mountains. This stuff, and the rest of it. '*Out of control,*' they had said. '*A danger to yourself and others.*' Even through my drunken haze, I know they were right. I mean, clearly they were.

'Here we are,' he says.

I blink. The world is spinning round me. Just me: not the sun. The city is quiet now. I hear a car revving in the distance. I have no idea where we are. I've just been letting Yannick lead me, and we could be going anywhere.

That thought sobers me right up. I look around. He's brought me to a backstreet in the dead of night. A bird is hopping on the pavement ahead of us, pecking at some dried-on food. There is no one else anywhere nearby.

I need to run, but I don't think I could. He would easily catch up and overpower me. I see an open window on an upstairs floor. I could shout. That's what I should do. Someone might look out of the window. That's all I've got.

Yannick puts his arm round my shoulder.

'I'm glad I met you, Ruby Robinson,' he says. I pull away. Prepare myself to scream, kick him, run.

He says: 'This is your place, right?'

I look up. We're in front of a door. It's the door of a tall building. A wooden door with a sign on it. I squint. Is it? The words come into focus. *Budget. Hostel.*

By magic, we have come to the right place.

'You brought me home!'

'I'll see you tomorrow with the tent. Good night, Ruby. It's been awesome hanging out with you. You speak excellent French. Drink lots of water now.'

He squeezes my shoulders, then walks off, turning to wave.

I try to control my breathing as I push the door. That was, I know, pure luck. The door is unlocked. I straighten my wig, give Yannick's retreating back a wave, pull myself together and go in. He could have done anything, and he walked me home.

A clock on the wall tells me that it's two o'clock. There's a woman half asleep at the desk, and she gives me a look that tells me she's seen drunk backpackers before and doesn't give a shit.

There are a lot of sleeping bodies in the dorm room. I bustle around, opening the backpack and flinching as my fingers touch nylon and cheap stuff. I eventually find Ruby's toiletries bag. (Why didn't we keep our own toothbrushes? It's gross using someone else's.) I take it to the bathroom and clean my face with a cheap wipe. It actually seems to work just as well as L'Oréal cleanser. Same goes for the supermarket moisturizer.

Back in the dorm, I stumble into a couple of beds and walk round, peering at everyone by phone-torch light because I can't remember which bunk is mine. They all look the same.

Someone says, in English, 'Can you please stop singing?'

I realize that they're talking to me. I was humming. What was it? A song from one of my old playlists that I'd listened to through Ruby's rubbish headphones on the train. A song that might as well be about me.

Britney. Asking me if I know that I'm toxic.

5

I wake up feeling so shit that it's quite comforting. My head is pounding and the acid in my throat makes me wonder how fast I can sprint to the bathroom if I need to.

Someone is walking around. Another person says, 'Sure, with milk, thanks.'

Milk. *Bleurgh.* I feel my stomach heaving, threatening, then tentatively settling.

I roll over and pull the duvet over my head.

It's proper daylight now and the room feels empty. I'm warm and comfy.

The third time I wake up, I scream because something touched my face with a thousand tiny fingers. I sit up in bed, head pounding and fuzzy, unsure where I am or what the hell is trying to grab me. My heart is pounding. My breathing is weird. I'm gasping for breath.

What's happening?

It takes me a long time, and the sound of someone laughing, before I realize that the thing that stroked my face is a purple wig, and the reason there's a purple wig on the pillow is because I'm Ruby Robinson.

Avignon. Some guy called Yannick. Wine, vodka, river.

I look around, trying to stay calm. Who laughed? There are two people sitting on a bottom bunk across the room, both boys. I remember striking a deal with Yannick, that he would buy the booze and I would pay. I wonder how much of my precious cash I've spent.

My phone is out of battery so I scrabble around to plug it in, and stumble out of the room, towards a bathroom, where I am treated to two awful sights. One is me, wigless and rough with bags under my bloodshot eyes. The other is a recently used, unflushed loo. Oh well. The smell makes my stomach heave and then I'm vomiting a stream of acid, and everything is a tiny bit better.

After a shower and a proper rummage through Ruby's clothes and make-up, I'm feeling almost cute in my wig and a dress I found in her bag. It has puffy sleeves and a very short skirt, and it's white with hot-pink flowers on it. It's a cross between a child's party dress and one of those 'sexy' fancy-dress outfits you get offered if you look up Halloween stuff online. Anyway, somehow it seems to work better on than off. I do the eyeliner flicks almost like Ruby does, and I'm ready to drink a million coffees and to find a bakery and eat all the croissants in the world.

Yeah, I shouldn't be spending, but Yannick's going to get me a tent. A couple of croissants will be fine.

Michaela is in the lobby of the building as I pass through.

She gives me a pissed-off look, but quickly replaces it with a smile. Maybe it's her accent, but she reminds me of the girls who go on Australian reality TV, in that she's super nice and laid-back on the surface, but I sense something darker and more interesting underneath. I reckon if I got to spend a bit of time with her I could recruit her as a sidekick, even though she's at least ten years older than me.

But she wants to take care of me. So I need to ditch her.

'Hey,' she says. 'Ruby.'

I give her an insincere smile back. 'Hey.'

'You OK? We were worried about you, before. Like – what was that? In the night? Did something happen?'

Oh God oh God oh God.

Although I'm used to sleeping in rooms full of people from the boarding-school years, I'm not used to those other people being adults. I cringe at the realization that my crashing in drunk must have woken everyone up and that they therefore all hate me.

'Sorry!' I say. 'Oh shit. I'm so sorry, Michaela.'

'What happened, though? I tried to ask, but I don't think you heard, and then I'm afraid I fell asleep.'

What happened? I try to find a way of framing my answer in a way that doesn't make me sound like a drunk. That doesn't make me sound like Tabbi Courtenay.

'I'm fine,' I say. She's still waiting so I sigh and carry on. 'I got chatting to someone and we went for a few drinks. Time got away with me a bit. It happens sometimes since ... Anyway, I'm really OK. Sorry to wake you. It won't happen again.'

Michaela is nodding. She wants to be my mum. It crowds in on me, flashing pictures into my brain. I hate anyone who makes me think about that woman. I edge away.

'Well, I'm worried about you,' she says, instantly becoming a better mother than my real one. 'I don't know if you're still on any meds, but you know. You have to look after yourself. Do your parents know you're here?'

I ignore the last part. 'Clean bill of health,' I say.

I'm starting to walk away when she says: 'Jack and I are coming down to the Med with you tomorrow. It's all arranged.'

I turn and give her a careful smile. I don't answer.

I stop and sit on a bench by the river. The soil is sandy, the sun hot. I rub a bit more sunscreen into myself and get my phone out to look at our Gmail. I haven't added it to my inbox: I have to go to the website and log in. Google hates me for doing this and sends me an email to tell on me, but in the end it lets me access it by typing in the password.

After all that, there's one solitary email in there and that's from Gmail, changing their tone and welcoming me in. I start typing a message, but it's too fiddly so I do it by dictation. I hold down the microphone and take a deep breath.

'Hey, babe,' I say. 'Hope you're doing OK. Look, I'm sorry I didn't tell you the full story, but since you don't really need any treatment you must be doing fine, and I hope you're looking at some nice mountains. I'm back in France, down south. I was on my way to Naples, but I ran into Jana and that guy and ended up jumping on a train that was about to leave. Anyway. Check in when you can. I guess you might not have your phone for a while. Um – yeah. Sorry. Hope the food's good and hope there's a spa.'

The punctuation comes out all over the place and for some reason it writes 'spa' as 'Spar' like the corner shop (it's unlikely there'll be one of those), but I send it anyway.

Down the road there's a bakery with a queue. I remember my sister telling me, years and years ago, that you can tell the good bakeries because they're the ones with local people in line for their stuff. I guess that's not rocket science. I know I need to stop burning through cash, but one sniff makes my stomach rumble, and I walk in anyway. I stand for ages behind women with baskets and a man with a baby strapped to his front. I keep checking the email, waiting for a reply from Ruby/me, but I know, really, that she'll be in no position to read or write emails. I hope she's OK. If I let myself, I could feel pretty bad about what I've done to her.

When I get to the front of the line, I fake having loads of friends by checking my phone before I order. Not that the woman at the counter could give any less of a shit, but it's my way of saving face.

'Three croissants, please,' I say in French. 'And –' (checking phone) – 'one pain au chocolat, one pain au raisin and . . .' Pause to scroll phone, checking the orders of my imaginary friends. 'A baguette?'

'I only have two croissants left,' she says. She looks at the clock on the wall. I do too. Yeah, it's the middle of the afternoon. These people are here for the new batch of eclairs and stuff. Those two croissants will be stale. I sigh, and try to focus.

'Yes,' I say. 'Sorry.'

I look at what there is and leave the shop having spent a ridiculous, actually eyewatering, sum on some chocolate eclairs, strawberry tarts, macarons and three baguettes. What can I say? Hangovers make me greedy.

Outside the shop I wander round the old streets until I find a bench in a little square. I tear bits off the end of a baguette and eat them, while checking my phone all the time. I chuck some bread down for the birds, but regret it when a hundred thousand pigeons turn up at once.

I write another email, typing it this time, suddenly really keen to hear from Ruby.

> You doing OK? Please do check in when you can.

Being hungover like this is making me feel strange. Like, did I *really* switch lives with a stranger? I eat half a baguette and a macaron, and realize I have no idea what I'm going to do with the rest of the food. I shove the boxes of stuff into Ruby's crappy little backpack and head back to the hostel.

The sun is shining again, and everything smells of flowers and dust. All that's missing is the sea. It's OK. I take hold of myself. I am all right. Ruby and I did something clever. I know she'll be busy right now. I don't know why I'm desperate to hear from her. I shouldn't be giving her another thought until August. Six weeks of freedom is a bit overwhelming, and it makes me want a drink, but I can't afford to be drunk for six weeks.

At the hostel I realize that I've accidentally done something nice. I crashed, drunk, into a bedroom I share with loads of other people and woke them in the middle of the night; and now I'm feeling remorseful, so I've bought them lovely expensive patisserie to say sorry. That, at least, is how I reframe it the moment I walk into the room and sense the atmosphere.

'This is so sweet of you,' says Michaela, taking a macaron out of the box. 'I mean, we really appreciate it, right, Jack?'

Jack can't answer because his mouth is full of eclair, but he gives a little shrug. I can see that he's furious about my hijacking his holiday. Two Chinese girls smile at me and split a strawberry tart.

'Some guy was looking for you, Ruby,' says Michaela. 'I wasn't here but Mei saw him.' She nods to one of the strawberry-tart girls.

Mei hands her half-tart to her friend and walks over to a bottom bunk. She picks up a large canvas package and hands it to me.

'He gave this for you,' she says. I take it.

'Tent,' says Michaela. 'So I guess you're all set for tomorrow. We should get a morning train. We'll get the TER – it's slower, and we'll have to change, but you don't need to buy a reservation. We'll be in Cannes middle of the afternoon. Find a beachy camping spot and we're all set.'

Yannick has done what he said he'd do. He's delivered me a tent.

The moment Michaela goes to the bathroom, I wink at Jack and the girls, then sling everything into my backpack. I fix the tent on to the bottom of it with some straps that seem to be there for exactly that purpose. I heave it on to my back.

'Tell her I've just popped out,' I say.

Jack grins at me for the first time and gives a little salute, and I walk straight to the station and get on the first train to the coast. I can't work out how to do it without taking a TGV, but no ticket person comes round, so it's free anyway.

6

I step off the train in Cannes. The platform is under cover, and it's only when I'm standing outside, in the very last of the day's sunshine, that I realize how hot it still is. All the same: Cannes! This is goals. I've shaken off Michaela and come to a place I know, a place that's still big enough to disappear into. The other places along this coast are nice: Antibes, the train's next stop, is full of happy memories for me, but it feels too small. Monaco is brilliant, but probably less so when you're poor. Cannes feels right.

I pull the backpack up on my shoulders, cross the huge road and set off towards the sea. It takes longer than I remembered to get there. At the Palais, I turn left automatically and start to walk along the Croisette, but it makes me feel weird because I've been here so many times as a kid and now everything has changed. The palm trees that line it, the welcoming bars and white-clothed tables between road and beach, the wild, addictive exclusivity of it all: none of that is for me, today. I head on to the beach by the Palais, kick my flip-flops off to walk over sand that is a bit too hot, then find a spot, put my backpack down and lean on it.

I look out to sea. It's calm out there, and there are three superyachts and loads of sailing boats out on the water. The swimming area is roped off to keep out the jellyfish, so it's full of people. Kids laughing, adults swimming, everyone having fun. I want to join them but I can't leave my bag. I tip my face up to the sun and wonder what to do. A sign says no one is allowed on the beach overnight, but I could sleep here anyway. I couldn't, though. I wouldn't be safe.

I stand up and pick up the bag, and then I walk around until my backpack starts to hurt and my head goes woozy. I realize that one of the hard things about being on the move all the time is that you have to have all your stuff with you, pulling on your shoulders and getting heavier every second. Also, if you live in a tent, you don't have a door to lock. I try to imagine myself pitching this tent on one of the Cannes beaches – a less obvious one than the one by the Palais – and I know I won't do it. Not just because Michaela might track me down, but because I'm scared.

I thought I was strong and brave, but I'm not. I walk around streets that I know, because I've come here on holiday all my life, and I feel the panic inside me growing and growing and growing. It's dark. I have nowhere to sleep.

I look up campsites.

I am gearing up to walk, but then the map offers me a local train to the campsite, so I take that instead. As I walk uphill from the station, the backpack yanks my shoulders and I think I'm going to die. I am so unfit, so hot and tired and hungry.

So scared.

Still, I get there, and, although the sign says they're full, I'm allowed to stay since I'm just one person with a tiny tent. They want ID, and photocopy my passport without noticing that I'm not the girl in the photo.

'How long do you want to stay?' says the woman. She's friendly. The campsite is cheap. There are discounts for a long stay.

How long do I want to stay?

I don't want to go to twenty-nine countries. I don't want to be constantly pulling my backpack on to a train, to be wondering where I'm sleeping that night. This campsite feels safe. No one knows I'm here. I speak French.

I take a deep breath.

'Three weeks.' I hand over a big wodge of my cash.

After half my time as Ruby, I'll either be ready to go somewhere else or I won't.

'Pitch three three four,' says the woman, and she gives me a flimsy map and marks the spot with a cross. She explains how to get there and draws a biro arrow that leads away from the nice views and the desirable pitches, and takes me behind the buildings and back and back until it stops at the far end of the far field, away from everything.

A Dutch family with four strapping kids (all younger, healthier, stronger than me) helps me fumble around in the dark to put up my tent, which is by far the smallest one I've ever seen. It says on the label that it's for two people, but I can barely squeeze in next to my backpack. Yannick added a sheet sleeping bag, and the Dutch people lend me a sleeping mat.

'Thank you,' I say to them. They are ideal neighbours. 'How long are you going to be here?'

'One week,' says the dad. 'Then we go round the coast to Italy.' In a week, I guess I'll buy my own sleeping mat.

I remember to tell them I'm called Ruby. The woman, Mila, brings me a metal cup of some kind of leafy herb tea, and even though I'd been eyeing up the wine box in the entrance to their tent I take it gratefully. It's a starry night. I am sitting outside my tent, drinking tea. I have made this happen.

There's one thing left inside the tent bag. I tip it up, expecting a rogue peg, and out falls a little bottle of vodka with a note stuck to it with an elastic band.

Tabbi! I wish you happy camping. Tell me when you're back in Avignon.

Yannick has added his phone number. I message him at once.

Thank you! Thank you for everything. My only friend in Avignon.

My only friend in France. My only friend.

We chat nonsense back and forth, and I feel like he's next to me again. I drink the neat vodka without realizing what I'm doing, and then it's gone and I wake up at 3 a.m., still dressed, half in a sleeping bag, my head fuzzy with drink.

I stand up and try to orientate myself. Which way was the toilet block? Or can I just do a wee on the grass? No. I am being sensible and mature here. I need to do this properly. I take Ruby's toiletries bag and use my phone torch to find the way.

Then I see that the sky is so beautiful that it's not even real. Above me, a billion gazillion stars twinkle away. I stand and stare for ages. I feel . . . calm?

I can do this. Maybe I can finally behave like a normal person, now I don't have to be Tabbi any more.

Or I could do the more fun thing. I could carry on getting through in the way I always do. Because, in the moment, that is easier.

7

A week later, I wake up in a tent full of sick, screaming because I'm in a car and I'm jamming on the brakes and I know this is it. I am done. It's over. My life as I've known it is over. It takes me a while to calm down, to remember first that this isn't real, and then that it is.

If my hair was long enough, there would be vomit in it, but luckily I haven't been wearing the wig. There's a stash of stinking empty bottles and cans around my head.

I can only remember bits of the past week, and I'd like to forget those too. I pissed off the lovely Dutch people so much that they complained to the campsite and they got moved to a fancier pitch, and I was nearly thrown out. On the upside, they told me to keep the camping mat. I found a shop in a backstreet that would sell me booze without ID. I have basically spent a week drinking because it stopped me thinking. Now, after that dream, my head is full of the thing I did – the thing that I have really run away from – and I'm trembling in fear about the fact that I might not be able to outrun it, to outdrink it, after all. So what do I do?

I know I've sent emails to Ruby. I can't look at them, so I just delete the lot from the sent folder and the inbox.

There's something else. Something happened last night. I try to focus. What was it? Something made me scared. It's another reason why this has to stop. I can't remember what it was. When I try to think of it, there's just black.

Having a blackout is not a good thing. It's scary. I curl up in my sicky sleeping bag and close my eyes. I'm shaking all over. I actually have to stop doing this now.

For the first time, a small part of me wishes I'd gone to the mountains.

Hours later, it's the smell that drives me out. That and the fact that I need a wee, and I might be about to be sick. I scramble out and breathe the air. It's nectar. There's a gentle breeze and it's fresh and glorious. I set off to the toilet block. I'm not wearing my wig. God knows what I look like.

I'm on the grass when a woman intercepts me. I try not to stop and talk. She grabs me with a hand on my arm and a surprisingly tight grip.

'*Excusez-moi?*' she says. 'Are you Ruby Robinson?'

I look at her. I don't say yes. She shrugs, already bored.

'There was a man looking for you,' she tells me, speaking French. 'I said I didn't know you. I thought that might be better. He didn't look friendly.'

I force a smile. A man? All I can think of is Jana's train-friend, for some reason, but it can't be him. He was interested but not *that* interested.

'Thank you,' I say.

'Be careful,' says the woman. 'I was like you once. You should take care of yourself.'

I have a flash of Ruby on the train. '*Maybe use a different name?*' she had said. She'd said her aunt and uncle might come looking for her. If they've tracked her down here, will we be busted? Can I just pretend to be someone else with the same name?

I turn back to the woman. 'How old was he?'

She shrugs. 'Like you? Maybe a few years older?'

Not the uncle. Not the train guy. Yannick? No, because he'd have texted. Nathan? The guy from Amsterdam? He's the only boy Ruby mentioned. It could have been him.

I thank the woman and run to the toilet block. I have a shower. I brush my teeth. I scrub myself until I can be fairly sure I smell OK. I dress in the cleanest clothes I've got. I put the wig on (not that it's a disguise any more) and set off, walking in the hot sun down into Cannes itself.

I have hardly any cash left. I'm shit with money and shit at life. No wonder they packed me off to get sorted out. I've never had to worry about cashflow because, through all the crap, I've always had a bank card that works, and, although the sensible part of me knows that it hasn't helped in any way, the rest of me knows that I threw my bank card into a bin to stop me using it and potentially ruining everything. I have never run out of money before: I've no idea what you do when that happens. What do you do when your bank card has gone to landfill, you've burned through your cash and you can't access your trust fund until August?

You confess. You go to Switzerland and switch back. You do exactly what you should have been doing all along and you accept the help. You accept all the help they'll give you. I'm destroying myself in a campsite in the French Riviera.

I could make some calls and hand myself in.

I'm walking around the backstreets near the beaches, the little pedestrian places that cars don't fit down (though mopeds do, as I find out from time to time). This is bad. This is really, really bad because I have no idea at all what it was I did during the blackout time and that's making me think of another blackout. Another thing that I did.

I'm close to rue Meynadier, the touristy shopping street, but walking along the smelly alleys where the bins are instead. I sit on a step and get my phone out. I google trains back to Zurich. I have to go back to Marseilles, back through Avignon, but I can do it. I could catch a train early tomorrow morning and be there nine hours later.

I know I have to. I tried running away, but everywhere I go, there I am. Changing my name doesn't stop me being Tabbi Courtenay, the girl who . . .

I look up, feeling eyes on me. There's a guy leaning against the wall, smoking and watching me. He wasn't there a minute ago. He's a man with scraggly hair and terrible skin, wearing chef's whites, and he seems to find the sight of me amusing. I like the distraction, and a man who hates me is catnip.

'Hi,' I say.

'Hi.' Somehow he manages to take the piss out of me using just one word.

I look at the door behind him. It's propped open. There's steam coming out and it smells amazing. I don't know I'm going to say it until I hear myself speaking my best French. Because I don't want to go to Switzerland if there's an alternative. Because this is a back alley where chefs go for smoking breaks and I like that.

'Is your restaurant looking for staff?'

He looks at me for a long time.

'You cook?'

'Not really.' There are things you can bullshit about, and this is not one of them. 'But I can wash up. I can talk to customers.'

'English?'

'Yeah. Actually, I'm Irish. I speak French, though.'

He nods. 'You do. Most of your compatriots don't. Yeah, they always need front-of-house staff. Bilingual is good. Do you do silver service?'

'I can learn.'

'What's under the wig?'

I pull it off. He laughs. I know my hair looks absolutely shit so I try to laugh too.

'I'll get a new wig,' I say, but he shakes his head. He looks at me hard.

'This is OK. You can tidy it up. It suits your face better than the purple.'

He points to the bags under his own eyes and I know what he's saying because I've been thinking it myself. He's saying that the purple of the wig brings out the purple in my hungover skin tone.

I laugh. 'I guess.'

He stubs his cigarette out on the wall behind him and drops the butt into a flowerpot that's full of them.

'OK then, miss,' he says when he's done. 'Come in and let's find out.'

I hang back for a second. Then I shove the wig into my bag and follow him.

The kitchen is a wild environment of steam and shouting and smells and heat. It appeals to something deep inside me. A boy a bit older than me is chopping a pile of onions. A woman is wiping the edges of some plates with a cloth. An older guy is throwing a burger into a pan. All of a sudden, I want to learn whatever it is that will let me stay here: these people all look really busy and I love that. I keep walking because my new friend hasn't slowed down. We go through a door and we're in the actual restaurant, which is much more orderly and smells of jasmine. After the kitchen, it's boring. The tables are mostly empty because it's the middle of the afternoon. It's more upscale than I expected.

My new friend just says, in French: 'Kevin, this young lady needs a job. She's bilingual. English-French.'

I want to say I'm actually not, but manage to stop myself just in time. I'm bilingual enough to be a waitress. I make myself do my biggest smile instead. *Please like me please like me please like me.*

Kevin looks at me for about five seconds then says: 'We

need a waitress, but a smart one. If you get a haircut, you can do a trial shift tomorrow.' I agree that I will.

Kevin is maybe thirty, but he has a young energy. I like him straight away. He's wearing a great cologne, and he has a face that looks as if it always smiles. I can imagine working with him. He's not the sort of adult who will tell me to pull my socks up and have a good think about what I've done. He's more the sort of person who might go out drinking with me.

'Deal,' I say. 'What time?'

'Eleven thirty. Lunch service starts at twelve.' He gives me another look. 'We'll give you a uniform. Wear black shoes. Smarten up or there's no chance.'

He walks away and I turn towards my new friend, whose name I never found out, but he's gone. I check the waiting staff. They are in pale chino-type trousers and light blue shirts with dark blue aprons. They look so posh and anonymous that I know that in my previous life I wouldn't have seen them at all. A girl with two French plaits gives me a grin as she walks past, carrying a tray of drinks. Another, with a jaw-length bob and a wine bucket, ignores me. I walk towards the front door, across the pale wood floor, through the clouds of jasmine and food and Chanel.

'Oh – excuse me?'

It's Kevin. I turn round, remembering to smile again.

'What's your name?'

'Ruby,' I say with a big smile. 'Ruby Robinson.'

Shit. I was meant to use a different surname. At least I didn't say Tabbi Courtenay.

'See you tomorrow, Ruby Robinson.' My new name sounds brilliant in French, though. Those two throaty 'r' sounds transform it.

I step out of the front door, feeling for a second like my old self. This place (I check its name: *Brise de Mer*) is exactly the kind of place we would have visited, back in the summers I spent here. Back in the days when I had my mum and my sister, and I was too young to have discovered what people seem to call 'substance abuse', but which I have always called 'fun', and I hadn't done anything bad at all.

It's a gorgeous-looking restaurant. It's clean and crisp, expensive but not outrageous, child friendly but only if they behave. Yeah. This is where we would have come. I look at the few pavement tables. They have pale blue tablecloths and padded chairs. Two women are sitting at one, drinking wine. I give them a *that looks nice* look and walk away.

So. I can postpone Zurich by one day at least. For now, I need to get my hair sorted out and find a pair of black shoes. I have small flip-flops and the pair of Converse. I would attempt to style out the Converse if they were black or even grey, but they're green so I can't. I have 120 euros left and that's it. I make a deal with myself: if I fuck up my trial shift, I'll use the train pass to get myself to where I should have been all along.

A men's haircut takes five minutes and costs eight euros. Everything about this is good. Unlike at my usual hairdresser's, you don't have to talk inanely about holidays for four hours, or wait it out in uncomfortable silence. You just sit there, they sort your hair out, you pay a fraction of the price you normally would (though a scary proportion of everything you own), and then you leave. You go into a clothes shop and grab some random things to try on just so you can look at yourself really hard in a mirror in private.

I have never looked like this before. It's weird, but the girl who looks out at me really isn't Tabbi Courtenay. She's not Ruby Robinson. This is some other version of me, a girl who has been there all along, but who hasn't been invented yet. A girl who will need a third name, who I should have named already. Maybe I don't want to be either of the girls I've been so far. The next one is going to be the best.

I have the very, very shortest of pixie cuts and I don't look so ill any more. My hair suits my face and my face suits the person I am now, because this person is trying really hard to avoid more trouble by saving herself. Her hangover is receding, and there's a weird freedom in knowing that it's the last one she's going to have for a while because there's no money left. Unlike the stupid purple-wig version, this one knows that it's serious. The barber found the longer strands of hair and coaxed them into symmetry and, weirdly, style. My bone structure actually looks quite nice and I can see that I've got a bit of a tan. This may be the very first time in my life that I've genuinely looked at myself and not felt disgusted. I'm not even wearing make-up, though I will tomorrow.

I don't try the clothes on. I just hand them back to the woman and leave the shop, smiling. On my way out, I swipe a pair of black pumps, size 38, from a basket by the door. For dinner, I have a slice and a half of pizza that some kid leaves on a paper plate at the campsite cafe. I hardly sleep. I miss alcohol. I am scared.

My trial shift goes OK – it goes well, actually. I model myself on good waiting staff I've encountered in the past. I smile. I take orders. I bring food out. I remember who orders what. I speak the right language to the right people. I manage not to take sips from people's drinks on the way to the tables. Everything about me is fake anyway, so it's easy enough to fake being a good waitress in such a way that the pretence becomes real, because actually what is the difference between someone pretending to be a good waitress and being one? Nothing.

'You're around for the rest of the summer?' says Kevin, before he offers me the job.

'Yeah.' Late August counts. 'I'll work as many shifts as you've got.'

'Then you're hired.' He grins. I grin back. I offer a handshake. He kisses me on each cheek. Kevin has no idea that he's just supplanted Yannick as my best friend.

For the next week, I work hard. It saves me completely. I don't drink. I can't get my tent properly clean, but I use the lingering smell as a reminder of what not to do. I have to fill in bank details for payment, but Kevin tells me I can get a thing called a Nickel card easily enough, and he's right. I get it at a tabac shop. I eat at work. I spend nothing and, after a week, I get paid and it feels like magic. I stay as far from the shop that I know will sell me booze as I possibly can. I realize that, screw them. I can manage without drinking, thanks. I can replace it with work, and keep myself busy and tired enough to feel that everything is OK. That I might be all right one day. I can keep myself busy enough and tired enough not to think about the bigger picture.

And then, when I'm starting to feel pleased with myself, Leonora walks through the door.

8

I'm having an excellent shift when it happens. I'm actually good at waitressing. One thing my weirdo boarding school upbringing has given me is an understanding of how to charm people and make them like you when you need to, so that if, for example, you haven't done your homework, or you've brought them the wrong starter, they will forgive you because you're sincerely and gorgeously sorry, and you make them feel good about themselves, in a way that is, for you, entirely self-serving.

The thing I'm coveting, though, is that kitchen, specifically the pastry section. It's run by Guillaume, the man I met on the back step, and I watch everything he does every moment I can. I love patisserie and I love the way he works. When I asked if I could help, he rolled his eyes and said no, he'd got me a job and what more did I want? But I'm still trying. I'm gonna keep asking until he gives me something to do, even if it's just weighing sugar or washing pots.

Everything in our dining room has that 'it's the seaside and you're on holiday!' aesthetic that you get in holiday rentals at home. It's a massive cliché, but everyone seems to go for it. The key thing is: it looks relaxed, but it's casual in the way a *Vogue* shoot is casual. Everything is where it is for a reason, and it all has to be done impeccably.

I arrive at work at five, and get straight to it. The moment I put on the chinos and blouse, I feel like a part of the *Brise de Mer* team and not the messed-up Tabbi-Ruby hybrid I actually am. We always have the dark apron over the top because those clothes are unforgiving, spills-wise. I change, check the bookings. Kevin says this entire week has been booked out for months, which means we have to spend a substantial amount of time turning away walk-ins. At six, when we open, the holidaymakers with little kids come in. Not the French ones (if they want to take their kids out, they just do it at the normal time and treat them like humans). It's the Anglo ones who come early so they can get the kids to bed and spend the rest of the night drinking on the balcony or whatever. I mean, fair enough.

The name Fairfax doesn't jump out. It doesn't even occur to me. It's not that unusual a name: I think nothing of it at all, beyond the fact that I'll be speaking English for that transaction. A German family comes in and their kids start throwing bread rolls at each other and I have to pretend it's fine while hoping they leave, or at least tell their children to stop.

Then the Fairfax party of three turns up. I go to greet them at their table, and there she is.

My sister.

She's the only person I love in the world, and she knows

what I've done and so of course she hates me, and in fact she already hated me before. Now I can't say a thing to her other than 'Welcome to the *Brise de Mer*.' I look at the man and the kid who are with her. I swerve my gaze away from eye contact.

I guess that man is her husband. They never invited me to the wedding, so I haven't met him. I was so upset when I realized she'd got married without me that I cried for hours and then went in search of self-destructive behaviour. He looks preppy, rich, dull. The kid, on the other hand, is interesting.

I didn't even know there was one. Seeing her, this little girl of about three, is a punch in the guts. She's cute. She looks like a dark-haired version of me. I remember that I, too, am now a dark-haired version of me.

Leo must be nearly thirty. I haven't seen her for six years, but I know her instantly. It's not even just what she looks like. It's the way she fills the room, the way she makes me feel. I look at her and I want to tell her everything. I want to get to know my niece. I want to cast off Ruby Robinson, surprisingly good waitress, and sit down and have dinner with them and say sorry. Sorry to Leo for the fact that I was a brat, and sorry in general for everything that came later. Instead I do some instant calculations. I feed it all into my brain and come up with this:

She won't notice me.

She last saw me when I was eleven. Rich people don't give a moment's thought to the waiting staff. She won't be expecting to see me. I may feel her Leo-ness enveloping me with everything I've ever missed, but she won't flicker because to her I'm a servant who brings dinner.

So all I can say is: 'Welcome to the *Brise de Mer*. I'm Ruby, and I'll be your waitress this evening. I'll give you a few moments to look at the menu, but meanwhile can I get you some drinks?'

I see Leo and Mr Leo looking at each other. I see them smiling and nodding. I crouch down to talk to my niece.

'Hi there,' I say. I look up at Leo. Our eyes meet. Something happens. It's a flicker. Then it's gone. 'We have a children's menu,' I say. 'It's on the back of the main one. Or of course your little girl is welcome to have anything from the main menu too.'

Leo is silent. Luckily Mr Leo steps in.

'I guess it's the French kids who go for the steak tartare and all that?' he says. American. Did I know that? I probably did. I was too busy being upset about not being asked to the wedding to care who the guy was.

I smile at him. 'It has been known,' I say. 'The main thing is, we always welcome families and so we'd love to accommodate your daughter with whatever she'd like to eat. Whether that's steak tartare or a bowl of pasta.'

They must have booked this place months ago. I homed in on a place where they'd reserved a table, and got myself a job. A classic Tabbi fuck-up.

The kid looks at me with a big smile. 'Please may can I have an ice cream?' she says. Cute.

'Arabella,' says her dad. Arabella: of course. 'Yes, darling, you can. But you need to have a main course first, baby.'

I am trying really hard not to look at Leo. My brother-in-law is doing all the talking. He orders a bottle of Chablis for them and an Orangina for Arabella, and I remember being Arabella, and teenage Leo taking me out for Orangina, and I want to cry. I'm waiting for Leo to say something that will unravel everything, but when she does speak she says: 'Better get some fizzy water too, yeah?'

And Mr Leo turns to me and says, 'Sure. The biggest bottle of sparkling water you've got. Badoit if you have it?'

'We certainly do,' I say. I go off to fetch their drinks and, when I'm far enough away, I turn and look back.

Leo is leaning forward, talking to Arabella. I stare for so long that, even though being good at my job is my absolute thing these days, I get a nudge from Kevin.

'Ruby?' he says. '*Ça va?*'

I wish I could hear what she was saying. I wonder how often, if ever, she thinks about me. She looked after me so much when I was small, and then she fell out with mum and I didn't see her any more. Because, even though I was eleven and had absolutely no idea what I was doing, I was the catalyst. I blew up our lives just by talking without thinking.

Then I blew everything up again even worse, but she might not know about that. I hope she doesn't know. I wish I could ask.

A huge part of me wants to run to her for a hug. Even though she didn't know she was doing it, she just broke our long silence by asking me for fizzy water. Though I think she said it more to her husband than to me.

'Sorry.' I force myself to focus. I hand the drinks order to Gilberto and go and fetch the starters for one of my other tables from the pass. As I'm unloading them on to a table of rich people, I realize what the stakes are here. I am supposed to be in Switzerland.

If Leo recognizes me, my life will be destroyed. If she tells anyone in the family that she saw me working as a waitress in Cannes, and if they believe her, it will all be over. They'll stop throwing money at me and smoothing things over.

There will be consequences.

I intercept Camille, one of the other waitresses. She's the one with plaits who smiled at me the first time I came here.

'Can you take over table seven?' I say it casually, as if it was a normal request even though it's not. She scoffs.

'No!' she says. 'I can't do that. I have enough in my head already. Why?'

'Someone I used to know.'

This interests her a bit. 'An enemy?' But sadly, she's not interested enough to change her mind. 'Good luck,' she says. 'You could always tamper with their food.'

I ask Kevin. He refuses too. I decide that, unless Leo takes a photo of me, I will deny it all.

Three minutes later, I pick up a tray that holds the Badoit and Orangina. I unload it on to their table, keeping my head down, and only Arabella watches me doing it. She's cute, with a blunt Amélie-style bob that makes her look like a tiny model.

80

'Thank you very much,' she says when I put her Orangina in front of her.

I imagine what this holiday is like for her. Sitting up at nice restaurants, long days on the beach. She'll spend some time in a kids' club, for sure. She has my old life, except she probably lives in Dubai. I hope they're not planning to send her to boarding school.

Neither adult thanks me for the water. I melt as far into the background as I can as I set up an ice bucket and bring the wine, at which point they become interested enough to engage.

I mutter, 'Who'd like to taste it?'

The husband says, 'Thanks,' and holds out his glass.

She doesn't look at me. *Thank God thank God thank God.* He tastes a bit and nods. I pour hers and then his. She says *merci* without looking at me (nevertheless! She spoke to me for the first time in years – that's weird) and I ask if they're ready to order starters. He orders for all three of them.

She's blanking me so much that it feels deliberate, though actually it might just be the way we were brought up. She knows you need to be polite to serving staff, but at the same time if she can get her husband to do it for her she'll go for that instead.

They stay for an hour and a half, and Arabella only gets handed an iPad an hour into it, which is pretty good going. Leo eats an artichoke salad followed by ceviche, and when the wine's gone she has a mint tea while Arabella and the husband (whose name, I finally overhear, is Graham) have ice cream and a cheeseboard respectively. Throughout the evening, Leo does not so much as glance my way, and I'm starting to think it might be OK.

I make a huge effort not to think about the last time we saw each other. I do everything I can to erase the memory of one of the few people I've ever loved saying: 'I hate you. I'm done here,' to me and my mum together. It was a plural *you*.

I obviously replay it in my head on a loop. Those words come again and again and again. They threaten to unlock other things, and I can't have that.

Long story short: I heard Leo and her then-boyfriend talking, and pieced together that she was pregnant. This was wildly exciting to me, and I didn't bother to focus on the details, specifically not the fact that she was keeping it secret and, most crucially of all, didn't want a baby.

I was so excited that when I heard my mother talking to her friend about someone else's baby I said, 'And Leo! I can't wait for Leo's baby!'

And the shit hit the fan for many reasons that I still don't understand properly. Leo did not end up with a baby, and she and our mum fell out so dramatically that she flounced out of our lives forever. Maybe that's where I got the idea from.

They have finished. Graham has paid their bill and added an excellent tip, so thank you, Graham. We've said thanks and goodbye. Arabella has said thank you directly to me, while looking me in the eye. She's a lovely kid: I am her aunt and I would like to be much more her aunt than I am right now. I would like to be the fun aunt, the one who buys presents and takes her to shows. I want to be everything to her.

I am not, of course, her aunt, because I am Ruby Robinson. I will, however, be her aunt again soon, and now that I know she exists I'm going to find them, when I'm ready, and sort this out.

This makes me gasp: it is the first time that I've been able to look at something I could do as Tabbi without dread. The first inkling of a positive future in my own skin.

They're standing up to leave, and I think I've got away with it. They're walking out of the door and I'm crossing the dining room with my hands full of ceviche for table five when Leo says something to Graham and turns back.

She walks towards me. I adjust my path to take me the long way to table five, to avoid her, but she's a missile. I deliver my starters, hoping the customers can't see my hands shaking. When it's all done, I turn round and she's right there. She's looking at me properly, up close.

'Tabbi,' she says. Her voice is low.

It takes everything I have to say: 'I'm sorry?'

'Tabitha – what are you doing here? Why are you working as a waitress and using a different name?'

Her voice. *Her voice.* She was my mother, really. She's the only person who's ever properly loved me, and I threw it back in her face without knowing what I was doing when I was too young to realize that life was complicated. Her voice is pulling me back through the years and for a second I want to hug her. I make myself step back. I step back again and Camille almost walks into me. Some of the drinks on her tray slop over the edges. It jolts me back into my professional self.

'Oh God,' I say. 'Sorry.'

I touch my necklace. I got it too recently for Leo to know it, but I tuck it into my shirt anyway. I take a deep breath and turn back to her.

'I'm afraid I don't know what you're talking about.' I remember to change my voice a bit. 'Sorry, madam. Do I remind you of someone? They do say that everyone has a doppelgänger.' I start to turn away, but she stops me. She actually touches my arm.

'Oh, come off it, Tabs. I'd know you anywhere. Don't be stupid. I know what you did. You're meant to be in some rehab place. How did you get away? And what are you doing here?'

I keep my face as impassive as I can. *Shit shit shit*.

Rehab. She said it. She said the word I've been avoiding, even in my own head. I try to breathe.

I cannot lose this job.

'Sorry, madam. I wish I could help.' Must not crack.

She stares at me. I force myself to return her gaze with what I'm hoping is a professional not-bothered look. I feel a little twitch in my face. I use all my powers to make myself believe that she's just another customer and look at her politely. I can't have her telling anyone that she saw me here.

I hate that she knows what I did.

I hate that she knows where I should be this summer.

I look away.

'I'm sorry. You'll have to excuse me.'

More heavy seconds tick by.

'Right,' she says. 'Fine. Look, Tabbi – I don't get this. You should be . . .' She stops. 'Wherever they were sending you. But message me, OK? Leonora underscore FF on Insta.'

Then she turns and walks out. I get through the rest of my shift because I have to. I take the little train home, looking over my shoulder. I start to realize that what I've done here might be more serious than switching places with a stranger for a laugh. There could be consequences. If I'm caught, there will definitely be consequences. Huge ones.

Massive. Unthinkable.

Later, I lie in my tent, looking up at the canvas. Did I get away with that? I mean, she didn't believe I was Ruby. That's for sure. She knows what I did. She said so. She knows where I'm meant to be, so what will she do now?

I look up her Instagram immediately. I stare at photos of bright sun and expat life. She has over three thousand followers so I figure she won't notice one more. I set up a fake account, naming it cherries and a bunch of numbers because the dessert special at work today was a cherry clafoutis. I follow her, and then follow all the suggested similar accounts too for camouflage, and mute everyone but Leo. My thumb hovers over the message icon.

Could I?

A day goes by and no one comes for me. Maybe Leo has convinced herself that it really was a doppelgänger called Ruby. Maybe she doesn't care enough to do anything. Maybe she makes a point of not doing to me what I did to her (ruining everything by telling on me). I don't know, but a day goes by, and another and another, and no one comes to drag me to Switzerland, or home to face some real consequences.

Although I want to think that this means I've got away with it, I'm pretty sure it actually doesn't, because at that point I start to realize someone is following me.

9

It's a warm night, cloudier than usual, and I'm walking away from the tourist centre of everything to the station for the last train to the campsite. Usually I enjoy the journey home. I like crossing the massive road to Cannes station. I like riding the nearly empty train. I like walking up the hill to the campsite. However, today I'm looking over my shoulder every few seconds, and have been ever since I caught sight of someone moving quickly away as I stepped out of the toilet block hours ago, this morning. There was a flash of movement, and then there was nothing. All my senses sprang into action. My lizard brain, if that's really a thing, has been telling me ever since that someone is following me.

I keep seeing signs. Little things. I sense movement behind me. I feel eyes on me. When I look round, there's nothing. Am I paranoid?

When I get on the train, no one else gets into my carriage. But that doesn't mean anything. There were others on the platform. I sit upstairs (I will always sit upstairs on a train if I have the chance). The other people up here are just two women, and an older man. Is it him? I walk to the end of the carriage, but there's just a guy in glasses standing by the door, looking at his phone. I go back to my seat. I'm knackered and I want to lie in my tent, but if someone is following me I don't want to lead them directly to my flimsy home. Who would Leo have told about me? She doesn't speak to our mother any more than I do, and she has no relationship with my dad, since he was just her stepdad for a few years ages ago. Maybe she's hired someone to follow me. She could have spoken to the place in Switzerland, though they would surely have told her Tabbi Courtenay is present and correct, because if Ruby had been busted I'd know.

Unless I didn't. I run it through in my head. Ruby gets there, finds that I've set her up, starts saying she's not Tabbi Courtenay. They don't believe her and roll their eyes at spoiled little rich girls and the things they say. Then, when a call comes in telling them that Tabbi has been sighted in Cannes, they think again.

No. That doesn't lead to me being followed. It leads to someone going to the restaurant and asking for me. Anyone Leo sent would find me at the *Brise de Mer*, not the toilet block.

Two stops later, I get off the train. I set off up the hill, by the light of the street lamps. I keep spinning around, but there's no one behind me. Still, there are lots of patches of darkness. There's movement on the other side of the street. When a man comes out of a house with a small dog on a lead, I almost scream.

At the campsite I buy a pizza and Coke and take it to my tent. I'm jumpy when I head out to the toilet block. I cannot be found because I would be in massive shit.

If they caught me now, they would send me to prison.

Fuck.

I can't sleep so I get up early and leave the campsite, with my work stuff and beach stuff in my bag. Luckily the restaurant has a laundry service that deals with all the uniforms so I just have to present myself at eleven with black shoes. Miraculously, my hair always looks fine because it's so short, and if I'd known a cheap, short haircut would be just as good as a 200-quid one then I'd have spent a *lot* less time bored in salons.

I walk into town and down to the beach. It's still early and the beach has rake lines on it. There are very few people here: a woman with a small child (not Leo, not Arabella). An older couple. A man reading a book. None of them looks interested in me. I change into Ruby's bikini. It's a bit loose, but even if it fell right off I'd just look like half the other women round here.

The water is warm and gentle and perfect. It comforts me. I swim out and out and out from the sandy shore and flip over on to my back. At least if someone follows me out here, I'll see them.

The sky is pale blue and perfectly clear. This really is a glorious place. I like my job. It keeps me too busy to drink or think. I float on my back and try to talk myself round. There's probably no one tailing me. I wish for a moment that a current would carry me away, out to sea, and deposit me on some other beach like a piece of driftwood.

It's not Leo. It's not anyone else either. It's me. The thing I did. The reason I would be in so much shit if they found me here. The thing I'm running from. It's catching up.

And I don't think I can bear it.

I work hard all day. Whenever there's a quiet moment, I find something to keep me busy. I polish already shiny knives. I wipe plates that don't need wiping. I triple-check the evening's bookings. I am the friendliest waitress, the fastest and the most efficient. I focus completely on being Ruby Robinson because that way I don't have to be Tabbi Courtenay.

Then I have to leave. I walk back through the old town with Kevin, trying hard not to spin round and see who's behind us, and then we get to the turning where I go left to the station and he carries straight on.

'Sure you don't want to come for a drink?' he says (I knew he'd be this guy right from our first meeting). I shake my head.

'I don't drink.' I say it firmly. It takes willpower.

'Of course. Well, let's at least get you that room,' he says, kissing me on each cheek.

'I've paid for the campsite,' I remind him.

'Until next week! Then you must move. You can't live in a tent. We don't pay that badly. Come look at the room in my neighbour's place.'

'Deal,' I say.

For a moment, I am about to ask if I can go with him right now, if I can stay on his sofa, if his neighbour might let me take the place instantly, at midnight with none of my stuff. There's no point asking him to walk me miles out of his way to the campsite because I sleep in a tent: I can't lock myself away.

There are numerous people who lie on the ground all around me. If I shouted, probably a hundred people would hear and statistically they can't all be arseholes who roll over and ignore the commotion. That's my security. It's pretty shaky.

'See if I can look at it tomorrow,' I say.

I walk into the campsite, reminding myself that no one real is following me, that it's the metaphorical thing that's trying to catch up and that I'm not going to let it. That's what I think, right up until someone grabs my arm and says, 'You're Ruby Robinson.'

The shock and adrenaline jolts me back into the moment, and all thoughts of metaphors and sleep are gone. Everything vanishes apart from the fact that a man is holding me by the arm and telling me I'm . . .

Ruby Robinson.

He's not calling me Tabitha. *Thank God thank God thank God.*

'Yes.' I say it fast, my voice coming out breathy. 'Yes. I'm Ruby Robinson.' If I'm Ruby, nothing terrible can happen. Ruby is straightforward, innocent.

'Finally,' he says.

I tug my arm away, and he lets go.

'Sorry to grab you,' he says. 'Don't run, Ruby. Just talk to me.'

I raise my hands in surrender and take a step back, and another. 'What do you want?'

Can't be the Amsterdam boyfriend. Can't be her family.

'You really are Ruby Robinson?'

Now that my heart rate is calming a little, I'm able to notice things. He has an English accent. He is about my age, wearing thick-framed glasses. I've seen him before.

'You followed me yesterday! You were on the train last night. You've been following me for . . . a while?'

'Yeah,' he says.

He looks awkward. Sweaty. Stressed. He's much taller than me. He takes a step so he's standing too close again. I edge away. He edges towards me, still looming. I look around. Where are one thousand other campers when you need them?

'Ruby – I guess you probably know this already, but I'm Tom O'Neill.'

He looks at me, expectant. His name is meant to mean something. Who's Tom O'Neill? Who is he to Ruby? She definitely didn't mention him. He's not bad-looking, but he can't be her ex because, if he was, he wouldn't think I was Ruby.

How did he know that Ruby was in Cannes?

I look him in the eye. He's looking right back at me.

'Tom O'Neill,' I echo.

'I know you got my emails. My grandmother is Maria.'

It hangs there. I'm not sure how to react, so I say nothing. How the hell is his grandmother a part of this? His *grandmother*?

'You're a stalker,' I say, going on the offensive, 'and I could go to the police.'

He laughs. 'The police! Amazing. OK, let's do that, shall we?'

I cannot, of course, have the police anywhere near me. And somehow he knows it. I look at him for a bit, and then I turn and walk off. He walks with me. I take some random paths between caravans and we carry on in silence until he says, 'I know where your tent is. You don't need to shake me off.'

All the same, I head to the closed cafe by the empty pool and we sit on the chairs outside. Mine is metal and its legs are different lengths so it rocks back and forth on the gravelly ground as I shift my weight. I listen to the cicadas and wait for him to speak. He doesn't.

'What do you want from me?'

He laughs at that, but not in a *you're funny* way.

'What do you think, Ruby?'

I shrug.

'Money,' he says, and at first I'm so relieved that I want to laugh out loud. So Ruby has borrowed money from someone's gran, and gone travelling. I don't have access to cash right now, but I will be able to sort this out. It'll make me feel good. Like karma.

'OK,' I say. 'How much?'

'You know how much,' he says. I wait it out, and he

huffs and says: 'All her savings. You owe my grandma thirty grand, Ruby Robinson. And I'm not going to leave you alone until we get it back.'

I email Ruby that night. Huddled in my tent, just me, the weird tent-filtered light and the faintly lingering smell of vomit.

> Ruby, I know you won't have your phone yet, probably, but when you get this PLEASE fill me in. A guy called Tom O'Neill has turned up and wants me to give him £30k. What? Why do you owe him that? He says his grandmother is Maria which I guess will mean something to you. He's not going to leave me alone until I give it to him. Please tell me what to do. Tell me what it's all about.

I send it, and I figure that now that she's been there for a few weeks the phones and internet rules might be relaxed. I keep checking for a reply, but nothing comes.

10

The next morning I wake covered in sweat, surprised that I've slept at all. Somewhere, across the field, there's the sound of a small child grumbling and the soothing tone of a mother saying whatever nice mothers say. I wouldn't know.

I poke my head out and breathe in the fresh air. It's weird how quickly I've got used to living like this: I had never slept in a tent in my life before and now I can hardly imagine a bed, floorboards, a door. Rooms. Indoor life. It feels strange and unlikely. I'm out of the tent, washbag in hand, breathing that dewy morning air, when I see that he's sitting on a fold-up chair behind the tent, waiting for me.

'Fucksake,' I say. I start walking to the toilet block, and he walks alongside me.

There are cars next to massive house-tents. There are bikes and surfboards. Mats that people leave outside overnight because they know it's not going to rain. Washing hanging on tent-ropes. Faint snoring. A lingering smell of suncream. The whole place is suffused with the essence of holiday.

All I have to do is scream. But I can't. I can't draw attention to myself, and to the question of whether I am, in fact, Ruby Robinson.

'You coming into the toilet with me?' I say without looking at him. 'Squeeze into the cubicle if you want.'

'Nah.' He takes the question seriously. 'I'll wait outside.'

'Let's go for a coffee,' I say when I come out, because I know when I'm defeated. 'You can tell me everything.'

We buy coffees from the site cafe, each paying for our own, and sit on a step, side by side. He takes a deep breath and launches into a speech.

'This isn't going to go away,' he says. 'I know to you she was just a gullible person on the internet. I'm sure you think that if she was stupid enough to go along with it she deserved to be parted from her money. But look – I wanted to make this real to you and so I've brought some photos. I'll do whatever I have to do, to get you to pay the money back.'

'To your grandmother?'

He sighs, irritated.

'Yes. Again – you know that. To Maria O'Neill, my grandma. Who has sent you over thirty grand because she believed you were an American soldier who wanted to marry her and yeah, I know that's stupid, but she's not stupid. She's naive, and she's lonely, and she doesn't necessarily *get* the internet. Now she's in deep shit, and I just need the money and then it can all be over. I mean, I can see that you've spent it – on the one hand, you're in the South of France, but on the other you live in a tent and work all hours. Which tells me the splurging has been done. But you have to get it for her, Ruby. This is an elderly lady who's destitute because you've stolen everything she had. Do I need to tell that restaurant? Because I don't believe you're just working a minimum-wage job. You have to be grifting. Are you stealing from them too?'

I feel sick.

'I didn't do any of that,' I manage to say.

It's true, but also, clearly, not. Because I totally believe him that Ruby did this. A part of me is impressed – was she playing me on the train, acting so ditsy and innocent? Who manipulated who? – but this is scary shit. That's too much money.

'An American soldier?'

He sighs, though he's got an alert eye on me the whole time. I look down at my coffee. It's a crap campsite coffee, but it feels like life support. I cup it in my hands.

'She didn't tell any of the family for ages and when she did she was in pieces. Our granddad died five years ago, and she's seventy-three and yeah, I guess more lonely than my mum realized. When we found out what had happened, we thought it must have been one of those – you know – Nigerian prince type things. But I have a friend at uni who's amazing at this stuff and together we traced you because . . . well, you had that moment of humanity, I guess, and . . . yeah, here you are. Younger than me. A kid.'

'OK.' I just want him to keep going, find out what I can. What was the *moment of humanity*?

'So, yeah, at that point we thought the fact that you

were young would make it easy. We thought you'd got in over your head trying something out, probably with friends. As you know, we messaged you and, every time we did, you blocked us. Then we found where we thought you lived. Some woman answered the door and said you weren't her daughter. She said you'd lived there for a bit, but now you were travelling. And . . . here we are.'

'She said I'd lived there for a bit?'

I try to square this with Ruby's story of her aunt and uncle. I run through what she told me. Her mother had her as a teenager, and she lived with her grandparents. They both died when she was nine (I didn't ask how and I wish I had, because now it feels like a convenient story), and she had to go and live with an aunt and uncle who didn't want her. That was what she said.

But from what this guy says it seems as if she just stayed with some people as a lodger. I guess she spun me a load of bollocks. Who even is Ruby?

I am running through the options, as fast as I can.

One: convince him that I'm not Ruby, but in a way that doesn't bring this whole scam crashing down. I have to make him believe that he's got the wrong girl, but without unravelling who I really am and why I'm here. Because no one can know that Tabbi Courtenay is not up a mountain in Switzerland.

Two: keep him off my back for a few more weeks, and then hand the whole issue back to Ruby. That's plan A, though it feels like a very long time.

Three: I somehow access enough money from home

to make him go away. Not thirty grand, but a couple to show willing. But I can't be in touch with home, and I can't access money because that takes me back to point one.

I feel cold all over. What do I do? I need to stop him coming after me for Ruby's shit, but without telling him anything about myself. I can't give a stranger the information that would blow my life into pieces and send me to . . . to . . .

I force myself to articulate the word in my head. *Prison*.

Unfortunately, I also say it out loud. Quietly, but he hears it, or reads my lips.

'It won't come to that.' His voice is gentler now. 'Just give us back the money. You won't go to prison. Honestly – in the eyes of the law, it's her fault. She sent you the money herself. It's not like you've killed anyone.'

I look away.

Deep breath. Focus on the problem in front of me. Get rid of this guy.

I glance at him and look away. He's actually cute, in a nerdy way. He hates me and he holds the power to destroy me: that's probably why I'm instantly attracted to him.

Ruby could access my cash. She has my bank card. If I told her how, she could get out a tiny bit of money, to buy her the time to get away from this guy again. And I do owe her. I've been living her summer of freedom while she's locked away for me.

This isn't her summer of freedom, though, is it? She was leaving out as much of her story as I was.

I turn to him.

'Look,' I say. 'It's complicated, but I'm not the person you're looking for. But I know who she is and I know exactly where she is.' He is looking sceptical so I carry on talking, as fast as I can. 'I can get you a bit of money. Because I feel bad for your grandmother. I can get you – fifteen hundred.'

He sighs. He looks up. 'Fifteen hundred? Ruby – you are exactly the person I'm looking for and it's pretty crap to say you're not. But yeah, fifteen hundred is a start. Five per cent. I'll take it. Look, this is my nan.'

He is holding out some pieces of paper. I realize they are actual photos, old-style ones with white around the edges. He's printed out real photographs to try to make Ruby feel bad.

I glance at them quickly and then away. Oldish woman, with a nice smile. In one of them, she's holding a baby. She's not even dressed like an old person: she's in an orange jumper that I might actually consider wearing, though probably only if I was going to a Scooby Doo-themed party.

I hand them back. 'She looks nice.'

'Yeah, too nice. I know you've seen her before. I know she sent you pictures like these, and in exchange you sent her photos of an American soldier that, when we reverse image searched, came up under the image category "handsome older US serviceman".'

Ruby – for fuck's sake. I can see the allure in a romance scam, but seriously? Conning a seventy-three-year-old lady into destitution is not cool. There are plenty of people with too much money, and this woman clearly wasn't one of them. Though who am I, really, to cast moral judgements on anyone?

'I'll get two grand,' I say. 'But the real Ruby's gonna have to access it for me.'

'Sure. Let "the real Ruby" do that.' His voice is flat. I admit it does sound weak. 'So when will you have the cash?'

I pause. What's the longest I can say? 'Give me a week.' He gives a little nod.

'How did you find me?' I say before I go.

He gives a little smile. 'Obviously I can't tell you that. Croissant?'

I shake my head and stand up. I need to go to work.

11

After that, Tom O'Neill is always there. He doesn't trust me not to leave the campsite and shake him off, and he's right not to. After work I go to look at Kevin's neighbour's room (it's shabby with a view of bins, but closer to the town and a huge upgrade from the tent), but when I leave the building Tom O'Neill is in the doorway opposite so I decide I might as well save the money and stay on the campsite.

On the way home from an early shift the next day, I snap. The afternoon light is golden and buttery, the shadows long. The streets are busy with people heading out to eat and drink. I finished work at six and I should have a perfect evening ahead.

But I haven't because Ruby's shit has followed me here. Is following me now.

I turn and walk right up to him.

'If you're so worried about your grandma,' I say, 'have her move in with you. Maybe if your family had taken more notice of her she wouldn't have got caught up with some scammy soldier.'

I don't even feel bad when I see that this has hit home. He takes a step back. Then his face changes and he starts swearing at me. Then he's shouting. It's the first time I have seen him losing control. The other people, in their holiday clothes and clouds of sunscreen, turn round and make disapproving faces.

I watch him with interest. How did he trace me here? It can only be through the train pass. That's the only thing there is. But it's all on my phone: the only time I've been into a ticket office was to make reservations I didn't even use.

I could make him go away if I had any spare money. If Leo had arrived after Tom, I'd have done things differently. I imagine Ruby's phone, confiscated, and I know that it's switched off and that's why she hasn't read anything in our Gmail account, but I could really do with her input right now.

I wonder what Tom will do when I don't come up with any cash. He's travelled all the way here. I guess he has family backing. There must be a next stage.

Every time I tell him I'm not Ruby, he asks who I am in that case. It's a reasonable question and one I can't answer. I flash, again, to the moment Ruby told me to use a different name just in case. *This* is what she was worried about. I wish I'd remembered to do it.

The only other person I can think of is Leo. If I could find her, I could admit that she was right and ask her for help. Could I do that? Would she immediately dob me in? It might be a risk I have to take. A last resort.

She gave me her Instagram, and I go straight to it, but it's not there any more. Her account has gone. There is no Leonora underscore FF. I know it was there. I saw it. I followed it. I set up an account specifically to follow it and now she's deleted it. Why? No one deletes their Insta on a whim. Do they? I look for her old account, the one I used to follow, but that's not there either.

When we came on holiday here, we used to stay for weeks. She's probably still in town. I need to find her.

Where to start? On our summer trips we never went near a campsite. I know Leo had a favourite ice-cream shop, Vilfeu just off the Croisette. I don't really ever go to the Croisette: it's not on my way to work or the station, and all that money and luxury feels a bit weird these days. But it's where I'll find my sister. She will one hundred per cent have been to Vilfeu with Arabella, but I can't stand outside an ice-cream shop all day in case she comes back because I have a job. Admittedly, though, the idea of Tom watching me watching the ice-cream shop is a bit funny.

I have to work out where she's staying.

Where did we stay before? Sometimes hotels, sometimes apartments. Always on or near the Croisette. The hotel I remember best was the Carlton. I walk there. I pass the Palais des Festivals, past a queue of people waiting to take photos on a fake red carpet with a backdrop of cardboard celebs. I pause to look at the handprints embedded in the pavements. We used to love these. Mine were always so much smaller than these prints. I walk past Julie Andrews. Catherine Deneuve. I crouch down and find that now, my hands are exactly the same size as Meg Ryan's . . .

Focus!

This bit of seafront is heady and gorgeous. I'm not the only one walking tonight. There are crowds of us promenading up and down. The ratio of curious regular people (now including me) to people who drip money from every pore (Leo) is strangely large. I never noticed all the normal people before.

I look at everyone I pass. None of them are my sister. When I get to the Carlton, a huge pale stone hotel that looks as if it could be made of sugar, I walk straight in. I don't allow myself to hesitate, to wonder whether I still belong. I just march past the doorman, who greets me impeccably.

God, I had forgotten the smell of these places. Somehow exactly the same, no matter where in the world you are. The smell of money, basically. It's not the same at the restaurant because there it's garlic and perfume. Here it's luggage and cash.

I flip back into being Tabbi Courtenay and tell myself that it doesn't matter that I'm wearing a cheap sundress with garish flowers on it if I'm in rich-person mode. I go straight to the loos and wash my hands and face in expensive handwash to give me a smell of belonging, then stride up to the reception desk.

'Hi,' I say in French. I channel supreme confidence. 'I'm supposed to be meeting my sister? She's staying here. Could I leave a message?'

'Of course,' says the receptionist, giving me a tight smile. 'What's her name?'

'Leonora Fairfax.' Every syllable feels weird coming out

of my mouth. 'With her husband Graham, and their little girl?'

She types on the computer. 'Are you sure she's staying here? I can't find the name.'

I fake a *doh* moment. 'Actually it might be the Marriott. Sorry!'

I feel her eyes on me as I walk away. I do the same at the Marriott and all the other fancy hotels along the seafront, and she's not at any of them.

'Where do all these people stay?' I ask Kevin in the lull between lunch and evening service, the next day.

He shrugs. 'Everywhere.' The thing I like about Kevin – one of the many things – is that he'll talk happily about any random thing without asking why. 'Some own houses down here. Some are in holiday rentals. You have no idea how much they pay for that stuff! And hotels – loads are in hotels.' He stops. Laughs. 'That is the least informative answer! I mean, you know this, right? Those are all the accommodation options.'

'Right. It's just – there was a family that came in the other day. The woman thought she knew me? I'm just thinking, maybe I do know her. She might be a friend of my sister's. I wondered if I could find her and ask.'

He shrugs, considering my story (momentous to me) to be underwhelming.

'Could be anywhere. Apart from where you or I live, of course.' He pauses. 'Easiest thing would be to look up the booking.'

'That can't be allowed!'

'Correct.'

Then a family walks in, asking if we can get them a table for ten tomorrow night. We definitely can't, but Kevin logs on to the booking system and gives every impression of trying really hard to work something out. He takes their number in case of cancellation.

Later, I pull a phone number off Graham Fairfax's booking. When I have a break, I go out to the back alley, the place where I first met Guillaume, and sit on the kitchen step. I start to compose a message. It takes my whole break to get it right and when I've finished it just says:

> Hi Graham. Sorry to message out of the blue, but I'm trying to reach Leonora. Could you pass on a message to her? My name's Ruby and we spoke in Cannes recently. If she could contact me on this number, it would be great. Thank you!

I send it. Two minutes later, I have to go back to work, but the next time I check my phone, hours later, there's no reply.

Tom is relentless. I start to feel I would be better off locked into a room in Switzerland. He's with me all the time, the devil on my shoulder. I wish I could tell him the truth, but he'd turn up where Ruby is and do his best to blow everything wide open.

On Friday, I sit outside my tent and beckon him over. He comes and sits beside me. It actually feels quite nice to be next to him. He's much taller than me. He's a total geek, but I grudgingly respect what he's doing for his grandmother. Also, I realize he smells nice.

'I got my tip money today,' I say. 'Here. Have it all.'

I hand it over. It's nearly three hundred euros, which is a lot of money, but he sighs.

'Ruby,' he says. 'This is one per cent of what you owe us. One per cent! Do you know what it's costing me to be here?'

I shake my head. I have no idea how the economics of Tom's trip work out. He sees me wanting to ask and answers before I say anything.

'My parents feel responsible for Grandma getting into this. They bought my rail pass. I'm working, believe it or not, when I'm not on your tail. Online stuff. Computer things. Flexibly.'

'That's why you have your phone in your hand all the time.'

'When you're at work, or asleep. That's when I get on with it.'

I nod. He is single-minded. Impressive. Out to right a wrong. I actually like this guy: it's a shame he has to hate me forever for something I didn't even do.

The next morning he follows me into town and to the beach. I sit on the sand. He does too. We both lean back on our hands. I put sunscreen on my face and pass the bottle to him. He takes it and does the same, pushing his glasses up on to his head. It looks strange when he does that. His face is different, with little dents on either side of his nose. I look out at the water. It's perfectly flat, perfectly blue. Glimmering in the sun.

Tom says: 'It's the weekend. If you don't come up with the rest of that two grand, it's going to have to be plan B. Sorry.'

'What's plan B?'

He looks pained.

'We already tried the police,' he says. 'And they won't do anything because she made the transfer herself. So that just leaves the *Daily Mail*.'

He might as well have punched me in the head. Of course the *Daily Mail* would go for this. It's the story with everything. Two crimes and an identity switch. The moment anyone prints my photo it's game over. The real story, all over the papers. My life ruined forever. Prison wouldn't even be the worst of it: the worst of it would be the shame. The fact that, for the rest of my life, everyone would know not only what I did (and why), but that I sent someone else to take the consequences and ran away to the South of France where I tumbled head first into somebody else's crime.

It would prove I'm not Ruby, but at the expense of everything else. Everything. The fact is: I didn't steal thirty grand from this man's gran. I did something worse. So I'll deal with Ruby's shit instead of my own. I chose to switch lives with her. I did. I clearly remember doing it.

It's been bruising and weird, but I love my job, and now, for the first time in my life, there's something I want to do. I want to learn patisserie. I want to come back to France and learn it properly. I could go to Cordon Bleu or whatever people do, or I could just learn on the job with someone like Guillaume.

I close my eyes. I could sleep here on the sand. It's more comfy than my tent.

It's hard, but working makes me feel better than drinking ever did. I did not expect this. I'm slowly suspecting that, luckily for me, I'm not actually addicted to anything. I was addicted to the feeling it gave me, the escape from my reality, and maybe I can make a better reality that I don't need to escape. When I do my job well, I feel brilliant. When it goes badly, I have friends and colleagues to share the pain. Friends. Colleagues. Things that regular people have: the parts of my life that have almost always been missing. I turn down drinks all the time and – newsflash – no one cares. They know I don't drink and they don't ask why.

All I need to do is get rid of Tom.

And then I open my eyes and sit up. I can get rid of Tom. I have a train ticket that will take me all the way across the continent, to anywhere I want to go, indefinitely, and I can use it to run down the clock until I can hand Ruby's mess back to her. I can get away from here and go somewhere new, get another job, settle in another place. I still have three weeks.

It's the scariest thought I've ever had. My breathing is coming weirdly because I know for certain that I need to do it. I can't let Tom expose me. I can't. Leo seems to have vanished. Graham hasn't answered, and Ruby's not online, and I have no backup.

Tom sits up too. He hates me to do anything without him. 'What?' he says.

I look at him. I look at him for a long time.

'Nothing,' I say.

I'll go tomorrow.

'I need a week off,' I tell Kevin that afternoon. 'Sorry. Family stuff. Emergency. I have to go tomorrow.'

Kevin's not happy, but he huffs and gets to work with rotas. These things happen and he will sort it out. When things are quiet before evening service, I go and stand next to Guillaume and watch what he's doing. He's pouring cream from a measuring jug into the bowl of a stand mixer.

'Do you think I could do this?' I say. 'For a job?'

Another chef swings past, overhearing. 'Yes! Join us in the kitchen,' she says. She's gone before I can reply.

Guillaume rolls his eyes. 'Sure,' he says. 'It's not a superpower, Ruby. It's about hard work. Can you do that?'

Well – no. I couldn't until recently. Now, though –

'Yes,' I say.

'The thing with pastry,' he says, turning the mixer on and raising his voice, 'is that people never realize it's the least creative part of cooking. These guys –' he gestures across the kitchen – 'they get a delivery of lovely fish. Invent a new dish to showcase the lovely fish. Write it on the specials board. Make up some gel or something to have with it. The right sauce. They're creating new dishes all the time.

Even a dish on the menu can change in its presentation, in the cooking of the different elements, from one night to the next. And this –' He gestures at his own station. 'This is the opposite. If someone orders an *île flottante*, they know exactly what they're going to get, and if it's different, they're disappointed. And, believe me, they won't hesitate to tell you so. It's about precision. It's about getting every single bit exactly right, and doing it over and over again.'

'That's kind of nice, isn't it?' I say. 'Reassuring.'

He nods, with half a smile. 'If you're really interested? Then why not? You've done well on front of house. Work the summer in your current role because Kevin would kill me if I poached his best waitress, even when I was the one who introduced her, but after that perhaps we could take you on as an apprentice. You're Irish, yes?' I nod. '*Voilà*. No Brexit worries.'

'Thank you,' I say. I am so desperate for this to be real that it's making me want to cry. He pats my shoulder.

'I know you're going away, but when you're back come in early before a shift and help me out.'

I finish work early again. I hug everyone goodbye and say I'll see them a week on Monday. I don't think I actually will, but I want to leave things open. I have to believe that it could happen.

Kevin walks with me to the station and hugs me goodbye.

'I hope everything's OK,' he says. 'With your family?'

'It will be.' I hug him back and turn away, feeling like crap. As I walk off, I really hope he's not going to shout something after me. Something about my week off, something audible to a lurking Tom who speaks enough French for that.

He doesn't.

'Do you know how much I hate doing this?' Tom steps on to the train beside me. We walk upstairs together and sit opposite each other, on a table by the window. 'Being this guy, I mean. Thinking about you all the time, knowing where you are all the time? Just stuck in this thing where I ask you for thirty grand and you don't give it to me.'

'Twenty-nine point seven,' I say. He doesn't bother to answer. We travel these two stops all the time. It takes ten minutes. Soon we're stepping off the train and walking up the hill towards the campsite.

'Want a night off?' Why do I say that? I'm as surprised as he is.

He looks down, half frowning. 'A night off?'

I inhale a deep breath of warm air. The stars are out above us. The night is perfect, and, although I sincerely hope Tom doesn't know it, it's my last night in town. The thought of heading back into the unknown, with no one on my side, is making my breathing go weird.

'Like the soldiers in the trenches at Christmas. A one-night-only truce. I mean, not one night . . .' I trail off. That sounded all wrong.

He doesn't reply for ages. When he does, he says, 'You mean that football game?'

I nod. We turn into the campsite. Sounds of birds, cicadas. Someone laughing. A baby, far away. We're almost at the back field, the cheap field where both our tents are located, before he replies.

'Sure,' he says. 'OK. One night off. Why not? It would be great to talk about something else. Shall I get some wine?'

I am tempted. Oh my God, I am tempted. A glass of wine, a truce, my last night in Cannes. Time with Tom that doesn't involve us rehashing the same conversation again and again and again. Wine would make me relax. It would make me happy. I have missed it.

I wouldn't stop. I would miss my train.

'You have wine,' I say. 'I'll get a soft drink.'

I don't have to look at him to see his expression.

'Seriously? When I first got here, you were drinking.'

I don't answer. I haven't the words to talk about this in a way that makes sense, that doesn't invite more questions. After a while, I look up. Tom is looking at me with the oddest expression.

'Sure,' he says. 'Coke? Fanta? Something like that?'

'Something like Fanta,' I say. 'Thanks.'

We sit on the grass near the swimming pool. I don't usually hang around in this part of the campsite, the most popular bit, the part that is legitimately the best, because I don't want to watch families being happy. Now, though, it seems charming. It's almost dark, but loads of children are still up. They're messing around in the pool, diving and jumping, throwing a ball, splashing like heck. They're noisy but in a nice way. It reminds me of the fact that I was once, too, a happy enough kid on holiday in Cannes.

The Fanta is sticky and orange and the sugar boost is exactly what I need. Tom's drinking one too. Neither of us quite knows what to say, so I dive in with what I plan to be a generic question to break the silence.

'Do you have any brothers or sisters?'

He puts his can down and leans back on his hands. 'Yep,' he says. I wait. 'Little sister. Flossie. She's – she hasn't been well. For years. Hopefully she's going to be OK, but it's been . . .'

'Oh God.' *Ruby! What have you done?*

'She's in remission, and she has to go for check-ups every year, but basically she's in a good place now. There's every chance she's going to be fine. It's just hard to dare to believe it.' He looks over at me with a little smile. 'But honestly she's going to be annoying me again soon. She was always so irritating, always wanting to hang out with me and my friends. We fought so much. Then suddenly everything changed. For me, I think the worst thing was seeing my parents going through it. Like, the people who are always strong for you suddenly on their knees. And your fourteen-year-old sister losing her hair. All that.'

I take a deep breath. 'Tom, I'm so sorry.'

'Not your fault. Oh, you mean about the money? Yeah, some of that was for Flossie. I didn't want to say that, though. I didn't want to weaponize her.'

I take a sip of my drink. The sugar is suddenly like sandpaper down my throat.

'I actually meant I'm so sorry for what your family's

been through with her illness. I mean, I think even Ruby would feel terrible about this. She can't have known.'

He sighs. 'Even Ruby? I know we weren't going to talk about it tonight, but if you'd just admit that you scammed the money, I'd respect you more. This split-personality thing is totally cracked. It does you no favours.'

'Don't. Football between the trenches.'

'Just – if you're not Ruby, who are you? If you weren't Ruby, you'd be shouting your real name at me.'

I hesitate. I could do it. I could tell him my real name. He could take it to the papers and my whole life could unravel. But he probably wouldn't.

'Have you contacted the tabloids?'

He looks away from me, over to the pool where three children are holding hands and taking a running jump at the deep end.

'No,' he says. 'Because of Flossie. The last thing we want is "brave sick teen" stuff all over the place. Floss would hate it. Gran would too. So, no. It was just a threat, really.'

I am a terrible person for being relieved.

'When you traced Ruby Robinson online, she didn't look like me, right?'

He shakes his head. 'She did. You did.'

'She didn't, though. I know Ruby. And she's honestly much prettier than me. She has these gorgeous big eyes.'

'You are so weird.'

'It sounds like it but it's not. I swear. Look – I know Ruby. It's a complex situation, but I was going somewhere I didn't want to go and we switched places. My real name is . . .'

Birds are going wild overhead in the very last of the daylight. Am I going to say it?

'Your real name is?'

Shall I?

I take a deep breath.

'Tabitha Courtenay.'

Silence. The sky doesn't fall down. No one comes to arrest me. Nobody drags me off to Switzerland, or to prison.

Tom shakes his head. He's done with me. I can see it. He knocks back the rest of his drink and stands up.

'See you in the morning, Ruby,' he says. I stay where I am on the prickly grass as he walks away.

12

The first train to Paris is at half past six, but since I have to walk the hour to Cannes station as the local trains haven't started yet, I leave at quarter past five. I wish I could take the tent with me. It's my home. The vomit smell has gone. It doesn't belong to me and now I'm not going to be able to give it back to Yannick's friend. However, there's no way I can take it down and pack it up. Tom is on this campsite, his tent five pitches away from mine. I'm pushing my luck as it is.

I'm going to shake him off by jumping on trains all over Europe. I'm running away without plans. Just travelling where the rail network takes me, beginning, today, with a trip to a random place on the map that I've picked because it's the furthest point from here on the rail network. I'm not using my bank card because I know Tom will trace it. I'll take out the whole balance in cash instead.

The early morning smells glorious. I'm going to miss everything. The warm breeze, the Mediterranean plants, the silky sea. It pulls me back. I want to stay here and learn from Guillaume. For the first time in my life, I have an ambition.

I walk fast to the centre of Cannes. I look behind me often. No one is there.

The platform is quiet. There's just me and a few people who look as if they're going to Paris for work or for serious travelling. There are high-end suitcases and backpacks. Families and stragglers like me.

I had to book this train because TGVs have compulsory reservations. If Tom is somehow tracking me online by my train ticket, he'll be able to follow me as far as Paris, but I hope not beyond.

When the train arrives there's a flurry of getting on at the right door, and people lugging cases and pushchairs. I find my seat, upstairs by a window, and squeeze my backpack into the overhead rack. Then I stare out of the window at the platform, desperate for Tom not to show up and jump on at the last moment. The platform is covered and shadowy. When everyone is on the train, the doors close and it starts to move. I'm almost certain Tom's not on it.

The seats are upholstered in orange. They're big and comfy and I'm tired, but I cannot relax. If he's followed me, he'll be walking down the train looking for me.

I don't dare stop concentrating until long after the train has slid out of the station. After we've been moving for over an hour, we reach Toulon. Since I've spent seventy full minutes staring at the door to the next carriage, waiting, and nothing has happened, I allow myself to relax a bit.

Two hours into the journey, I start to yawn. I don't have anything to do or to read so I plug my phone in to charge and attempt to internet stalk Tom's sister. There's not much there, though I do find a gofundme for Flossie O'Neill without any photos, with a message about it being a place for their friends to help them out. I feel like the worst person in the world.

I try to track down my own sister with no success, and look up Ruby's old social media, which all seems to be deleted. When I find myself too close to my previous life, I put the phone away and pick up a free railway magazine. I read a bit of marketing stuff about how amazing French trains are, and then I close my eyes and wake up in Paris.

I rush to the metro, and after buying a couple of second-hand books at a shop near the Gare du Nord I start taking trains north. I get a train to Brussels, a train to Cologne, a train to Hamburg. The German trains are weirdly unreliable, like British ones, but I make progress all the same. I get off trains, check the screens and move to the right platform for the next one. I sit on benches and read. I buy railway baguettes and eat them slowly. I could live like this, I think. Always on the move, never having to stop and exist in a place. I like passing through.

The reverie ends when I arrive in Hamburg at 1 a.m. on a delayed train, and need a place to sleep. My budget is tiny, but I have found a dorm bed online in a hostel for thirty-five euros, though I can't book it because I only have cash. I am terrifyingly off-grid. The hostel is close to the station:

I just hope they'll still have a bed now and that they'll take cash, since the alternative is to sit on the platform until morning and I really, really don't want to do that.

I pull my backpack on and get my head down. I've memorized the route to the hostel, though of course it doesn't work because I go out of the wrong station exit. Hamburg Hbf is unsurprisingly massive. It seems to have a huge, closed shopping mall right inside the station and it feels like the kind of place, late at night, that would have zombies.

I walk around the deserted station, following a red-tiled floor in wrong direction after wrong direction. All the shops are closed and all the people who got off my train have melted away. I feel like a person in a disaster movie, the one who dies first because she's reckless and stupid. There are people living here, sitting in the doorways, and I feel bad for them as well as alarmed for myself. I keep looking over my shoulder. If Tom had invisibly followed me, now would be a great time for him to show himself.

When a bearded man approaches, I want to scream. I get ready to be mugged and try to work out what to do if he takes all my stuff. I'll get a job in Hamburg, somehow, and get back on my feet. I've got Ruby's passport and most of my money in her money belt, and I've never felt so grateful for it.

'Some money?' he says.

My hand shakes as I take a five-euro note out of my pocket and hand it over.

'Can you show me the exit?' My voice is shaking too, just like my hand.

He points behind me and round a corner, and two minutes later I'm out on the street. I regulate my breathing and almost run to where I think the hostel should be. Cars pass by fast, their lights dazzling me before it goes dark again.

The building in front of me is intensely cool and designer so I think I must have the wrong place, but no, it's the hostel. I walk in and nearly collapse with relief. There's a hard-looking woman on the reception desk and I almost run over to her.

'Do you have a bed?' I say it in English because I don't speak German. She replies in perfect English.

'You haven't booked?'

'I know. Change of plans.'

'We have one.'

They have one bed left – but it's in a mixed dorm and they won't let me book it as neither Ruby nor me is eighteen and it's not allowed. The woman is tough as old steak and won't budge on the rules.

'The thing is,' I say, 'I've just travelled from the South of France, and –'

'Why did you do that?' She gives me a raised eyebrow. I'd love to be able to raise one eyebrow like that. 'I'd have stayed there.'

'So I've got a train to Copenhagen in –' I look at the clock on the wall behind her – 'eight hours. I just want to be safe. You're saying I'm too young to sleep in a mixed dorm because of safeguarding, but that means I'll have to sit in the station all night.'

She shrugs. 'Yeah. I can see that's not necessarily sensible.

But what can I say? I don't make the rules. You would be allowed in a female dorm, sure, but we don't have a bed.'

I look around. The reception says it's open twenty-four hours. There are huge windows to the outside. There are sofas that don't look the most comfortable, but they would be OK. If I just sat here, would she throw me out?

I look up. She can read my mind. She gives a massive sigh.

'Ten euros and you can stay on the sofa, use the bathrooms and have breakfast. But you have to be up by half past six. I can't let the other guests see that it's possible to doss down outside the dorms. I'm only doing it because you're a young woman on your own. It's against all our rules.'

She glares as if she properly hates me. I'm glad that somewhere in there lurks a heart of gold.

I give her my best Ruby-smile. 'Thank you so, so, so, so much!'

She takes my passport, gives the photo a sceptical look. I look at her. I've practised the face Ruby is doing in the picture. The woman frowns slightly then shrugs. The Ruby in the passport picture has a dark bob. I now have a dark very short pixie cut. We're very clearly not the same person. She knows that. I know it. She can't be arsed to do anything about it and I love her.

I hand her ten euros. She leads me to a sofa that's not visible through the massive windows. I get out my sheet sleeping bag and then, somehow, it's half past six and someone is shaking my shoulder.

13

I step off the train and look around. This is it: the furthest point on the Interrail network and a very difficult place to get to indeed. It's taken me days to reach it, train after train after train. I've boarded trains that I wasn't meant to catch with this pass. I've dodged ticket inspectors. At one point I had to buy a separate ticket because all the seats allocated to Interrailers were taken. It's been exhausting, and I'm as certain as I can be that Tom hasn't come with me.

So here I am. An idea that was just a distant place on the map is real. An actual place, rather than 'not-Cannes'. The station is small, the land around it flat. I pull my backpack on and step down from the train. Here I am, in the Arctic Circle.

Not many of us get off here, but at the same time it's everyone on the train because this is the end of the line. A couple of people are waiting with hotel signs, but most of the other passengers just melt away. Two other backpackers have arrived together, both boys, and, as we step straight from the platform to the road, I edge towards them in the hope of some company. One's shorter than me and the other is just a little bit taller. They both see me.

'Hey,' says the short one.

'Hey,' I say back.

They don't seem to mind me walking with them. I can feel myself starting to spin out at the weirdness of this, the giddiness of my flight. I am sick of being on my own. If they don't want me attaching myself to them, they need to say it to my face because I certainly won't be taking a hint.

We start walking together. It turns out we are booked into dorm rooms in the same hostel. It's quite a long walk, but I'm used to walking round with a backpack on now. When I was Tabbi, I wouldn't have been able to do this.

The boys are Japanese. They're called Ichiro and Takanori and they are besotted with each other. I settle easily into their company. I don't have to talk, though they sweetly switch to English for me. I just like having people with me.

'How long are you staying here?' says Ichiro. The air is cold on my face. This is a different world from Cannes.

'I only booked two nights,' I tell him. 'And that's all I can really afford. After that, I'm heading back south. My trip is mainly about going on as many trains as I can.'

They nod as if that's not at all weird.

'How about you?' I remember to add.

'Oh, we're staying a week,' says Takanori. 'We're obsessed with this place. I want to stay up all night and watch it never get dark.'

That stops me in my tracks. 'Watch it never get dark?' I should have thought of that. I noticed the light evenings during my days of travelling north but didn't really think about them.

'There might be some . . .' I watch Ichiro searching for the word and wish I spoke Japanese. 'Twilight!' he says triumphantly. I grin. 'But no darkness.'

No darkness. That sounds like what I need.

Kiruna is relatively small, and flat, and it's got something magical in its air. It's cold, which I guess I should have expected, but since it's August I somehow didn't. I assumed the whole of Europe was sweltering right now, but this is the Arctic and it feels like the wind is coming straight from the North Pole.

I'm going to need a coat.

The buildings are blocky and functional, low to the ground under a huge pale sky. When we find the hostel, it's friendly and straightforward. I get a bottom bunk in the female dorm, which is as expensive as that first room I stayed in in Avignon, and I sling my bag on to the bed, unpack the warmest of Ruby's clothes and put them all on. They're nowhere near warm enough: neither of us was expecting this. Why did I even come here? Why didn't I go straight to the Greek islands and lose myself there? Just by looking at the extremes of the map, I've landed myself in a place that's expensive and cold. I could have picked up another tent and gone somewhere cheap and hot.

Ichiro and Takanori have booked a double room, and I agree to meet them for a beer later on, though I think they're just being nice and, of course, I will not actually have a beer. They are on the trip of a lifetime and probably don't want me tagging along. Still, I'll go. I'll crash their date and drink tap water at their table.

I stand at the reception desk and look at the leaflets. Lots of them say 'Lapland'. I check the map and discover that it's true: I'm in freaking Lapland! I'm also in Sweden. Lapland, I discover, is a province of Sweden. No wonder it's cold. Everyone but me is wearing those expensive Gore-Tex-type jackets. I have a sweatshirt and a light raincoat. One pair of jeans.

The guy who checked me in looks like a Viking. He has flowing light brown hair, a beard, a smilier face than Vikings probably did. I try to look nice. Be sweet like Ruby was when I met her. Ditsy.

'Hey again,' he says. 'Can I help?'

I give him a big happy smile.

'Yeah. Um, maybe. Do you happen to have a coat I could borrow? Like, in lost property or something? I didn't really know I was coming here. I'll give it back in a couple of days?'

He looks at me for a while, then laughs.

'You didn't know you were coming here? I love that. Sure, we've got a pile of stuff people leave behind. As long as you return it. So – how do you visit us by mistake?'

I run through potential answers in my head. In the end, I settle on an edited truth.

'I just wanted to come as far north as I could on an Interrail ticket,' I say. 'And see what happened.' He nods.

'You're actually not the first to say that.' He goes into

a back room and comes out with a bright blue coat with a fur-lined hood. 'Just give it to me when you leave. If I'm not here, leave it in your dorm and it'll find its way back to lost property.'

I want to kiss him, but I don't. I set off in my wonderful new coat and walk around the town. I find a sign telling me that the Ice Hotel is 20 kilometres away. I look it up and find that it's open in summer too. I thought it would have melted by now. Tabbi Courtenay would have visited this town just to go to the Ice Hotel and post it on her socials.

I keep walking. It's strange to be at the end of the line. I look at the huge sky and wonder how far the North Pole is from here. Probably still quite far.

I walk down to the water. I walk and walk and walk because I'm scared to stop. I can feel it following me. Not Tom O'Neill. He'll never find me here. Not him, but the other thing. Tom was actually a distraction from that. He filled my mind with other people's problems and kept me going.

There's a bench beside the water. I sit on it and stare out across the grey lake. I think it's a lake but it's huge. The ground is stony and scrubby, and the plants that grow are tough little things that look like they have spikes. I stare at the water and then, in the far north of Europe, at the furthest point on the rail network, it happens.

It catches up with me.

I've always told myself and everyone else that I had a proper alcohol-induced blackout that night, but I didn't.

I can actually remember.

I came home when no one was expecting me. I saw something awful happening. I needed to get away and I had never felt worse about myself. I drank half a bottle of vodka, took all the drugs I could find (mainly my mother's diet pills). And I got in the car.

I got in the car.

I did that. I made those decisions. I knew what I was doing: I wanted to destroy myself, and I didn't care about anything or anyone else. I got in the car and I drove into Central London. I must have been driving like a maniac because I was one. I'd only had three official driving lessons and even driving sober on my own would have been illegal.

I kept driving, and I was crying too and playing loud music. I was playing the Beastie Boys: I didn't even really know them, but I'd heard of them and I wanted something beastie. I was shouting along with a song called 'No Sleep Till Brooklyn' when there was a motorbike ahead of me, and I didn't want to hit it. I was going too fast to stop in time so I drove up on to the pavement.

I jump to my feet. I can't do this. I walk and then run towards the centre of Kiruna, and when I see a shop called the Coop I go in. They have loads of booze for sale and even though I haven't touched it for weeks – even though I've been pleased about that, have made proper efforts to keep it that way even when it was socially awkward – even though I know this is the worst thing in the world I could do, I do it anyway because I need to stop thinking.

I realize I won't get served because the signs say you have to be twenty to buy alcohol. Twenty! I pick what I want anyway (a wildly expensive, yet comparatively cheap, spirit called brännvin) and remember how Ruby got that wine on the train. The other Ruby.

I wait outside the shop. When a man who's maybe forty or so approaches, I step into his path.

'Excuse me?' He looks round. 'My friends and I really want a bottle of brännvin.' No idea if I pronounced it properly, but he seems to know what I mean. 'But we can't buy it because we're too young, so . . .'

He smiles and shakes his head. 'Sorry, my dear. I'm in the police.'

I laugh and wait for him to come back out of the shop, just in case, but he shakes his head and walks off, laughing. The next person is a middle-aged woman. She refuses because it's illegal. I get lucky third time round and soon, with the help of a gym-bunny guy of about thirty, I have my booze.

It's an old friend. It's my worst enemy. I don't care what it is because I'm back there. I'm in the middle of London. I'm driving beside the Thames, window down, yelling along with the Beastie Boys. I'm crying. The car is swerving.

I run to the nearest bench and open the bottle. I have to blot this out right now.

I stare at the bottle. I'm going to do this. I am.

If I do, I won't be able to stop. I'll drink until I black out and everything will go wrong again in ways I can't begin to imagine. And yet it's better than being here. Better than being in that memory. That truth. Why did I come so far away? Why didn't I just go to Italy or Spain, or somewhere else in France, and get another kitchen job? Why didn't I keep busy?

I raise the bottle to my lips.

Someone touches my arm.

Someone says, 'Ruby – I don't think you should do that.'

14

Tom O'Neill takes the bottle from my hands. He puts it down next to him and looks at me for a long time. I look back. He is different here. He's looking at me in an entirely different way.

'Ruby,' he says. 'I mean Tabitha – whoever you really are. Let me help. Whatever you need, you're not going to find it here.' He winces. 'Sorry about the cliché. It's true, though.'

I am so relieved I want to cry. The tears prickle at the back of my eyes, and I try to hold them in but what's the point? I let it all out. I cry and cry and cry. I try to reach for the bottle again. The smell of it is pulling me in. I touch its smoothness with my fingertips, but then it's gone.

Tom puts an arm round my shoulder. What's he doing here? I sniff and wipe my face on a tissue he produces from somewhere. Finally I can speak.

'All right, Oprah,' I say. 'How the hell did you do that?'

His arm is still round my shoulders. This is so totally weird.

'How did I do what?'

'Find me, first of all.'

There's a moment's silence. Then he speaks.

'Honestly? Don't hate me, but when you were at work a while ago I put a tracker in your backpack. By the way, just after you left, I figured out that you were telling the truth. You're not Ruby Robinson.'

I have questions, but I don't bother to ask them. I could be outraged about the tracker, but I'm not. He has just stopped me from doing something that I know, really, would have been a terrible idea. I still want to do it, though.

Then I realize what he said.

'You know I'm not Ruby.'

He nods. 'Yeah. And so I wanted to say – I'm really sorry. Oh my God. I can't believe what I did. I grabbed you in the street. I sat outside your tent. I followed you. I was a total stalker who made your life hell, and I didn't even have the right person. I am fucking mortified, I can tell you. After you told me your name that night, I looked you up and . . .'

I look into his face. It's a nice face. His glasses suit him. Like me, he's not dressed for the weather. He's looking at me with something different in his eyes. I think of our last conversation, our football-in-the-trenches moment. This feels like that, but better because now it's real.

'So,' I say, through tears, 'you knew you had the wrong person, but you followed me anyway?'

'I couldn't leave it like that. First I had to tell my parents that all that time I had the wrong girl. So, yeah, I'm not their favourite kid. They've cut off the money. When I told them I needed to find you to say sorry, they just called me a loser, which is fair enough. As far as my parents are concerned, I've just added loads of cash into the loss column, after promising them I'd get Grandma's money back. I've spent absolutely loads, earned a bit but not enough, and all I have to show for it is your tip money, which I'm going to give back just as soon as I can.' He pauses. 'One good thing, though. Flossie thinks it's hilarious. Making my sister laugh means a lot.'

I lean on him. I like the bulk of him. I realize that no one has touched me like this, or even at all, for ages.

'Look at us,' I say. 'Pair of losers. Keep the tip money.'

I reach across him for the bottle, but he grabs my hand and stops me. I don't mind him holding my hand.

'When I offered you wine,' he says, 'and you said no, that was the right thing for you. When you were drinking, in Cannes, just before you got that job? I heard you being sick in your tent and then you didn't even come out. Not even for a breath of air. It was a bit scary – I almost went in to check on you, right then, but you started humming so I could tell you were alive. Being sober suits you. I watched you change. It was . . . nice to see.'

I cringe. 'So – tell me what happened when I left. What did you do?'

He stands up. 'Walk with me? It's too cold to sit still for this long.'

We walk around, out of town, along the lake.

'When you ran away,' he says, 'I was super annoyed. I waited outside your tent for ages. Then I started to worry. It took me ages to unzip it and check on you because that seemed a bit too much even for me. And then, of course, it was empty. You didn't even leave a note.'

I nod. I had contemplated leaving a note, briefly.

'You weren't at work. You weren't anywhere. I checked the tracker and found you halfway to Paris. So I followed you. I didn't do it by train, though. How did you even do that? I couldn't see how you could get the right bookings on an Interrail Pass. I waited until I could see that you were heading north in Sweden. I knew you'd be going to the end of the line, so I got some cheap flights.'

The air is cool in my face. About fifty per cent of me wants to get back to that bottle of spirits. The other half is so grateful to him for saving me from myself that I want to marry him right here, right now.

'To go back to your question, though,' he says, and for a second I am overwhelmed with fondness for this guy, for the formal way he speaks. As if he's being interviewed on Radio 4.

'To go back to my question?'

'I did what you told me to do ages ago. I looked at all the pictures of Ruby Robinson I'd saved from her social media. She's deleted it all now, but when I saw the pictures I had to face it. She looked a bit like you, but she wasn't you. Sorry, but I had some pics of you, some stealth ones I'd taken.'

'While you were stalking me.'

'While I was stalking you. Yeah. I put them through loads of different bits of software. All of them said they were different people. They all pointed out the bone structure, the features – everything that was basically different. And, although I hadn't believed it when you said it, I did when it was tech. Sorry, but there we go.'

'Fair.'

'I tried to remember the name you'd told me. I knew it was Tabitha, but I couldn't remember the surname. I just knew it started with C. So I got to work, and after a while I found you.'

We stop and look at the lake. I don't ask him what he found. I know the worst thing has been hushed up and papered over with money, but I'm still scared. Things get out. If there's something interesting or shocking, it ends up online.

He doesn't know it. He can't: I'd see it in his face.

'This place is wild,' he says. 'I mean, cheers for bringing me to the coldest, most expensive place in Europe.'

'You're welcome. Did you know it's actual Lapland? I thought it was a country, but it's part of Sweden.' I try to remember what the leaflet said. 'And Finland too, I think.'

'Does Father Christmas live here?' He looks excited, like a kid. It's adorable.

'Yeah. Must do. The Ice Hotel is just down the road.'

'Is that where he lives?'

'I guess? Why wouldn't you?'

Five minutes later, we pass a man wearing lots of layers of clothing. He has a big white beard and is wearing black boots and a dark red coat. We can hardly contain ourselves, and as soon as he's out of earshot we collapse laughing. That was him. It was definitely him.

'So,' Tom says when we've calmed down, 'Tabitha Courtenay. I guess you're another victim of Ruby Robinson. How did she grift you into swapping lives?'

I look away. I look out across the surface of the grey lake.

'I can't tell you that,' I say. 'Not yet. Let's just say, she did it so well that I thought it was my idea.'

I see him starting to say something. I see him deciding not to. I turn and begin walking back to the hostel. Tom comes with me. We stop outside.

'Would you like to hang out together a bit?' he says. He is looking into my eyes. I look back at his. I keep wanting to look away, to protect myself, but I don't. This guy likes me. He's seen me at my worst (almost my worst), and he still crossed a continent to straighten things out with me.

I take a deep breath.

'Yes,' I say. 'And can you please tip that alcohol away for me?'

That night, we stand outside under the midnight sun. It's bright, bright daylight. Tom reaches for my hand. I step closer to him.

15

I'm only working the lunchtime shift this afternoon, so we don't need to wake up until half ten. That's the thing with living in a building: the sun can rise and babies can cry and kids can shout across a field that they want to go to the beach *right now*, and you don't have to know anything about it.

The sun is coming in round the edges of the blind. I yawn, roll over and check my phone. Ten thirteen. That's nice. I roll into Tom, next to me in the bed, and sling an arm over him to wake him up. He grunts.

'Today's the day,' he says. I kiss the back of his neck and get up because I need the loo. On the way to the bathroom, I put the kettle on.

We are living in that room in Kevin's building while I juggle waitressing shifts at the *Brise de Mer* with one day a week learning from Guillaume. Tom does his IT job and also washes pots in the evenings. We live in a tiny room that manages to contain a couple of kitchen units, a small double bed and some cupboards, and we are paying all our own expenses and saving towards Ruby's debt because we both feel we have to do that. Our windows all look out over the bins. There's a bathroom that has a loo and the world's most pathetic shower. The whole thing is more luxurious than a tent, more comfortable than a sofa in a hostel reception area, a lot more private than the various dormitories I've spent nights in. It's cheap but still expensive, and I love it.

I flush the loo and stare at myself in the spotty mirror as I wash my hands. I look quite healthy now. My hair has grown into a reasonable shape. My skin is clearer and tanned. My eyes are sparkling. Since Tom found me in Kiruna, life has been better than any rehab.

I know this can't last because I'm still avoiding the big thing. Tom knows there's something, but he doesn't know what it is. I cannot look it in the face, can't give it a name, can't take myself beyond the point at which I swerved up on to the pavement to avoid the motorbike. But I know I will. It's in front of me, blocking the way. My time is running out: soon I will have to get therapy and find a way to live with it. I'll find the people I need to find, and do what I can for them.

Meanwhile, this is my last day as Ruby Robinson. I'm setting off this afternoon: tomorrow I'll arrive in Zurich and become Tabitha Courtenay again. Tom and I have talked about it endlessly. He knows everything that happened on that train: we've been over it again and again because he's obsessed with how much he hates the real Ruby. He wanted to come to Zurich with me, to confront her, but I've persuaded him not to, because Ruby will know by now what I've done, and I don't want Tom to hear it from her.

As soon as I'm Tabbi again I'll tell Jana, or whoever

is meeting me at the station, that I'm not going back. I'll speak to my dad if I have to: I'll tell him that I appreciate all his help and that now I'm going to France for a while. Because I won't be sulky or bratty, I might get away with it. If they do force me to go home, Tom will follow as soon as he can. He was only here for Ruby, and now he's only here for me.

I step back into the main room and look at my boyfriend. I feel my mouth smiling as I watch him rolling over, half awake. The last thing I expected from this summer was a boyfriend, but it seems I have one. He's totally unlike Barney, and all the better for it. Tom is dependable. He was only ever trying to help his grandmother, and threatening me never suited him. Emotionally I've been very cautious, but at every stage he's turned out to be exactly what I need. He doesn't hate me at all, and I still like him.

'Coffee?' I say.

He rolls over, smiles a sleepy smile at me and mutters, 'You're amazing.'

I get the cafetière out and start to make it.

Half an hour later, we're back down on the beach. We always end up on the beach. Sometimes it's packed with people. It's never empty because this is August in the South of France, but it's less busy now that the peak French holiday season is over. There's a feeling of things winding down. The queues at the ice-cream stalls are smaller. I bet there are more grassy spots at the campsite. We find an empty patch of sand easily, and there's more space around us than usual.

Tom spreads out our cheap little mat.

'There you are, *mademoiselle*,' he says. I kiss him and sit down.

'*Merci, monsieur*,' I say.

I put sunscreen on my face, even though I did it before we left home. I take off my T-shirt and hand it to him so he can do my back. I have a bikini of my own that fits me now. I like the way his hands feel as he rubs the cream into me. I never imagined something so complicated as a relationship could feel so easy. Maybe being Ruby is, finally, better than being Tabbi ever was. Having a boyfriend who likes me, who respects me, is incredible. Tom listens to me. We're equals. I've been doing it so wrong up to now.

I'm still wearing that star necklace. Tom asked me about it once, and I just said, 'I bought it for myself.' I told him the truth. That shouldn't be a massive revelation (telling the truth and letting someone know the real you can be OK), but it is. I didn't tell him how much it cost.

'Wish you'd let me come with you today, Rubes,' he says. He wanted to start calling me by my real name, but I've asked him not to. It's too confusing, when everyone else knows me as Ruby, for him to start calling me Tabbi. Though after tomorrow I guess I'm Tabitha again. Weird.

'I know.' I take the bottle from him. He turns round so I can do his back. I squirt the cream, and he winces at the cold. 'It really would just scare her off. I'll find a way to get your gran's money, I promise. Even if she has to scam it off someone else.'

His head jerks round. 'Not that.'

'Someone who could afford it?'

He shakes his head. 'Not even.'

'To entertain Flossie?'

'Hmm,' he says. 'Maybe.'

I'm a bit excited about reclaiming Tabitha Courtenay. It's the first step to facing up to myself. And right now I'm on a beach in Cannes with my boyfriend.

'I wonder what Ruby's doing now,' I say. 'Getting ready to leave, I guess.'

'Getting ready to pay her debts.'

I nod. This bit makes me feel sick. I have to make her listen to me. I don't know Ruby at all. She might not give a shit about Maria. In fact, she definitely doesn't or she wouldn't have taken all her money. She might continue not to care when I tell her about Flossie.

He's promised his family he knows where she is, and since we're paying into a fund for his grandmother every week, his parents are less angry than they were before. I've been chatting to his sister on FaceTime. She loves the whole adventure.

'As soon as they let me travel,' she said the other day, 'I'm going straight to Cannes.'

I lie back and look up at the sky. I become Tabitha when I step on to the train this afternoon. Not now. Right now, everything is straightforward.

16

As the train slides underground into Zurich station, I feel myself shaking. I'm ready for this, but I'm scared. I need to take the good bits of my Ruby life and bring them into Tabbi. I have a plan, all written down in my notebook on this journey, and at the hostel I stayed at last night.

And I have Tom waiting for me. Once I've got all my Tabbi stuff back – my passport, mainly – I will finally be my real self, in a functional relationship. I love it that he is back in Cannes, doing his web-design job, waiting for me to become my original self, so we can be . . . real.

As soon as we've switched back, I'll call my dad. I'll tell him I'm fine, that my rehab has been great. Much as I don't want to, I'm going to have to leave Cannes soon. For one thing, Tom has to go back to uni in Birmingham. For another, the moment I give up that Irish passport I won't be allowed to work in France any more. There are still two weeks on the Interrail Pass so Ruby can do what she likes and we'll probably never see each other again. It's weird to have spent a few hours with someone, then lived their life for six weeks. I don't feel great about the chances of her paying the money back.

I'm not going to finish my A levels. No thanks. I don't need them to be a pastry chef. I'm going to learn to cook, and sort my head out.

And – the big thing. The thing that's hanging over me. When I'm Tabbi, I will deal with it. I know I have to. I'm almost ready.

I step down from the train. I'm starving but I'll wait. It won't be long: in a couple of hours, I'll have access to my real money. Money I haven't earned. *That* feels weird.

I notice straight away that Zurich station is different today. It's madly busy. There's music playing from muffly speakers that people are carrying. I see a group in Baywatch costume. A couple wearing butterfly wings. Women in fishnet tights and tiny skirts. Men in garish cotton trousers.

I take the escalator up to the main concourse. It's wild up here. Loud, busy, full of people dressed for . . . something. This does not feel like it did before.

I see the clock where we're meeting. I find a table at a coffee shop called Yard Bean, and sit with a coffee and a pastry and watch the people going past, and wait. I can see the meeting point from here. If she's early, I'll just walk over.

Two hours to go. A very drunk woman sits at my table, giggles, burps and closes her eyes.

One and a half hours.

A couple wearing leather shorts sit at the next table. They nod at me, so I lean over.

'What's happening today?' I say it in English, waving around at all the people, the costumes, the music, the sleeping woman opposite.

'Street Parade,' says the man. I nod as if I know what that means.

'You should come,' says the woman. I smile, but I'm not in the market for a street parade today. I finish my coffee and watch the clock. Bet it would be fun, though.

One hour.

Forty-five minutes.

With thirty-seven minutes to go, I realize that she must have her phone back by now, and I log on, once again, to that empty Gmail account. It contains a needy-looking eighteen messages from me, and none from her. Why hasn't she messaged? Maybe she hasn't been allowed her phone until today. I wonder how to broach the fact that I've hooked up with the grandson of the woman she scammed and that I'm on his side.

Ten minutes before our meeting time, I go back to the counter and spend almost the last of my cash on two hot chocolates with squirty cream and marshmallows. I want all the sugar I can get because of my nerves. It shouldn't be surprising that Switzerland is as expensive as Kiruna, but somehow it is. I sit back at my table and wait, sipping one drink, holding the other, Ruby's battered backpack at my feet, until, with two minutes to go, I pull the bag on to my back and walk to our exact meeting spot.

I stand there and wait. People walk past me with glittery faces, pink hair, platform shoes. None of them are Ruby.

Five minutes late.
Ten minutes late.
I start to drink her sticky chocolate.
I finish it. She should have been here half an hour ago.

I locate the next train to Paris and go to its platform. I wait half an hour longer. I realize I'm almost entirely out of money, but that's OK because soon I'll have my bank card.

I check my phone. There are five messages from Tom, going from Nearly time! Thinking of you! to ???? photo please! to Is everything OK???

I keep waiting. The thing with staying in a station for ages is that no one else does. When you get to a station, you think there are loads of people there and that you're the one on the move, but actually, if you stay for hours, everyone else leaves. Of course they do. It's a station and, in this case, they go to Street Parade. There's a notice next to the Paris platform that, even with my bad German, I can decipher as saying 'Today is Street Parade, the biggest techno party in the world'. I'm glad everyone is so happy. I like the energy here. I just don't like the fact that Ruby's ... nowhere. Maybe she's been distracted by the world's biggest techno party.

I study everyone who gets on to that Paris train, and not one single one of them is Ruby Robinson. I mean, I'm not stupid. I know she's a player. I guess she might have extended her stay up there to avoid the consequences of her scamming for as long as possible. As I didn't tell her where she was going, she won't care about inconveniencing me.

I look up the place and it turns out to be a two-hour drive from Zurich. I don't, of course, have a car, nor am I ever going to drive again. There's probably a bus, but I just spent almost my last cash on two hot chocolates.

Was I picturing it as the end scene of a movie where two girls have a re-meet cute, hug each other and switch back, having learned from the whole experience? Why yes, I was. I should have guessed she wouldn't make it that easy.

Jana's not here. I'm not sure what this means. If Jana's not here, maybe Ruby has changed the arrangements. But why didn't she tell me?

I start to spiral. If Ruby doesn't come – then what? She's probably found a way to take my money. I don't really care about that, but I do need to become myself again. It's time to go back to real life. To make Tabbi Courtenay make sense.

I guess if she's not coming to me, then I'm going to have to go to her.

I look the journey up on the Interrail app. I can use my pass to get a train, to Interlaken, via Bern, then a local train to Grindelwald. There is one leaving in nine minutes, so I run to the platform and jump on it. I have a generic thriller I picked up on the beach, about a hitman, and although the Swiss scenery out there is spectacular – rocky mountains, wooden chalets, bright turquoise lakes – I barely look at it. I force myself to read because I have to stop my mind racing. This does not feel good.

I text Tom.

> She's not here. Going into the mountains to find her x

He answers:

Oh shit. Take care!! Want me to come? xx

I take a deep breath. I really do want him to come, but I force myself to write:

Not yet. Thx tho. That means a lot xxx

I hesitate. I want to write a term of endearment. Darling. Sweetie. Gorgeous. I feel too self-conscious. Maybe I should try one that could look a bit ironic. I edit the last message before I send it.

Not yet. Thx tho. That means a lot, babe xxx

I smile as I send it. He immediately replies:

I LIKE BEING YOUR BABE.

Grindelwald is the most spectacular place I've ever seen. It's high up in the mountains, and surrounded by bigger mountains. The last rays of the day are shining from a deep blue sky, giving everything long, gold-tinged shadows. The air feels so fresh that it's cleaning the insides of my lungs. I stand on the platform for a moment and take it in. The buildings are dark wooden chalets. People walk past me, all of them knowing where they're going. Everyone has backpacks, clumpy boots, shorts, walking poles. If I was coming here on holiday, I'd be happy, but I can't stop yet. This is not the end point. I walk into the picture postcard ahead of me, and I keep going, into the falling night.

What if she's gone down to Zurich while I've been travelling in the other direction?

What if I get to the place and she's not there at all? There's only one way to find out. I stand outside a hotel and hook up to their Wi-Fi to check the map.

It's a ten-mile walk from here, but it'll be dark before then. I set off anyway.

17

It's half past ten the next morning and I'm standing, exhausted, halfway up a mountain, outside a place called the Zen Lodge. The sound of cowbells chimes all around the mountain. It's weird to think that I should have spent the past six weeks in here, shut away, doing a detox it turns out I did actually need. I should have been having intensive therapy, which, again, would have done me good. I'm never going to regret my gonzo rehab because it's been the best summer of my life. But this place might have sorted me out too, with less drama, less fun, less Tom.

Instead of being here, I've lived in a tent, got drunk, got sober, got a job and travelled through and to, I think, six or so countries. I've looked my own sister in the eye and told her I'm not me. I've ended up with exactly the right boyfriend, and a very temporary home. I've decided what to be when I grow up and set off along that path. I've stood under the midnight sun in the Arctic. I've persuaded a German woman not to throw me out on to the streets in the middle of the night.

Who am I kidding? I've done all of that without confronting the Thing. Inside this Zen Lodge place, they would have forced me to deal with it. I'm glad I didn't go.

And, apart from Leo, no one even seems to have noticed that I'm missing. Every now and then, I check for her Insta, but it's still not there. Graham Fairfax never answered my text. I have logged into my own previous account a couple of times, ready to find awful things, but that's been pretty much empty too.

No one misses me. No one is thinking of me. I knew they wouldn't, but it's still a punch in the stomach.

I take a deep breath and look around. I'm wearing the closest thing to mountain clothes I own: Ruby's jeans, tied at the waist with some string. I'm only just starting to warm up after my weird night. The landscape here is surreally beautiful. The bright sun is lighting up every little crevasse of the mountains around me. There are patches of snow high up on some of them. They are rocky up there, with dark green trees and hallucinogenically green grass lower down. The Zen Lodge is screened by trees, but that just means you can't see it from Grindelwald. The stony road that leads to it swoops around and approaches from the other side. And that's where I am. Tired, aching and stiff, ready to reclaim my life from a master grifter.

This building, behind its locked gates and its fence, looks like a luxury hotel. I want to take a photo of it, but I only have one per cent battery since I ended up sleeping in the woods last night and even in Switzerland the mountains don't have chargers on them. I stretch and try to remember how people do yoga.

This place is part wooden chalet, part cream plaster. It would look amazing covered in snow, but as it's summer it's standing in a field of bright green grass and colourful flowers. Even the drive looks expensive, as it's made completely from white stones. The 'Zen Lodge' sign is discreet, and there's absolutely nothing to say that it's a fuck-off luxury rehab specializing in troubled under-twenty-fives. It looks, from the outside, like a five-star hotel or a hedge-fund manager's second or maybe twelfth home. It also looks like it's saying, *Go away – you don't belong.*

It's wrong about that. I do belong. It's going to be strange going back into that world.

I stand still and listen, but all I can hear is the constant sound of cowbells from somewhere nearby. There's no movement in the building. The gates are locked, but as there are cameras on each gatepost I expect someone already knows I'm here. I look up at the windows and although I think I see a movement behind one, it stops and maybe it was just the light. I do some stretches before climbing over the fence easily enough and walking up the drive. I listen to my footsteps crunching on the stones, with a backing track of cowbells.

Long before I reach the door, it swings open. A man in chinos and a white shirt is standing there. I know he's a security guy. He's dressed to match the luxury setting, but he's all business.

'Can I help you?' Flinty-eyed. Speaking English, but not

a native speaker. Not actually wanting to help me. Wanting me to leave.

'I hope so!' I say in my jolliest voice. 'I'm here to see ... Tabitha Courtenay.' That was bizarre. I'm used to me being Ruby. I'm not used to her being me.

He gives me the tiniest smile.

'She's not available.'

I took six trains to get here and then I walked over the mountains like the Von Trapp family. I slept in the forest (weirdly well as I was so tired, though I woke up freezing) as it turns out even a hostel bed was going to be over £40 anyway.

I'm not going to turn round and walk meekly away because Tabitha Courtenay is *not available*.

'Is she still here?'

He shrugs. 'Guest information is confidential.'

'Didn't she leave yesterday?'

Nothing.

I look for a name badge. This feels like a situation that might go better if I could call him by his name. He doesn't have a badge. If he has a name, which presumably he does, I'm not allowed to know it. It bubbles up inside me: this is *my* world. *My* rehab. They don't get to treat me like scum.

'Here's the thing.' This is the point at which I would have said his name, but never mind. 'That girl isn't Tabitha Courtenay.' I pause, but if you looked up the word 'unimpressed' in the dictionary, there'd be a picture of this guy's face right now. 'That girl was called Ruby Robinson. I'm Tabbi Courtenay.'

He looks at me for a while, then makes a signal of some sort, and an actually uniformed security guard comes over. Are they taking me seriously? Is this guy going to invite me inside? No, and no. The new one steps towards me. Too close. He's going to throw me out. I shout as loudly as I can. I don't go quietly. 'She's an imposter,' I yell as if she was trying to get the Tudor throne off me. 'We switched places! We need to switch back.'

The security guy doesn't even look at me. He grabs me by the top of my arm and walks me down the drive. I struggle but he knows what he's doing, and I can't move. Seconds later he dumps me outside and closes the gates with an electronic thing. They swing and then *clink* shut.

I have no idea what to do, so I just walk a little way away. When there's a rock between me and anyone looking in my direction, I sit behind it and wait. Shit.

I text Tom.

Bit of a hitch, babe, but working on it.

The phone dies just as I'm sending it.

I try to work it out. Ruby can't have gone home, to my real home, because she's not me. She can't step into my life because she's the wrong person. Our six-week swap ended yesterday. Didn't it? Maybe it didn't. I've been all over the place. I could have the dates wrong. That would be easy.

That's bullshit. Of course I don't have the dates wrong. Right up until it died, my phone said it was 23rd August. The one thing I actually know about Ruby is that she's a thief.

If anyone could have managed to access my trust fund, and run away with it, it would be Ruby Robinson.

I'm exhausted and aching. I think of my bedroom in London, of how comfortable it was. How cosy. In fact, home, the place I always thought was boring and loveless and a total pain in the arse, now feels incredible. A house, close to London, with my own huge room, with a carpet and heating and a duvet. Multiple pillows. My teddy bear. My everything.

I touch my necklace. That's from my world. That's my proof.

I am thinking of duvets and my teddy, Alice, and then I wake up. Tragic that the thoughts of comfy home things have lulled me into falling asleep on some stony mountain grass using a literal rock as a pillow, but they have. I wake up, aching even more, and do some more stretches as I try to work it out. My back is annoyingly spasmy. I force myself to stay in what I think is an approximation of a downward-facing dog while I count to a hundred, but it still hurts.

She must be still in there, or the guy would have told me. Would he, though? I don't think he wanted to talk to me at all. I'm so disorientated that I'm still second-guessing myself about the date, rather than knowing I'm right. I start trying to tally up the weeks in my head, but I can't do it. Everything is fuzzy.

I realize I have no food or drink, no phone and pretty much no money.

I hear the car coming long before I see it. I hide behind

the rock and watch. It's a black one. The gates open and it glides in. I don't dash in after it because I know what would happen and I can't be bothered to go through that again.

I'm hungry. I don't have a plan, except to wait here and hope Ruby comes out.

So that's what I do. I wait, and then she appears.

She walks out of a side door and heads in a different direction, across the sloping grass, uphill towards the mountain, away from me. She's in the lodge grounds, but the fence is just made of wire, and I can easily see her through it. I run alongside the boundary towards her. From the back, I can see that she's dressed in a pink tracksuit and trainers. My tracksuit. New trainers. Her hair is a bit longer and better cut than mine, but essentially in the same style. Then she hears my footsteps and turns and I see that it's not her at all.

Or is it? This girl's face is covered in bruises, and I wonder what the hell has been happening. Is the bruised face the reason she's still here? You shouldn't get a bruised face in a place like this. Or should you? Just how harsh is it?

What did I do to her?

I say: 'Ruby!' I say it loudly, but she just turns away from me and looks straight ahead. She keeps walking.

I shout it again, louder. The mountain air is harsh in my lungs. I walk right up to the fence and shout her name again. She gasps and steps back.

Yes. It's Ruby. The fence is between us, but we're less than a metre apart.

'Ruby,' I say. 'What happened to your face?'

The bruising is horrible. She has two black eyes. Her face is all swollen, and up close I can see that she has a bandage across her nose.

'I'm sorry?' she says. She looks at me through her bruises. Her lovely eyes look different under all the swelling. 'Can I . . . ?'

She looks back towards the lodge, as if checking who's watching.

'Ruby,' I say. 'Look, I might have got the day wrong, or else you've stayed longer because –' I indicate her face. 'Whatever has happened to you, I'm so sorry. But anyway I'm here. We did it! When will you be ready to leave? I need my bank card. I'm so completely out of cash. I'm absolutely starving.'

She looks at me. It's hard to read her expression.

'I'm sorry to hear that,' she says. Her voice is polite. The voice you use to a stranger. She takes something out of her pocket. 'But – why are you calling me Ruby?'

That's when I know, really. I know what she's doing, but I let myself pretend.

'Ruby! It's me – Tabbi. What have they done to you?'

If I'd come here, would I be bruised and confused? Was this, even after everything, a lucky escape?

She's holding a walkie-talkie radio, and as I wait for an answer, she presses a button.

'Can I have some help?' she says. Her radio crackles and there's some movement in the grounds of the lodge.

I talk faster. 'Ruby. Just give me my bank card or some

cash, and tell me when we can switch back. I can wait a few more days if you need to recover. Are you OK?'

Someone is approaching. My heart sinks as I realize it's the man who threw me out earlier. The uniformed one.

'I have no idea what you're talking about,' she says. She looks me in the eye and says it to my face. She even uses my voice. 'None at all. But – I can see you need money, so take this. I like helping those less fortunate, so let me do this for you. And then you have to leave me alone. I mean, thanks for being concerned about me, but I'm fine. I think it's you that needs to get some help. But this . . . I don't think this is the place for someone like you.'

The security guy is nearly with us. She pushes a banknote through the fence. I take it and shove it in my own pocket.

'What's happening?' the man says to Ruby as he runs up to her.

She turns away from me. Her voice wobbles. I see her lip quivering under all the facial carnage.

'I don't know,' she says. 'I should have listened to you. Sorry. I don't know what's happening, but she's freaking me out. I gave her some money . . .'

He puts a hand on her back and leads her away. He turns to me as they go.

'You'd better not come back,' he says. 'I'm calling the police.'

She's given me one single banknote, but, when I look at it, it's 1,000 Swiss francs.

One thousand francs.

That's an enormous amount of cash. It's nearly a

thousand pounds. How can there be one note that's worth that much? It cheers me up, in a temporary way, distracting me from the bigger picture, and despite the fact that this is MY FUCKING MONEY I am pathetically grateful. I'm starving and thirsty. I can get some food, right now. Can I? No: I'm halfway up a mountain. I'll have to walk for ten miles to get back to Grindelwald first.

Ruby looked me in the eye and told me that she didn't know me. The fact that she gave me a huge amount of money proves that she knows she's lying: otherwise, what with her injury, I'd have wondered if she'd got amnesia. She is trying to pay me off. She's been where I am right now – been living on her wits with no money.

I stand on the mountain and look around. Then I take a deep breath and, weirdly comforted by the nearby cows and their bells, I set off, back down the mountain.

She's tried out my life and she wants to keep it.

She won't get away with this. I just need to find some fuel to fortify myself and then I'll be able to work out my next move.

PART TWO
Ruby

18

Six weeks earlier

I am running away from everything, in the process of a calculated disappearance, when I see the girl. She's in the same Eurostar carriage as me: a teenage girl, about my height and with my approximate colouring.

When I was talking to my old colleague Alex about running away, all fake casual as if I didn't mean it, she said: 'Find someone else who's away from home and swap lives?' She was joking, but it stuck. Right now, though, I am not intending to swap lives. I am focused entirely on stealing a passport. The Eurostar has all its border controls in London and everyone on this train has already passed through them, so this is a good moment to steal someone's ID. From now on, I am in the Schengen Area, and that means twenty-nine countries with no passport checks. I just need some ID, and then I'll change the name on my Interrail Pass. Surely that's allowed. If it comes to it, I could get a job in Paris as soon as I arrive and save up. My mind races as I let scenarios play out. Wash up in a restaurant, save all the euros, then live a new life as whoever the train girl is.

I'm never going back. If I can steal this girl's passport, I will use it to build up a new identity. I've researched it and, as long as I look enough like her for the first things (getting a bank account mainly), I think I'll be able to do it. If she's British, then her passport will be irritatingly restricted in Europe, but I can ... I pinch the skin on my arm, trying to keep myself here, to make things happen rather than getting obsessed with future problems as they scroll out in my head. I am in ultra-planning mode. I have to make this work. One thing at a time. Get her passport.

I can see her from my aisle seat. She's about five seats down.

The chances of it working are small, but if I don't try, they are zero. I know she has a passport on her so I just need to get it.

I walk down the carriage, acting as if I'm heading for the loo. I pause by her seat and smile. She doesn't look up from her phone. I spot the guy next to her. Bums. He was out of my eyeline before: she's travelling with her boyfriend, which means I have to distract two people. I walk past the loo and keep going until I reach the Eurostar Cafe and then I buy a bottle of water, ask for a paper cup, carefully pour water into the cup and head on back.

It's harder than you might think to spill water on someone on a train that is running smoothly, but I do it. I fake a trip just as I get to her seat and chuck water all over her. She screams and looks round, hating me. Her boyfriend leaps up and glares, hands in fists as if he wants to fight. I try to roll with it in a way that will bring me closer to her passport, but all I can do is say, 'Oh my GOD, I'm so

SORRY!' I choose an over-the-top persona and inhabit it. 'I'm such a klutz! Let me help,' I say.

I cast around, looking for something to dry her with. This is the part where she might get some tissues out of her handbag and in all the flurry I could lift her passport.

It doesn't happen, though. She's pissed off at me and wants me to go away. The boyfriend unzips his bag and brings out an actual towel, and they both turn their backs. I stand there for a moment, but her handbag is on her lap and she's hunched over it. I would have to tackle her to get to it and that would end badly.

Back in my seat, I think hard. I check my phone. Nothing. Taking someone's passport will be possible. People lose their passports all the time. Once I've done it, no one who knows Ruby Robinson will ever see her again. So I have to do it.

I try again. I pour some more water into my paper cup, and walk in the other direction. There's no one in the next carriage who could possibly be any good so I carry on all the way down the train. After lots of bumping into seats and trying to squeeze past people carrying coffee, I see another girl. One who also looks a bit like me, but this time with wonderful blonde hair. She's grouchy, grumpy, closed in on herself, twiddling her hair round her finger. Most people on this train are excited, but this girl isn't. I look at her for as long as I can. She's rich. Her hair is gorgeous and expensively cut and she's wearing a shimmering dress that I think is AllSaints. Even her flip-flops look fancy. More than the individual things, though: everything about her screams money. She exudes it. She can afford a replacement passport without even noticing the cost.

There's an older woman beside her, reading a book; I can't tell if they're together.

I slip into a free seat behind them, an aisle seat next to a woman on a laptop who ignores me. I check my phone. Still nothing. I realize the two in front of me are together when they start to argue. I listen. The girl is English, petulant. Wherever they're going, she doesn't want to. They speak English, but the woman has a German accent. They're not related. The woman is getting increasingly irritated by the girl's attitude, and rightly so as far as I can tell. This girl is a brat. A rich brat with a passport.

They are heading to catch another train. I don't know where it's going to, but it's leaving from the Gare de Lyon. The girl wants to get the metro because she says it's only two stops. 'Why can't we do that? It'll be fun.'

'We have to take a taxi,' says the other woman. 'It's tourist season. The metro will be hellish. Plus, those are my instructions. Taxis wherever possible. Not public transport. No one wants you running away again.'

Interesting. I look at my phone. Nothing.

I, sadly, am not going to be crossing Paris by cab. If the metro is hellish, I'll take my chances. I have £200 in the bank, 2,000 scammed euros in cash, a two-month rail ticket, and no plans apart from leaving Ruby Robinson, and specifically Frank Brody, Maria O'Neill, Linda, Eileen and, most of all, Tom O'Neill behind.

I know that this girl is the one. She has money and so

whatever happens she'll be fine. If I steal her passport and pretend to be her, she'll just spend a hundred pounds on a new one and carry on. I'm pretty sure I shouldn't try to cross a border on a passport that's been reported stolen, but I'm equally sure I can walk around with it in my pocket, use it for ID and then get a new one with the same name on it and a new photo. It's weird to think that although I have no idea what this girl's name is, if things go well I might be using it by the end of the day.

I get to the Gare de Lyon in less than fifteen minutes on the RER, which is like the metro but an actual double-decker train. The girl was right: it was two stops. The woman was wrong: it wasn't remotely hellish. When I get there, I locate the taxi drop-off point and wait for them, taking my black wig off so they won't recognize me from the train, though neither of them so much as glanced my way. They arrive twenty minutes later because going through traffic is actually quite a lot slower than travelling under the ground. I fall into step behind without them noticing.

All my senses are on high alert. I'm doing this.

They don't talk for a while. Then they stop by the departures board and look up.

'There it is,' says the older woman, who looks like she'd rather be anywhere but here. 'The ten fifty-two to Zurich. Platform eight.'

The girl looks sulky. I have no idea what the dynamic is. It's not mother and daughter, though the ages would fit. I think it's minder and charge, even though the girl looks about eighteen.

'I'm not going,' she says. She looks around, searching for a way out.

'Yes, my dear. You are.'

I put my wig on, get on to my Rail Planner app and reserve a seat on that train, which sets me back twelve euros. I still have no message from home. Then I stay away from them both, observing from a distance. I watch them get on board, in first class, of course. I watch them inside the train, walking along an upstairs carriage. Once I'm sure they're there, I walk to the other end of the train and find my seat. Even second class is nice, though it's busy, and best of all my seat is also on the top deck. I'm not even planning to sit in it, but there you go. Upstairs on a train is cool. A guy drops into the seat next to mine, nods hello and puts his earbuds in.

I watch Paris receding. It surges inside me: I'm doing this. I've run away from home. I left Matthew and Claire a note promising they'll never see me again, and they won't. I didn't say anything to Frank, because he doesn't deserve it. I've just walked straight out of his life forever. Let him wonder.

Then I take the purple wig out of my bag. I pull off the black bob that I've been wearing up to now and shove it down the side of the seat, where it looks like a dead animal. I put on the purple and make the earbuds guy move to let me out. He doesn't look up.

At the end of the carriage I pick up my own backpack from the luggage storage and pull it on to my back. It's not heavy, because I didn't have much to bring.

There's no one guarding First Class so I just walk up the steps and straight in. I fluff out the wig and amble down the lovely empty carriage. And I soon see that it's too empty. She's not here.

I watched them go up the steps. I saw them here. There are a few people, but they're young business-type guys, plus an old man with a bald head.

I walk slowly to the end of the carriage. It's mostly unoccupied blue seats. When I'm most of the way down I see some stuff on a table. I stop and look at it, and I recognize the girl's leopard-print handbag. A water bottle on the table. There's nothing else.

That bag might contain her passport. I'm about to pick it up and go back to my seat when the door at the other end of the carriage opens and I hear the older woman saying something in a disapproving voice. I walk quickly away before I'm busted.

I wait a while. I walk along the downstairs carriage underneath and come in through the same door they did.

The girl is sitting on her own at the table. The other woman is a few rows back, reading. I turn and grin at my mark as I pass. She's already looking at me, seeing me for the first time with no idea that we've been travelling together for ages, that fifteen minutes ago she almost caught me stealing her bag.

She speaks first. She says 'Hey'.

'*Bonjour*.' I make sure I say it in the most English accent possible. Her eyes light up. She wants to talk: excellent. My plan had been to turn back as if at an afterthought, flash her a wicked grin and ask if I could sit in First Class with her for a laugh. Turns out I don't need to.

'*Enchantée*,' she says. She uses a deeper, posher voice than when I was eavesdropping. Then she was whiny. Now she's trying to impress. Not sure why, but I'll take it. I sit opposite her, get my phone out and put an earphone in. I have wired ones because they're cheap. I look at her AirPods on the table. Covet them.

I dart a glance to her face. She's as keen to connect as I am. Interesting.

'Off to Switzerland?' she says, which, since we're on a train to Switzerland, seems like a reasonable punt.

I put the earphone down. 'Interrailing.'

'Oh my God,' she says. 'That's immense! How cool. On your own?'

I do a big sigh. Stare out of the window, and try to be non-specific while I work up a story. 'Yeah,' I say. 'I guess so. Now.'

Things get better: she gets out the Haribo and I accidentally eat loads because I'm greedy, and because train food is expensive so I haven't eaten for ages. She feels sorry for me being hungry, and so she gives me the nicest sandwich in the world.

'I'm Tabbi,' she says. Tabbi. Seriously? *That's* my new name?

'Short for Tabitha?'

'Yeah,' she says, 'but no one calls me that. It's either a witch or a cat, right? I mean, I know Tabbi is a cat too, but what can you do? I spell it with an i at the end.'

'I think it's cute,' I say. 'Hi, Tabbi.'

I'm definitely not one of life's Tabithas, but maybe I can abbreviate better than she does. Beth? That feels more like me, and it goes more under the radar. It's a normal name that sounds a bit like the middle part of her fancy one.

'My whole family is obsessed with the idea that their kids have to have stupid names. They could never be the sort of people who call their kid normal things like –' She stops. I want to laugh out loud. Her obvious panic about the fact that she might be about to say my name makes me like her a lot. 'Sophie?' She looks at me, anxious. A part of me wants to introduce myself as Sophie just to see her face, but of course I don't. Frank's current girlfriend is Sofie. She's welcome to him.

I put Tabbi out of her misery, adopting a silly, dizzy persona so she'll think she's in charge.

'I'm Ruby,' I say. 'Is that a normal name? I guess it is. And you want to know something? This isn't my real hair.'

We chat about our travels. I improvise a boyfriend in Amsterdam, because it's better than the truth. She lies to me, pretending she's going to the mountains because she's stressed. I see it on her face. I heard her telling that woman she wasn't getting on the train, heard the woman say she had tried to run away. Wherever she's going, she doesn't want to be there. Where, and why? Also, no one gets escorted across Europe against their will just so they can relax in luxury. I watch her face change as she talks, start to see that she looks out of the window when she's making things up.

When it's my turn, I tell her that I'm going to Switzerland

because I love mountains. I'm not really sure what else there is: it's the only thing that occurs to me. Anyway it seems to land. I watch her having an idea. I have an idea too. I hope it's the same one.

This girl is very, very rich. And about as happy as I am, i.e. not at all happy.

There's a man coming after me. He's not coming after someone called Tabitha.

We keep talking. She gets out some vodka in a water bottle. When she gives me her bank card so I can nip along to the bar and buy more supplies, I pause.

She literally gave me her bank card.

Honestly, if the train was pulling into a station, I'd be off, and I'd go on a spending rampage, then steal a passport from a French person. I decide, though, that if she hands the card over this easily, the rest of it is going to be a piece of piss. I will use this opportunity to prove my credentials as someone she can trust and just buy the stuff we agreed and take it back to her. I become Ruby, the sidekick. The girl who does as she's told. The ditsy girl who can be manipulated. I even say 'Everything happens for a reason', then worry that it was overkill.

Within an hour, Tabbi thinks that switching places is her idea. I'm not sure exactly where she's going, but I'll take it. In an excellent twist of fate, there's no one there who actually knows her. It's like the universe is demanding that we do this.

It's right there in her eyes. No way is this just a holiday (given the vodka and oxy, I have a suspicion that it might involve some clean living), but whatever it is it will come with a degree of luxury that I've never known before, and it will be a hiding place for me. If I can't get out, Tom O'Neill won't be able to get in. Whatever it is, bring it on.

I get her to download the app and log into my ticket, and tell her to go wherever she wants in Europe. Her face lights up. She thinks she's played me.

We're not a brilliant match, looks-wise (the first girl on the Eurostar was better), but I think it's close enough, and when you're wearing a garish wig people don't see anything else. If I'd still had my dark hair, it would have been a different matter: no one would ever have got us mixed up. Tabbi's face is narrower than mine and more delicate. She has bone structure. I have a big smiley mouth (not used much for smiling lately, but there you go) and my face is more . . . I don't know. Less thin. All my features are a bit bigger. Frank once told me I looked like a cartoon character and even though he claimed he meant it in a nice way, and I'm sure he did, it's stuck with me. Not a real girl. No mother, no father, no family. No boyfriend. Not even a real face, just one someone has drawn on. The only part of me that looks real is my nose, which I like because it's more interesting than the cartoony stuff.

'You'll have to cut your hair off,' I say.

She nods at once, serious-faced. Jeez: she *really* doesn't want to go to the fake luxury hotel. If it's a no-booze yoga retreat or something, I'll be fine with that. Hell, I'm also fine with prison. I don't give a shit what it is if it gets that scary guy off my tail.

I give her my scissors and razor and she goes off to do it.

Not gonna lie: she looks awful when she comes back. Her lovely hair was doing the heavy lifting. When the wig goes on, it helps a million per cent.

All I have to do is look like her until the bored woman who Tabbi says has never looked her in the eye has gone. Mission: escape Jana. It's hilarious. Something that should be impossible, but that I suddenly feel we might be able to do after all. We have to fool her for five minutes. I can do that.

I remember to tell Tabbi to use a fake name. Hopefully that will keep my shit away from her. With any luck, she'll be fine.

19

Tabbi takes my bag and vanishes, and suddenly I'm mooching on the main concourse at Zurich station. Standing with Tabbi's entitled attitude and no hair, wearing her shiny long dress and sparkly flip-flops. Just another spoiled rich girl, waiting, bored, for the next luxurious thing to happen.

This place is wild. The ceiling is high and the station is airy. Everything is clean and shiny. The air is hot in a way I've never even known before. I look up. Above my head the ceiling is glass, and this whole place is filled with such gorgeous light that it's like standing in an Instagram filter.

There's a bright blue sculpture suspended from the ceiling. It's a woman with gold wings, curvy and gorgeous. I wander over to have a closer look, and read the info. It's by Niki de Saint Phalle. I've never heard of her, but I like her. Nearby is the big clock. That's where we'll meet, in six weeks. I go and stand under it, imagining being my future self, wondering what I'll do. What will have happened to me by then.

'You could have waited,' Jana says in almost unaccented

English, appearing beside me. I keep my head facing away from her. She pauses. 'You look so different.' I freeze, ready to deny it. Still not looking at her. Of course I look different. I am different. I am totally exposed. 'Your pretty hair! For Jesus Christ's sake. I suppose it suits where you're going.'

OK. Not ideal.

I risk a glance at her. She's looking over at the blue sculpture. Not at me. I am barely breathing. Could she actually not notice? I smell like Tabbi's perfume and I'm wearing her dress and wheeling her pink case. Is that all it takes?

I have all her stuff. I have one of her bank cards, in case I need to pay for anything, and she has the other, which she's only going to use to grab a load of cash at this station and then she's throwing it away to avoid leaving a trace. I have her leopard-print handbag (it's actually horrible) and it contains the thing I wanted most of all: her passport. Her case, next to me, will definitely contain lovely clothes and expensive toiletries.

The main exit is ahead of us. There's a clear line directly to it. I could be far enough from Jana before she reacted and out of the door and away before she started to chase me. I could get away from her, even with this massive case, which I am no way leaving behind.

I play it out in my head. I run with the suitcase. I get out of the station and as far as I can. I jump on a bus or a tram or into a taxi, ride it randomly and go and hide at the back of a McDonald's or something. Jana calls the police. They pick me up. Jana finally notices that I'm the wrong girl.

Everything unravels. I lose the passport. I lose her bank card and her stuff. If I run, I'm banking on outrunning the Swiss authorities. That's unlikely.

Deep breath. Stay here for now.

'Soz,' I say. I use Tabbi's deep voice and keep my gaze firmly fixed on the big blue woman suspended from the ceiling. Best to keep the talking as minimal as possible, and *soz* feels like a Tabbi thing to say.

'Well. Where are they?'

She looks at her watch, then around the concourse. She isn't questioning me! Tabbi is right. (*I* am right. I am Tabbi.) This woman doesn't give a shit and just wants to get away. I want to ask what her plans are. Why are you so desperate to get away from this job, which was an easy mission? Are you hooking up with the guy you met on the train? I try not to smile. You had one job, Jana. One!

I focus inwardly so hard that I feel myself *becoming* Tabbi. I calm my heart rate just by thinking about it (I can check that later on the Apple Watch I am now wearing). I close my eyes for a second and let a wave of *I am Tabitha* wash through me. Open them. Feel more Tabitha than even Tabbi could possibly have felt. Haven't seen my dad since I was a tiny kid. Mum is a bitch. I embellish a bit: no real friends. I miss my sister Leo in Dubai. All I ever want is to feel normal because I have no fucking idea how lucky I am or what normal is like for most people. I am unthinkingly rude to people and I don't even realize it. That's me.

Jana sets off towards the big clock. I follow five steps behind. Safer that way. She stops, looks around and huffs.

Someone wants to go to the bar. I want to say that to antagonize her, but manage not to.

The old guy Jana was talking to on the train is over there, waiting for her at a coffee shop by the exit. I keep scanning the crowd. There aren't many people here, on the main concourse. OG Tabbi has vanished: good.

I spot a man walking towards the clock. He's holding a whiteboard that has the word *Courtenay* written on it in loopy Euro capitals, and Jana hasn't seen him yet. My new surname looks classy. I bet people spell it wrong often, though. Courteney. Courtney. Whatever.

This is it. Either I tell him I'm Miss Courtenay, or I put as much distance between me and this man as I possibly can, as fast as I can. If I can find myself a space in which neither of them is responsible for me, then I'm in business.

I turn to Jana. 'Thanks,' I say. 'There he is. Bye!'

I grab the suitcase and walk away from her, hoping that she takes the opportunity to wash her hands of me. Just goes off with that guy she met on the train. Lets her hair down in Zurich, if that's a thing that people do. If she believes her job is done, this moment is my opportunity.

I can tell, though, by the squeaking of her shoes, that she's just behind me. I speed up.

Fuck it.

I grip the suitcase tightly and bolt. Because of Jana's train guy, I don't go for the main exit, but I nearly make it to a side one. I take off at top speed. My legs are not expecting it, but soon they are pounding towards the outside world.

Taking me out into Zurich. I'll get away from here, disguise myself again, make a new plan. Be free.

I'm almost out when a hand grabs me round the top of my arm, much too tightly, so tightly that there's going to be a row of bruises there, and yanks me back. I struggle. I kick out and pull away.

Then I'm on the ground. On the actual ground. I'm lying on my stomach with one of my arms up behind my back.

'Miss Courtenay,' says a male voice. He has a slightly American Euro-accent. A lot of steel in his tone.

'Hey,' I say. 'OK, can you let me go?'

'. . . Can I?' he says.

'Please?'

Silence.

'I won't run away.'

Silence.

'I promise I won't run away.'

He loosens his grip, and I twist round and size him up. He's quite old but obviously wildly fit. He's wearing a white shirt with rolled-up sleeves and a pair of expensive lightweight trousers. He's like someone from the past, from a Wes Anderson movie. Rosy cheeks. Slicked-back hair. Your basic Swiss guy, but turbo-powered. I shift around to a sitting position.

'Sorry, Miss Courtenay.' He's speaking with a lot of courtesy considering what's just happened. 'I'm afraid coming with me is compulsory. If I need to compel you, then, believe me, I will.'

Bastard. 'You don't need to compel me,' I mutter.

Now Jana is with us. Laughing. She speaks to him in German, assuming I don't understand, but I've just done a German GCSE: everyone assumes British people can't speak any other languages and they're usually right, but not this time. My French is quite crap, but my German is fine.

She tells him I'm a pain in the butt, that I cut all my hair off on the train for no reason at all, that I made a friend on the journey from Paris and thank God for that because it gave her a bit of peace to read her book. When she says that bit, she looks over at the man who's waiting at the coffee shop. She wishes this guy luck with me, says nothing to me at all, and then she's gone.

I struggle to my feet. Lots of people are watching and pretending they're not. Two kids are just staring at me, while their parents try to get them to keep walking. I give the children a little wave. A small bow. It's what Tabbi would do.

Jana has gone. I guess we did it.

'My name is Albert,' he says in English. 'I'll be accompanying you to the facility.'

There's no parking at this station so we have to get a taxi to Albert's car. On the way to the taxi rank, I think I glimpse real Tabbi outside the station, but then I'm in the cab and she's gone.

I look out at urban Switzerland as we go. My arm really hurts where he grabbed it. I wonder whether Tabbi's rich dad would sue him for me. It's all so foreign out there. So exciting. There are trams. Big buildings. A blue, blue sky.

Church spires. People on bikes. A world that is normal to the people who live here, but not to me. I stare and stare and stare. My heart is thumping. Too soon, we're at the car park.

Albert has a big silver car with blacked-out windows. I've never been in anything like it. He puts Tabbi's massive case in the boot and then holds the back door open for me. It feels a bit doomy. A bit prisony.

What am I doing here? Where has she sent me?

I look around, just in case, but there's no way I can escape this man. Getting in involves taking a massive step up because this feels like a mountain car. I lean back. It smells of new car and that is like a drug, or maybe that's still the vodka and wine talking because although I faked taking that pill I definitely did a lot of drinking. There is a click from the doors. I try to open the one next to me. Nothing happens. He's shut me in with child locks. Fair.

Albert drives out of the car park and on to a main road. I look at the city around us, at Zurich. There's a tram going past. Tall buildings with lots of windows and slate roofs. Trees. I try the door again. If I could, I would open it and take my chances in the traffic.

When we're out of the city and the silence starts feeling a bit much, I lean forward.

'Albert?' I say.

I look at the countryside. Green and grassy. The further from the city we get, the more impossible it is for me to break away. The more the fear is closing in. I have given up my train ticket, for this. For what? No idea.

'Tabitha.'

He seems more relaxed now that we're on our way. Happier. He must be glad to have me in his mobile prison. I imagine him feeling pleased that I didn't do a better job of bolting, even though, in a sense, 'I' did. Tabbi bolted properly, and I am her dupe. I hope she's going to have fun out there.

'Actually, can you call me Beth?'

'Beth?'

'Yeah. I hate the name Tabitha. It's stupid.'

'I think it's charming.'

I ignore that.

'So if you take the middle bit of it, you can make it into Beth. That's what I'd like to be called now. Please.'

'OK,' he says. 'Beth. Yes, if you like.'

'What's it going to be like up there?' My voice is a lot smaller than I'd like. It's very un-Tabbi. Though that doesn't matter any more because, whoever I am now, that's Tabitha Courtenay.

'Have you seen the brochure?'

What brochure is going to say 'we'll torture your child'? Actually, probably lots. Those boot-camp places. They're a thing. My mind is leaping all over the place. This had better not be boot camp.

'Kinda, but I wasn't really ... concentrating. And brochures aren't always what ... you know.' My voice is wobbling. How intense is this going to be? What the fuck am I letting myself in for? Getting up at five and running a marathon? Digging holes? Is it going to be Camp Green Lake? Military discipline?

'I can see you're on edge, Tab– Beth. Nervous. It's understandable and normal, and you are far from the first person to attempt to run away from me.'

'How many have succeeded?'

There's a laugh in his voice. 'How many do you think? But I can assure you there's nothing to be worried about. Your parents have sent you here because they're concerned for you, and you're going to be getting the best possible care and attention. I can assure you, you'll be in a very different place by the time you leave.'

Yeah, because I'll have been electrified into submission and starved and tortured. I probably won't even remember who I really am.

'You think?'

'Everyone's scared when they arrive. It's always fine.'

'My parents don't care about me.'

He doesn't answer for ages, and then he says: 'It's feelings like that that can be behind the reason you're here in the first place.'

'Deep,' I say.

He laughs and in spite of everything I do too. Even though he pushed me over and basically sat on me, Albert is the only person I know in the entire world right now, and it's fair to say my Stockholm syndrome is setting in.

I sit back and look at the scenery, and even though it's becoming more and more green and trippy – even though there are actual mountains out there – I want to be sick. I wasn't even lying when I told Tabbi I love mountains. I do, in theory – it's just that living in Norfolk, the flattest place in the world, a county that has been cosmically ironed, I've never seen one. And here I am. They do something to me, inside. In my chest. They make me feel small and insignificant and scared.

No: I told *Ruby*. I am Tabitha now. I need to stay in character, even inside my head. She isn't Tabbi for the next six weeks. I am inhabiting her life and inventing Beth. She is me, I am her. I am the rich girl headed to the facility. And, the closer we get, the more certain I am that Tom O'Neill isn't following me any more.

I take some deep breaths and check the Apple Watch. My heart rate is eighty. Not great.

It takes two hours to get there and most of the time we're going uphill. We drive through little towns, past forests, green grass. At one point we drive for a long time beside a blue, blue lake. I can't look away from it.

'Where's this?' I manage to say.

Albert looks round. 'Lake Lucerne,' he says. 'That city we just passed through? That was Lucerne.'

A while later, there's another lake, and this one is so spectacular, fringed with mountains, shining turquoise in the sun, that I forget everything else and just want to look at it forever.

'OK,' I say after a while. 'What's this one called?'

'Lake Brienz.' He pauses. 'We're nearly at Interlaken. Between the two lakes. This one and Lake Thun. At Interlaken we take the road to Grindelwald, and then we're nearly at the lodge.'

We go up and up and up. I can practically see the air getting thinner outside the window.

'Is it going to be cold?' I guess I've got the right clothes since I didn't pack them. I smile, again, at the thought of all the awesome stuff I must have in that suitcase. Even Tabbi's travelling clothes are more expensive than anything I've ever worn before.

'No,' says Albert. 'It's very warm. In the winter, it's a different matter.'

It's going to be difficult to run away, but when I get there I'll review the options.

Either this is the greatest heist anyone has ever pulled, or I've made the worst mistake of my life.

20

The 'facility' looks like a haunted house from a horror movie. It is up a mountain, a huge house on a slightly flatter patch of land, with a slope downhill towards Grindelwald on one side and a steep climb on the other, and it's all surrounded by grass and flowers. Grindelwald must be hours' walk away. This is the most remote place I've ever seen, and I'm actually here.

I take a moment to stare at the mountains.

'So you get snowed in? In winter?' I say as we stop at the electric gates. There's no snow because it's summer, but I can see some high above us.

'Sure,' says Albert. 'We have to clear the road ourselves or we're cut off.' He laughs. 'I mean, we have snowploughs. We're not out here with spades.'

He presses a button on a remote control and the gates swing open. There are cameras high up, turning slightly to follow us down the drive. The fence around the edge is not particularly high or sturdy. I could definitely get out of here.

He drives right up to the building. I open my window

and hear the sound of our tyres on the drive, and distant bells. Albert stops the car, and just as I am about to open my door and get out someone opens it from the outside and there is a woman standing there, looking at me. She's younger than Albert, maybe in her thirties, though so Botoxed it's hard to tell. She has a steely look about her. She is literally wearing a white coat.

If I ran away, she and Albert would bring me back without breaking a sweat. I should do it when they're not focused on me.

I look around. There's just me, Albert and this white-coated woman. Clear air, mountains and a fancy-looking prison.

'Tabitha Courtenay!' says the woman. 'Welcome to the Zen Lodge.' She does not use a welcoming tone.

I notice the sign by the front door, a tiny plaque with ZEN LODGE written on it in a serious font. Zen people don't wear white coats. I get out, feeling, for a second, a tiny bit rock star standing on a Swiss mountain in my lovely dress with my chauffeur pulling my bag out of the boot. I pause, fill my lungs with air that is, actually, cooler than I expected. I picture Frank's face, if he could see me now. Sofie's. Ruby Robinson, chauffeur-driven to a luxury resort in the Swiss mountains.

I take Tabbi's handbag, say goodbye to Albert (I want to cling on to him and beg him to take me back to the station, but manage not to) and follow Nurse Ratched in through the door. We leave my case on the doorstep. I guess someone else will bring it.

The smell: vanilla, a bit of jasmine.

The entrance hall: shiny, tiled. High ceilings, and a rich-people air that I haven't ever experienced before, and which, in spite of everything, I like very much. There is gentle classical music playing. Last year I temped in a posh hotel and even though I literally never visited the rich-people parts of it because I was a kitchen porter, washing up for twelve hours at a time, I glimpsed just enough on my way in and out of the windowless kitchen to know that it was nothing like this, because there is nowhere this exclusive and posh in Norfolk, or if there is it's very well hidden.

And now I am walking among them. I'm on the other side of the divide.

I look down a corridor. At the other end of it there's a boy. His hair sticks straight up. He's wearing baggy trousers and looks like a busker. I can see at a glance that he's here for the same purpose as me. He feels me watching him and looks round. We give each other a little smile and wave and then the man who's chaperoning him leads him away.

The woman (she hasn't told me her name) turns to glare at me, and I realize that it's because I've stopped walking. Because I am looking around, taking it all in. Maybe it's going to be OK. Perhaps this is about to be the best six weeks of my life.

We keep walking. Through a door, along a carpeted corridor. Through another door. Another carpeted corridor, this one less fancy. There are closed doors all the way along it, with numbers on them. There's no music here, and the silence is so heavy that it's a thing, a cloudy monster stalking us through the building. Engulfing me. I imagine the documentary about me. '*And after that she was never seen again.*'

At the end of this corridor there's a lift. The mystery woman, who becomes still less friendly the further into the building we go, presses a button.

'We going up?' I know, stupid thing to say, but I want to make her look at me. To say something.

She nods. Doesn't look. Doesn't speak.

The lift is small, and not as nice as it should be. It's like a lift in a shopping mall. Functional, non-luxury. Mirrored. I check myself out. I do actually look good. I'm glad to be shot of my stupid wigs, and my short hair looks better than you'd think. As the woman presses the top button, 6, with a manicured fingernail, I discover that this dress has pockets. I love a dress with pockets. I put my hands into them and find something. It's small and compact and unmistakably a pill. I pull it out and look at it.

The woman has swiped it out of my hand before I can do anything. I'm pretty sure it was half an oxy. Probably the one Tabbi pretended to swallow on the train as I was pretending to swallow mine. Dammit, I would have taken that right now. She holds it up with her long nails and looks at it, then at me.

After that, the journey to floor six takes a ridiculous amount of time. When you're in a lift with someone and they're carefully putting the half-pill they just swiped from you into a little plastic bag they just pulled from their pocket, time does kind of stretch out. What would Frank do? I try to fart, but I can't manage it.

Frank. I was doing well at not dwelling on him.

And then we're there, in an attic that is absolutely nothing like the rest of this place. The floor is bare floorboards, the ceiling low, and no one has bothered to pump this part of the building with jasmine: the only smell is bleach. Nursie leads me to a door at the end, with the number 12 on it, and unlocks it with an actual key.

A key. This is it. This is my cell.

I look up and down the corridor. No point even trying. I follow her in.

It's a small single room. There is a narrow bed, a little table next to it. A window with a blind. A small TV screen high up on the wall. A door that probably leads to a bathroom. I walk to the window. Mountains. It's like a painting out there.

I smile. 'Thanks,' I say. 'Now what?'

She shrugs. 'Your bag will be checked and delivered. *Carefully* checked. At six o'clock there's an introductory meeting downstairs.'

'Introductory meeting?'

She doesn't bother to confirm. My heart is beating so hard I can't concentrate. Is it really beating harder and faster? I guess it is: priming me for fight or flight. I had a go at flight. There's no point fighting: I'd lose. I check the Apple Watch: 112 bpm.

'I thought this was meant to be luxurious.' I am trying

to be like Tabbi. 'Didn't my family cough up for a suite? I don't like it here. I want to leave.'

'Change into loungewear,' she says, 'and come with me for initial testing.'

I look at her. She looks back. I send red arrows of fear and dislike to her. She sends a vague disdain back, but mainly boredom.

'What loungewear?'

A huff. The thought-bubble over her head says *spoiled druggy brat*. God knows what Tabbi's dad is spending on this. This woman hates me in the same way and for the same reasons Jana hated Tabbi.

'Bathroom,' she says.

I decide to lean in, to play my part.

'Seriously? I have clothes. I can provide my own *loungewear*, thanks. Just give me the bag.'

She huffs out her breath and points to the bathroom door.

The bathroom is tiny, with a shower, a loo and a very small basin. Not even a bath. It's not that different from the train loo, where this all began. On the back of the door is a hanger with a pair of grey pyjamas on it. I laugh.

'Is this prison?' I call out. Silence. 'Is it?' My voice is shakier this time.

I change into the pyjamas. There is no mirror so I can't look at myself, but I know that, in my prison outfit and with my short hair, I must look like someone who's been locked up for her own good, which I guess is what I am. As

Tabbi, I'd be shocked to be so unstylish. As Ruby, I can't focus on anything coherent. As Beth, I'm going to go along with it and hope they don't fry a bit of my brain. I'm going to invent a Beth who is stroppy and outspoken.

'Nice,' I say, stepping out of the bathroom. I've left my dress on the floor just to see if someone's going to pick it up for me. I try for a sneer. 'Very stylish.'

She gives me a look of amused contempt and nods towards the door. I stay still. She stops, huffs and motions for me to follow her. I don't go.

She grabs me by the wrist. Her fingers are cold and strong. I let her lead me along. She takes three vials of blood from me and sends me into a meeting room.

21

'My name is Tabitha Courtenay and I'm an alcoholic.' No part of that sentence is true, but it makes everyone laugh. That's what I wanted, as part of my new persona, but as soon as I've said it I realize I've got it wrong.

The girl next to me, who has pink hair with dark roots, just muttered, 'Jamie,' looking at her lap. Now, though, her head whips round and she stares at me. The guy next to her in the circle, the one with the wild hair, said, 'Cosmo,' and then gave a big sarcastic smile at everyone, ending with me. All these kids really are in trouble, and their energy is downbeat. Whereas I have escaped the thing that was coming after me and the only drug I've taken lately was that booze on the train. The thing that's spinning me out is the fact that I did this. I set off to make something happen and it did. I targeted a stranger, and now she's not a stranger any more. I wanted her passport, but I have ended up with her life.

I'm still not sure what the hell I have walked into. But, when I realize that no one will be able to find me here, I also feel elated. And the more I look at these people, the more ridiculous they become.

I feel like an AI learning on the job. I hunch over a bit and try to be more like the rest of them. The room is big, scented with vanilla, and outside the huge window there is part of a mountain, with bright green grass in the foreground. An actual cow wanders past from time to time.

There are six of us and we all arrived today. Six of us and a woman called Emma who's in charge. Emma, who's about forty maybe (again, hard to tell with the Botox), rolls her eyes at me, but doesn't say anything. The boy next to me says, 'Viggo.' Viggo manages to look preppy even in his rehab uniform. His hair is blondish and perfectly styled, and he's wearing the kind of glasses that American professors wear in movies when they talk about 'getting tenure'. The girl next to him, who has lip fillers, whispers, 'Laila,' and the small boy beside her mutters, 'Clement,' and we're done. These are apparently the people I'm going to be living with for the entirety of my life as Beth.

'Tabitha,' says Emma as soon as we've all done the intros, 'since you seem to be enjoying yourself, maybe you'd like to go first. Tell us a little bit about why you're here.'

Shit. I look around. I have no idea what to say because I have no reference points with these people's lives. I still don't know what this place is. I draw back into myself, copying Jamie next to me, and shake my head. Emma indicates that I have to say something.

'I didn't want this,' I say. 'Or need it.'

There's a little flurry around the group. No one actually says anything, but the way they breathe feels like agreement.

'They *made* me.' Tabbi would be petulant. I can be petulant too.

The silence stretches out. No way is she getting me with that trick. If you want someone to keep talking, you make an awkward silence and wait for them to fill it. I can do that. I wait it out. I win.

'Anyone ready to be a bit more expansive?' Emma says in the end, and Laila starts talking. It's as if she's been waiting for her opening. I sit back and listen. She has an American accent. I start to target her passport. I could do that voice. I could get lip fillers.

'I'm scared to be here,' she says. 'Like, I'm actually crapping myself? I mean, I don't know what I'm gonna do without ... you know. Everything. Like, who even am I? I'm ... really, really scared.'

It hangs in the air. She looks like she's going to cry.

Emma leans forward. This is what she wanted. 'You're not alone, Laila. You're in the right place. These people around you: they understand. You're doing this together. For the next six weeks, you guys are a unit.'

They all nod in a sage way so I do too. Laila starts telling a story of drink and drugs and unwise behaviour, and I focus on every word. So it *is* rehab. We're here to stop us drinking and taking drugs. In that case, it's going to be a piece of piss since I already don't really do either. I mean, I drank vodka and wine on the train, but that's because I was targeting Tabbi.

She gave me vodka because she wanted it to show up on these blood tests. Also, the oxy.

I wonder what exactly Tabbi did that has brought me here. I know I'm going to have to tell her story soon. I know she doesn't speak to her mum, and that she doesn't know her dad at all, and that she was sent to boarding school and hated it, so I start crafting a vague story of being an unloved rich girl.

There's more money in this room than I've imagined in my life. I could pay off my debts using everyone's pocket money, and obviously I'm gonna have to give it a go. I should stand out as the intruder here, but I don't because we're all wearing the same outfit. My home-made crew cut pretty much fits in too and is actually more authentic than my old shaggy hair would have been. The moment I cut it just before I left Matthew and Claire's seems so impossibly distant that I can't believe it was only a couple of days ago.

I push it away. Cosmo's hair is sticking up so he looks like a cartoon character with his finger in an electric socket. Clement is peroxide blond with dark roots, but still looks about nine. I glance around the circle and for a second I imagine that we are all stand-ins, that every single person who was meant to be here switched with a stranger on the way. I have to stifle a smile.

I tune back in to Laila.

'. . . and I started stealing when I was high,' she says. 'That was bad. It wasn't about cash. It was about doing something messed up. And getting away with it. Like – I've stolen so many fucking things from shops. Sometimes I throw them away. Like, dump them in the trashcan right outside.'

Cosmo turns to her. 'What, sending things to landfill? People like you are why the world is fucked,' he says.

She laughs. She doesn't give a shit what he thinks. I need to try to be like that. I guess I am, a bit, like that. Time to rejoin the conversation.

'What about you, then,' I say, 'Mr Perfect? Why are you here?'

Cosmo gives a little smile, but doesn't answer. The preppy boy, Viggo, does.

'I used to nick things too,' he says. 'But I did it for money. Is that better or worse?' He pauses but no one answers. 'My family wouldn't give me any more cash. I did it for drugs. Lifted things, sold them online, bought zing.'

We all nod. I don't know what zing is, but obviously I could hazard a guess. I don't get not needing money. I don't get needing drugs. I feel like a schoolteacher, having no idea what drug we're even talking about. I imagine myself pushing glasses down my nose and leaning forward like a judge, asking, 'Are you referring to ecstasy, young man? Or amphetamines? Cocaine, perhaps?' Zing sounds like speed, but what do I know? I realize my life hasn't been as messed up as I thought. These people are ridiculous.

'You OK?' Cosmo is looking at me.

I stop smiling. 'Sure.'

'You just looked happy again for a moment there. Kind of stands out.' He gestures around him.

I don't know what to say. I give him a grin and say: 'It's kinda funny, isn't it? All our families sending us to be locked up. Like, expensive prison for messed-up kids. It's gonna be a weird summer, for sure.' I look at him hard. Did I get it right?

He grins back. 'Yeah. When you put it like that, maybe. Nice to meet you properly anyway, Tabitha.'

'Sure,' I say. 'And call me Beth.'

Jamie, sitting between us, clears her throat. 'Hello? Get a room,' she says. I lean back. After Frank, the last thing I want is any love interest ever again. No thanks.

When Emma comes back to me, I just say, 'Same,' in the most final tone I can manage. When I have to elaborate, I say, 'Just the usual stuff.' That won't do the job either, it seems. 'I used to steal things too, like Jamie and Viggo. I hate my family. They hate me. I don't speak to my mum and I don't even know my dad, though he's coughed up for this. I went to boarding school when I was little, and I just kinda turned to drink and drugs for something to do. I wasn't happy, and it helped me feel better.'

I lean back, look around the circle. That sounded fine.

'Yeah, but what about the rest of the story?'

That was Viggo, sitting on my right. I turn to him.

'Rest of what story?'

He gives me a little grin. His eyes are greedy for information. Sparkling.

'You know, man. You're Tabitha Courtenay.'

I try to pick up clues from his face, from his eyes. He's looking at me intently, and I try to work out what he's expecting me to say. My mouth goes dry. Everyone is looking at me. Even Cosmo, the laid-back one, is interested in this, and I have nothing.

Laila breaks the silence. 'What are you talking about? You're being weird, Viggo.'

If Tabbi did something notorious, then I guess it hasn't crossed the Atlantic at least. I hope Viggo might explain it to her, but everyone is still looking at me. My heartbeat speeds up. I shake my head and stare at the ground. I need to wait this one out. The silence goes on and I keep staring. I can hear everyone breathing. There's no noise from outside. There's a cow looking in at the window. I guess this place is soundproofed or we'd hear her cowbell. All our chairs are on a big rug. It's so deep that you pretty much sink up to your ankles when you walk on it.

Focus.

Emma steps in. 'Back off, Viggo. This is day one. Tabitha will talk in her own time.'

Viggo mutters, 'Sorry,' and Cosmo steps in, talking about his life at English school in Paris, describing how he drifted towards the druggy set. 'It was just something in me,' he says. 'I didn't have any terrible trauma or anything like that. Like all of us here, I'm incredibly privileged. But it was, like, the moment I first smoked I felt I was coming home. I wanted to try everything. I, like, *had* to do it all. And I knew that it wasn't going to stop. I was obsessed. I hated it. Unlike you guys, I actually asked to come here.'

That takes the attention away from me. Everyone is amazed, so I surmise no one else was done with their awful behaviour. I sink back into myself and stop listening.

What did Tabbi do? How come she's the only one they already know about?

I go back over our hours on the train, looking for clues. What heat am I taking here? I can hold my own so far, in this room full of too-rich idiots, but ... what do they think I've done? I don't even know what kind of thing it is. What makes you notorious in this world? Why am I more notorious than them? If they hadn't taken away my fucking phone I could google her, but they did so I can't.

I'll have to stay in denial for as long as I can and see what I can piece together. Could I message the real Tabbi on our Gmail account and ask? There has to be a computer somewhere in this place.

I'm working out things to say ('I'm not ready to talk about it in the group', 'What did you hear anyway?') when I realize that the session is ending. We're free for twenty minutes, until dinner. Emma explains some rules.

It turns out that rich-kid rehab is right in the middle of the Venn diagram of school, prison, posh hotel and the kind of kids' holiday camp you see in American movies. For the next six weeks, we will all have to do loads of therapy, together and separately, but outside of that we are allowed to walk in the grounds (never beyond), play table tennis, Scrabble, chess, read books, watch DVDs. We're not allowed online at all, and we won't be given our phones back until just before we leave.

'Is there a spa?' says Jamie.

'No,' says Emma. 'No spa, no pool, no gym. You can get plenty of exercise from walking.'

There's a bit of mild grumbling as we stand up, but no one really cares. I try to mirror their uncomfortability with the clean-living side of it, but actually it's the digital detox that's freaking me out. I keep reaching for my phone, but I won't get it back until the day before we leave. For months, it's been my way of keeping myself safe. If there's nothing creeping on to my phone, I'm all right. If there's a message from Maria O'Neill's scary Tom guy, then I'm not, and there have been messages from him all the time. Even now, I have no idea if he knows I'm here since he generally seems to know everything. In my head, he is terrifying. Frankenstein's monster, pursuing me across Europe to make me pay.

And it's not only the big stuff: I miss my phone for everything. I grew up with it as my only companion. If I could have made it sentient, I'd have done so in a heartbeat.

I don't know who I am without it. I don't know if I can do this at all.

22

I sit in my room and breathe deeply. I can't keep this up for six weeks.

I can't do it.

I don't know what to say, or how to be.

I have no idea how to fit in, as Tabbi. I don't know what I don't know. When I bought a rail pass and set off, I was planning to shake off Tom O'Neill, the bastard, and steal a passport to melt away completely. I imagined I'd sleep in hostels and on beaches, living off my wits. I was not expecting to find myself faking it among the super-rich.

There's a wide window sill and I sit on it and stare out. The window is a sash one and it only opens a fraction. Specifically, it doesn't open wide enough for a human to fit through, and I bet if I tried to smash it I'd find that it's made of some million-pound fake glass that doesn't break and has to be torturously mined by distant children. However, it does bring in air that smells insanely fresh, like mountains and flowers. I breathe it in and try to work out how to run away. I can't see the town from here, but I know it's there. Grindelwald. We drove through it, and I could definitely reach it on foot. I have Tabbi's bank card. I could buy myself a new rail pass, first class this time. I could do my plan A, but with more money and a new identity.

I could probably walk straight out of the front door.

I could do it now. I don't even have to sleep here for one night. I stare out of the window and run through it all in my head.

Soon I'm thinking about home, wondering whether they've even noticed that I've gone.

When I decided to go, I had to do it quickly because Tom O'Neill messaged me my own address and said he'd see me soon. I was so sure that Frank wasn't going to help that I didn't even tell him. There was no point: Frank and I hate each other now. We'd been in it together, right up to the point at which he changed the rules, kept nearly all the money for himself and dumped me. Then Maria O'Neill's son (I'm guessing) suddenly popped up. Where had he been when we were running Lance Silverman? If I'd had any idea that there was a tech-brilliant family member on the case, I would never have let it get to this point.

It's my fault he found me. I did a stupid thing. He tracked me down online and started sending threats, demanding money I didn't have, that I'd never had. I had no one on my side, and I needed to get away. So I did, and now, somehow, I'm here.

If I stayed, I'd be secure for six weeks. I stare out of the window at the trippy landscape and try to weigh it up. Run away with Tabbi's identity and vanish, or stay here, knowing that I'm safe from my stalker.

This place is full of money. Could I walk away from that? I could stay and work out how to get it. Jamie is no good to me as I'm too white to use her passport, so my focus is on Laila, and America.

Claire and Matthew won't care if they never see me again. Who am I kidding? They'll be delighted. They've had me living with them for seven years, since I was nine, and there hasn't been a day when I thought they might have liked or wanted me in any way. Although I'm not an orphan, I might as well have been because the only thing worse than being an orphan is having parents who are still alive, but who just don't want anything to do with you.

Everything about me is accidental. I shouldn't exist. The only reason I do is because my teenage mother had no idea she was pregnant until it was 'too late'. Her parents took me in and, even though I'm sure a surprise baby wasn't what they'd had in mind, they were the best. Maybe that's why I'm not as completely messed up as I should be. I called them mum and dad, though they were careful never to let me think that they were my parents: everyone else had a Mum and Dad, and I wanted them too. Some people probably did think they were older parents: Grace and Matthew were fifteen and eighteen when I was born, and Mum (Grandma) was forty-eight so it would technically have been possible. And my grandmother was, for nine years, the centre of my universe.

She gave me my ruby necklace. It's a real ruby: it's the only nice thing I've ever owned and I will never take it off ever (Tabbi thought it was her idea that we should keep our own necklaces, but I was never, ever going to switch). I saw the woman I was meant to call 'Auntie Grace' occasionally, and even when I was young and clueless I could see that she winced – practically retched – at the sight of me. She basically hated me and so I have always had to hate her back. I don't like hating people, least of all my own actual mother, but she kinda gave me no choice. I have no idea who my biological father is, but since she was fourteen when she got pregnant it's safe to say he was either a kid or a bad guy.

When I was nine, everything changed.

I should have been in the car that day, but I'd been invited for a last-minute sleepover with my friend Cat, so when they were hit by a drunk-driver as they pulled on to the Norwich bypass there was no one in the back. The back of the car, like the front, was crushed and for a long time I wished I'd been in it. A part of me still does.

I had to go and live with my Uncle Matthew and his wife, Claire. They didn't want a kid – actually, they did, but not this one.

I take deep breaths of mountain air. It's easy for me to picture how it went. Claire would have been the first downstairs that morning because she always goes down and makes tea for them both. Two sugars for Matthew, soy milk for her. She would have gone into the kitchen and found my note on the table.

> *I'm going away. Don't worry. Thanks for looking after me.*
> *Ruby*

She would have picked it up, looked at it. Smiled a bit. Made the tea and taken the stairs two at a time.
'She's gone.'
I picture Matthew smiling.
'Finally.'

I blink hard and try to force myself to be fair. They weren't exactly *mean* to me. They didn't lock me up or make me clean the house while they laughed and got ready to go out to the ball. They *did* find my existence irritating and considered themselves quite the saints for 'taking you on and keeping you in the family'. They never went to parents' evenings, never showed any interest in what I was doing, but they did let me eat. They did buy what I needed.

It got much worse a couple of years ago when they tried for a baby and didn't manage to have one. You'd think that might have meant that they noticed that they did, in fact, already have a child who was right there, living in their house, but it didn't work that way. It took them both from putting up with me until they got a proper child of their own to actively hating me.

I was thirteen at that point, and I heard every word of the discussions.

'Send her into care!' That was Claire. 'They'll look after her. That's why it's called *care*. We've had her for four years. We've done our bit.'

'Can't,' said Matthew. 'It says in the will. That we would have her if anything happened to them.'

Matthew wears a suit. He is completely boring, except when it comes to me. Every time he looks at me, he gets angry. He hates the fact that 'we're the ones cleaning up Grace's mess'.

They didn't send me into care at thirteen. I decided I'd better work out how to look after myself. And here I am. A new person in a new place.

I don't like Beth Courtenay right now, but I could work on her. I could make her better than Ruby Robinson, and much better than Tabbi Courtenay. Whatever Tabbi's secret is, I don't care because it doesn't belong to me.

I'll stay here one night and see what happens.

I walk into dinner late in the hope of swerving a few social gaffes, but when I get there everyone's just sitting at a big table, and it seems relaxed enough. I adopt a fake chilled air. The food is chicken with jacket potatoes and lots and lots of salad. It's amazingly nice, and thankfully there don't seem to be any complex mealtime rules here that Tabbi would have known and I don't. I eat two platefuls. I drink loads of water. I can't believe how much better this food makes me feel. There's even pudding, some kind of apple pie, and I have a big slice of that too. Everyone else is digging in as well.

I look round the table. *Yeah. So far so good.*

'Not gonna lie,' says Jamie, 'this is not as bad as I thought. When I got my nose done, the food in the clinic was much worse than this.'

'You got your nose done?' Cosmo rolls his eyes. 'I mean, of course, but why?'

She shrugs. 'Didn't like it. It's cute, don't you think?' She turns sideways. Her nose looks ... fine? I dart my eyes back to Cosmo, but he's already lost interest.

'What was it like?' I lean forward and risk it. 'Getting a nose job?'

She gives me an assessing look. 'Yeah, I can see why you'd ask. It was great! In and out on the same day, and it healed in a few weeks. Go for it.'

'Excuse me!' I'm laughing, though, because she was so spectacularly rude.

'Yeah, do it,' says Viggo to me. 'And yeah, I expected some kinda boot-camp place. Like, getting us up early to go for a run. Breaking us down, like the army. I thought it was gonna be torture. It actually seems like it might be chill?'

I remember to stay quiet. Observe and feel my way. Still, as they join in with stories of friends being sent to boot camps, I start to relax. Their stories are entertaining, if clearly exaggerated, and I start to work one up in my head in case I need to offer it.

'Excuse me,' says Jamie, holding her glass up. 'Excuse me! I need some squash if I have to drink water.'

There are a couple of kitchen people around. One

disappears, then comes back with a metal bottle of *sirop* with French writing on it. He slams it down beside her without a glimmer of friendliness. She doesn't care.

'Cheers,' she says, and she tips as much of it into her glass as will fit.

'What's wrong with water?' Laila is refilling her glass from the jug. 'Seriously, this is, like, Swiss mountain water. It's amazing. It actually tastes *nice*.'

Jamie shakes her head. 'I hate water.'

Cosmo leans forward. 'You can't *hate water*, Jamie.'

'No? Watch me.' We do all watch as she picks up the nearest glass, Viggo's, and takes a sip. Her face scrunches up and she puts it down, saying, 'Yuk!'

This draws me in. 'But it literally doesn't taste of anything! That's why it's *water*.'

'It does,' she says. 'It tastes gross.'

Everyone laughs at that, even silent Clement. We all look at him. We wait for him to speak. He doesn't. I hold my glass out for a squirt of *sirop* and I have to admit that, even though the water is lovely, water with *sirop de grenadine* in it is nicer. *Sirop de grenadine*. I file that away in case I get to use it at some point.

By the end of dinner, it feels as if the group is settling. We have all arrived today and will all be doing the same six-week programme, and everyone is bonding. Viggo fancies himself as the alpha guy. Cosmo's the one I'd like to be friends with. Jamie and Laila are already besties, but they're happy to be friends with me too. Clement's the silent outsider. Which leaves me ... the girl who's frantically observing, second-guessing and trying to fit in. Working out who to target and how to do it, ready to bolt the moment it goes wrong. I wonder what Tabbi would have been like with these people. I hope she's all right out there.

'You OK?' says Cosmo as we stand up at the end of dinner. I haven't been this full for ages. Definitely days, but also probably weeks and months.

'Yeah. Kinda relieved about this place.'

Viggo jumps in immediately. 'I mean, yeah, I bet.'

I glare at him. 'I wasn't talking to you.'

We look at each other for a while. Although everyone is moving, for me it all stops. I try to read his expression. His eyes are dark brown, his hair glossy. He thinks there's something particularly bad about me. I must have done something crazy.

'Whatever you think you know about me,' I tell him, 'you don't.' The truest thing I've said in ages.

He raises his eyebrows. 'Sure,' he says. 'Well, it's day one. Like Emma said. You'll talk about it when you're ready.'

23

It's day four before I discover what it is. Why I, as Tabitha Courtenay, am notorious even in a group of teenage drunks and druggies.

First of all, I realize that no one here is actually addicted to anything. This is an intervention: it's more of a behaviour thing than a medical one. There's no *Trainspotting*-style cold turkey, no agonizing rehab. This is a gang of privileged teenagers who needed to be shut away to nip their behaviour in the bud. They tested our blood when we arrived, and mine proved I'd been drinking. Not that anyone, for one second, seems to suspect that I'm not Tabitha Courtenay.

Once I'm certain that there's going to be no boot camp and no electric-shock therapy, that the worst thing we have to do is chores, I settle in. I'm always ready to bolt, but I'm also working up a plan for a heist. These guys have way too much money: I think my best bet is just a straightforward sneaking into their rooms and taking things, just before we leave. They don't value their stuff enough to be bothered about it, and if I can manage to get out first I'll be long gone before anyone suspects me. And anyway, why would Tabbi Courtenay nick stuff when she already has everything?

It's a fine if simple plan. I'll leave Viggo's stuff alone so it looks like it was him: he deserves it. Meanwhile, I discover that I can get my hair sorted out a bit here, and even better than that I can get these horrific eyebrows shaped properly. Tabbi mangled them in a way that makes the beautician wince, and I have to act like I did it myself while I was drunk (which, to be fair, is the exact vibe they're giving). I love it when they're done. I never bothered with eyebrows before, but from now on I totally will.

Bigger plan: I'm keeping an eye on Laila. If I could get my hands on her US passport, I could do anything.

I hang out most with Cosmo, and a bit with the girls. I stay away from Viggo and talk to Clement when he'll let me, though he's still an enigma who sits and plays chess on his own in the downtimes, moving from one side of the board to the other to be both people, turning down anyone who offers to play a real game with him. I keep an eye on everyone's reactions to me, but I can't make any progress on Tabbi's secret.

Until I do. I'm in an individual session with Emma when it happens. So far I've got through these by channelling my feelings about Maria O'Neill. I say things like, 'I have massive regrets, Emma. If I could go back and change things, I would. I don't know how to make it right.' Often (in fact, every time) I end up crying and there's nothing fake about that. I just have to remember to stop short of saying what it is that I have actually done.

This time, though, I give it all that, but then she says: 'Yes, Beth. We've covered all this. So now I think it's time to look at practical steps you could take to feel you've dealt with it. And the first one is naming the thing you did.'

She looks at me hard. My gaze slides around everywhere. The wooden desk. The tiled floor. White walls. A window that only has sky outside it. Deep blue with a wisp of cloud. I can't look her in the face because the story I want to tell her is one thing, and whatever she's expecting to hear is another.

'Go on,' she says quietly. 'You can say it, Tabitha.'

The silence is heavy. It goes on and on. This time I have to be the one to break it.

'I ruined someone's life,' I say.

'Yes,' she says. 'You did. Tell me what happened.'

I think back to where it all began.

Frank and I were sitting, hip to hip, on the low wall, brainstorming. I was leaning sideways on him and he had an arm round my waist because those were our innocent days. Two oddballs, happy together. More than happy. In love. Obsessed. Delighted to have made a weird little world together. I hated school but I loved Frank.

'I would, though,' he said. 'I would totally deal. I just don't know where to get it. How do people do that?'

I smiled, even though this whole thing was making me feel weird. Little creatures, eating me up from the inside. Frank needed money. He needed a lot of it. He would do anything to get it, and I was really hoping we were about to come up with a brilliant plan.

'Ask the careers woman?'

'Oh yeah. Hey, miss? Do you have any info on how to get into sales? You do? Great. I was thinking I'd start out with marijuana.' He said the word in a teacher voice, pronouncing every letter including the j. 'Then maybe move up into the class As?'

I assumed the teacher role. 'What you need to do, young man, is pick your A levels carefully. Are you aware of a TV show called Breaking Bad? Watch that for research. Focus on chemistry. Then an access course in basic dealing, and you'll be all set. It takes hard work and dedication though, young man! You're going to have to pull your socks up.'

It was stupid, but we both laughed until we almost fell off the wall.

'I'd get killed by the other dealers, wouldn't I?'

I side-eyed him. 'Life insurance?'

'Fake my own death?'

We considered it. We'd already discounted any kind of heist. We couldn't rob a bank because of course we couldn't. Gambling was – spoiler alert – risky. And the bailiffs were coming to Frank's house soon, unless he could do something about it. Unless he could access about twenty thousand pounds, Frank was going to lose his family and his home.

'How's your dad?' I said.

'Shite.'

Frank was the eldest of three boys, but he only lived with one of his brothers and one of his parents. His mum had left when his littlest brother was born, taking the baby, but their grandparents stepped in and got a judge to stop her taking the older two. Then the grandparents washed their hands of it all and moved to Spain, leaving them both with their dad and his drinking problem. Frankie had spent the years since then trying to keep things together, both hating and longing for his mum. That was what had bonded us in the first place. Happy days.

'The boy's not going into care.' That had always been his mantra. He needed to keep Mick at home at all costs. Sometimes I'd wondered whether foster care might have been OK, because when I'd looked it up it seemed like he'd go to live with a family who would make sure he had a comfy bed, a warm home and food, and Frankie wouldn't have been responsible for those things any more. One time I started to say it, but stopped when I saw Frank's face.

We did the only thing we could. We carried on brainstorming.

'If we stole twenty grand, we'd get caught,' I said. He nodded.

'And we don't know how to, like, hack into things and transfer the money out. That stuff they do in movies.'

'You're good at that.'

He shakes his head. 'Not good enough. Working on it, but not yet. Maybe I could do a bitcoin scam.'

We looked at each other. I could see he was on the edge. We didn't know enough about bitcoin, but . . .

'A scam could work,' I said. 'Not bitcoin. Everyone knows about them. What about a romance one? One of those ones where people pretend to be in love and get the other person to send all their money?'

He nodded slowly. I could see his mind whirring.

'Keep talking,' he said.

'I didn't mean it to happen,' I say to Emma. 'I just got sucked in.'

What the hell. I'm sitting here with access to the kind of therapy I would never in a million years be able to afford in my normal life. I may as well use it.

'Tell me about it.' She's using her special therapist voice.

'OK. I will. You have to promise not to interrupt, though.'

'Of course! I promise.'

'Even if what I'm saying seems weird? Even if it's not what you're expecting?'

She smiles calmly. 'Yes, Beth. Even if that.'

I take a deep breath and tell the story. Saying it out loud makes me shake all over, but I do it. I take myself back there.

Frank and I worked hard on researching scammers. I read up on it obsessively. I listened to podcasts about people who'd been scammed. I found out how it happened. Meanwhile Frank worked on the money side of it. Assuming we made it work – how would you have that much money land in your account when you're sixteen without the bank taking a very close look indeed?

We sat outside to swap information in low voices. It was drizzling gently and most people had stayed inside after lunch. The water was making my hair so mildly wet that one minute it was dry, and then it tipped over into rats' tails. I didn't care.

'It's possible,' he said. 'Don't worry. I'll take care of that. There are loads of ways to have money under the radar.'

'We don't need to split it fifty-fifty,' I said carefully. I pushed my wet hair behind my ears. 'But if we're doing this I'll need a proper cut. This is a big risk for both of us and I need funds to get away from Matthew and Claire.'

He kissed me. 'You're gonna have fifty per cent. Absolutely not hearing otherwise. We have to solve all our problems with this. All of both our problems.'

We had that conversation. We did. He agreed to it. I was owed half the money we made. We were a partnership, in it together.

We sat on that wall in the rain and invented our guy. We found a stock picture of an old dude, who was still OK-looking, wearing an American military uniform. After five minutes' brainstorming, we named him Lance Silverman. Lance for the military, because it's a weapon, and Silverman because he was a silver fox. We set him up with a Gmail address and a Facebook account. Then we had to go in for afternoon lessons.

Later, Frankie fiddled with the settings and made it look like he'd been on Facebook since 2006, and we filled in his profile. We scraped together forty dollars and bought him 2,000 friends, and then friended him ourselves with ten new accounts that exchanged banter with him on his wall. Frankie went back and filled in some happy birthday messages dated April 22nd every year.

We had ourselves an avatar. And that's where my shame properly begins.

Over the next couple of weeks, we targeted loads of people with friend requests. Some of them accepted. We started conversations with those people. Most of them ignored us. It was like Squid Game: *people fell away at every stage, but, instead of getting closer to winning the money, the contestants who remained were heading towards losing it all.*

The closer we got, the worse I felt. I carried on, but I started to realize that we wouldn't actually be able to go through with this. Because the people we were targeting were not the gullible rich people who, I had imagined, would never send Lance more than they could afford. These people were naive, and lonely, and trusting. The only mistake they made was believing a word we said. Whenever I found that someone had blocked us, I felt relieved.

The three we ended up with were Linda, Maria and Eileen. All white women, all in their sixties and seventies. Two UK-based, one in Australia. They were all delighted with their handsome new boyfriend Lance. They started to write messages telling us things I really, really didn't want to know. They told us about their traumatic divorces (Linda), the day their husband died (Maria) and about never meeting the right person and feeling that there had to be something wrong with them (Eileen, in Australia).

In chemistry one day, my phone vibrated in my pocket and I opened it under the table to read the latest message. It was from Maria, who lived in Basingstoke, wherever that was.

'OK,' she said. 'My love, I've arranged to withdraw the money to buy you out of the Secret Service. I know you'll pay it back as soon as you can access your US accounts. I wish I could give it to you forever, but I need it for my granddaughter. I'll tell you about her when we're together – it's a difficult story. So I trust you, my darling. Lance – I never thought I'd find love again.'

I took a screenshot and sent it to Frank, across the room. I watched him get his phone out and open it stealthily too. A few minutes later, I saw the reply appear.

'Our wedding day will be the best day of my life,' Lance had written. 'And every day that comes after it will be just as wonderful, my love. Your granddaughter will have everything she could ever dream of.'

I didn't feel good about this any more. We had done it, had got to the point where she was ready to send us money. I was pretty sure we were about to ruin her life, and God knows what was going on with her granddaughter. A difficult story – that rang all the alarm bells. Scamming widows out of their savings felt grim.

'Ruby Robinson!' Dr Jones was standing in front of me, hand out for the phone. I looked down at it. I locked it and handed it over gladly.

'That's a detention,' she said, striding back up to the front of the room and putting my phone on her table. 'So. Moles, anyone?'

Frank caught my eye from across the room. He winked. I shrugged. I was shaking all over. We had to end this. We had to do it now.

After detention that afternoon, I sat in my bedroom and looked at Maria's profile. I looked at it from my own account, from Ruby Robinson from Sprowston, on the outskirts of Norwich. Maria didn't have things locked down at all. Lance was very locked down by this point: we couldn't allow any of his girlfriends to write on his wall.

I checked her friends list. I found a guy called Benjamin O'Neill, but I couldn't see his page. Maria didn't have anything on her wall about grandchildren, but she did have loads of links to fundraisers for sick kids, and that didn't make me feel any better.

I clicked 'message' on her profile. It opened up Messenger. I started typing.

'Maria,' I wrote. 'Don't send your money. It's a scam.'

The phone shook in my hand. I looked at the words. This, I knew, was the right thing to do. But if I did it I'd mess up Frank's future, and his brother Mick would go into care. I was desperate to send it and I knew I couldn't. I had to care more about my boyfriend than I did about a woman who would send all her money to a stranger on the internet.

My finger hovered over it. We were in too deep. We would be in massive trouble if it came to light, which it would. Could I tell her just to send a little bit of money? Enough to buy Frank some time and give me something for my escape fund?

The door slammed downstairs. I jumped. My hovering finger hit send.

My heart pounded in my chest and my hands shook.

Shit shit shit.

I'd sent the bastard message by mistake! Delete delete delete. *I gasped for breath as I tried to focus. Go to the message. Focus. Find the right thing. Unsend: there it is. Unsend for everyone, please. Oh my God.*

I did it. I clicked unsend for everyone and then I inhaled. Unsent for everyone. Never sent. Gone. I wasn't sure if she'd get a notification about that, but if she did at least she wouldn't be able to see what the message had said, unless she was online right now. Was she?

I guessed not because later that night Frank called me. He was over the moon: she'd followed his instructions and made the transfer. She had sent Lance Silverman £28,534.

'I'm sorry I wasn't able to round it up to the thirty,' she wrote. 'But this is what I have, my love.'

I'd actually forgotten I was sitting in a sunny therapy room in Switzerland. I was back in Norwich, staring at the screenshot. It wasn't going to his bank account, of course. It was in some online anonymous thing, but it was ours.

Emma is looking confused.

'Tabitha,' she says, and I can tell she's choosing her words carefully. 'Beth. This isn't why you're here. You know that. Did you do this romance scam too? Because this is not at all what I thought you were going to talk about.'

I just give her a little nod. Now that I'm Beth I didn't do that scam. I didn't part Maria, and also Eileen and Linda but mainly Maria, from their money. I didn't do that because I'm not Ruby. Thank God for that. Whatever Tabbi did, I'll take it.

'What were you expecting me to say?'

The question sits in the room for a long time. *Please tell me please tell me please tell me.* This is the moment for it, when I'm feeling shit about Maria O'Neill. When I'm ready to own anything Tabbi can throw at me.

'As you know,' she says, 'I've been waiting for you to tell me about the accident.'

Here it is. I take a punt. My voice is still shaking from thinking about Maria, sending us way too much money.

'The accident,' I say, 'that happened when I was drunk. High.'

Emma nods. 'Yes. The accident in which you killed a man.'

24

The moment I discover what she did is the moment any admiration I ever had for Tabbi turns to hate. I hate having to be her. I hate having to sit in the group session and take responsibility for something I didn't do, something I would never, ever have done. Something far worse than conning a widow out of her savings.

I hate her for doing the most horrific thing in the world. Drunk-drivers are the worst people, and now I'm having to pretend to be one. Tabbi did the thing that took my grandparents away from me. A drunk-driver killed them and messed up my life. Tabbi might as well have done it to us herself.

At that moment she becomes my enemy. I drop my plan to scam the others in here because now I just want to focus on Tabbi. The gloves are off. I'm sitting right here, living her life, and I'm going to take her down.

I piece it together pretty quickly. Most of it makes sense. Her boyfriend, Barney, dumped her. She pretty much told me that on the train. She didn't mention the fact that she flounced away, got drunk, took whatever drugs she had to hand and then went off in her mum's car. Hit a guy, killed him, drove off. Somehow got away with it.

I don't have much experience of drinking, none of drugs and none of driving. The thing I really can't get my head around is the killing part. I want to vomit when I think about it. I can't believe that the girl I met on the train actually killed a human being. Someone had been alive and now, because of her, they weren't. Why is she not in prison? No wonder she had to be escorted on the journey.

I don't understand how she killed someone and is paying for it with . . . six weeks of mild rehab.

With Emma's support (or rather insistence), I tell the group about it.

'So,' I say, as I start, 'I'm not sure I can get through this, but I'm gonna try. First up – I hate myself.' They all nod, serious.

I think of my grandparents. The massive loss. The ruined lives. Theirs, obviously. Mine. Matthew's and Claire's too, in the sense that they were forced to take in a kid they didn't want. The fact that I still can't think about the people who were my mum and dad, no matter what the biology said, without crying.

I think about them. I cry. I remember that I'm Tabbi, and I know those tears need to look like remorse, but actually I'm crying hot tears of hate for the person I'm impersonating. How could she? How could she get away with it? And send me here to take the heat while she swans around Europe on my passport?

I tell them the basics. Dumped. Drunk. Followed my

worst destructive urge. I tell them I have no memory of the accident because that's the safest way to do it.

'I know you all know this,' I say. 'And I appreciate you. For being nice to me when you all – nearly all – already knew this. I hate that I did this. I just didn't care what was happening right then. I guess I set out to destroy myself and yeah. I didn't even manage to do that.'

I'm trembling as I say this stuff. They probably think it's guilt.

I stop. Sit back. Look at the ground.

'You didn't destroy yourself,' says Viggo, 'you destroyed someone else.'

'I know,' I say with a glare. 'I'm a monster. I get it.'

'Er,' says Laila, 'no offence, Beth, but – how come you're here? Didn't you have to go to, like, court?'

I just shrug and say, 'My dad sorted it,' and they all accept that.

After the session, Emma takes me away for another chat, and I cry and tell her that I hate myself.

'I don't know how I got away with it,' I say. 'I really don't.' Literally true.

'Um – you *do* know, Tabitha,' she says. 'Your mother gave you an alibi, as did your ex-boyfriend. No one was able to prove that it was definitely you, rather than someone using your mother's car, particularly when the car was swiftly reported stolen. Your family were able to smooth it over with a good lawyer, but they insisted you spend the summer here.' She looks at me, looks hard into my soul. 'Beth – you know this. You've done well in facing up to everything else. Do you have memory lapses?'

I don't know what to say. I just shrug and say, 'I guess I had a blackout. Like I said on the first day, maybe I'm an alcoholic.'

Once I've dealt with that, I start to settle in for the duration. The six of us spend all our time together, and, apart from Viggo, I like them. They don't seem to hate me, and I do despise them a bit for that, but I try to deflect Tabbi talk and focus on everyone else and their much more trivial backstories.

In group sessions, there's always someone like Emma listening, but they hardly ever join in. They just let us chat, and bond.

I never used to be one of those girls with loads of (or any) friends. I was fine before my grandparents died, but after that I didn't know how to talk to anyone any more. I felt too different. My old best friend Cat and I drifted apart, and anyway we went to different secondary schools, and I couldn't make friends with anyone new because everything in their lives was so normal, and I couldn't join in.

Once we got to about thirteen, boys started noticing me for the wrong reasons and I didn't like that either. A bunch of them began asking me for nudes all the time. Obviously I never did it. The girls just thought I was weird and, whenever I got the chance to join in, I would somehow say the wrong thing. I kept my head down, blocked all the boys, and then finally met someone else who was an outsider too.

After that, I didn't need anyone but Frank, right up until the point where he double-crossed me and took the money.

And now I am, for the first time, part of a group. It may be a messed-up group of wildly ridiculous, overprivileged teens, and they may all be horrified by the thing I've done (not as horrified as I am) but nonetheless they accept me. Cosmo is particularly lovely.

'We can all see how sorry you are,' he says. 'And we're here to be your friends, no matter what.'

I try, again, to imagine Tabbi being forced to own what she did, and I know why she was so desperate to run.

Cosmo, Jamie, Laila, Viggo, Clement and Beth. A weird little gang. I might still steal from them when I get the chance, but mainly I want to bring Tabbi down.

We spend our days outside, walking. And inside, talking. We are given jobs to do (we mainly do laundry: endless grey tracksuits). It's unexpected, considering it's rehab and that I'm very much an imposter, but apart from having to own Tabbi's stuff I'm almost happy. Cosmo and I are soon at each other's sides the whole time.

My hatred for Tabbi becomes a solid thing simmering at my core. I'm like a nuclear reactor. Like a nuclear reactor, I could do something dramatic. I start to plan.

One afternoon I go for a solo chat with Emma.

'You're doing so well, Beth,' she says. 'I know you're struggling with forgiving yourself, and I'm glad that you've confronted the consequences of your decisions. I hope you're encouraged by the fact that the group have accepted you.'

That's a more complex question than she knows. I'm glad the group have accepted me, Ruby Robinson. I despise them for accepting me, Tabitha Courtenay, so easily.

'I'm pleased you're planning to atone by volunteering. I think that will be a very positive thing for you. How are you feeling about going home?'

I shake my head. 'Nah. Just gonna stay here.'

We share a nice moment. Emma nods.

'Going back to your old life isn't straightforward, and if there's the chance for a fresh start – school-wise, home-wise – then that's what I'd recommend. Which leads me to a question that might surprise you . . .'

At that point she pauses. I give her my best smile. Yes, Tabbi can do some volunteering. She can volunteer forever. She needs to atone for the rest of her life. I'll commit to that for her. She's gonna need a new passport, though, because I'm going to keep her identity. I'm not giving up Beth. She can get a new Tabbi passport: she'll be fine.

'It might surprise me . . . ?' Whatever it is, I'm going to agree. It'll be some plan for future Tabbi. I'll be far away by then.

'Well – I know it's been a while, but your father has been in touch, to see how you're doing, and he's delighted to hear about your progress. He's going to be in Europe next week and he'd like to visit you. Here.'

Her words hang in the air. It takes a while for me to process them.

Shit.

This man might not have been in Tabbi's life since she

was small, but he's been bankrolling everything she does, and there's no way he'll mistake me for *his own daughter*. For one thing, she must have been exaggerating when she said she hadn't seen him since she was three. For another, he will have seen photos. She's his daughter! Of course he will. He's probably got those awkward school photos in his study or whatever. He knows what Tabbi looks like. In a world of social media, there's no way any parent could accept an imposter as their own child. After drifting along, almost allowing myself to believe that I'm Beth, I'm suddenly pulled up to a screeching handbrake skiddy stop.

We are fucked.

'No,' I say. 'I don't want to see him. I'm not ready. Also, can I have my phone back?'

She sighs. 'It's OK, Beth. I know it hasn't been easy, but we're all so pleased with your progress. It's like you're a different girl.' I give her a quick look, but she doesn't mean anything by it.

I run with it. 'I *am* a different girl,' I say. 'I feel like – this sounds crap, but I feel like I've just been growing up or something. Like – I did something horrific that I'll never be able to undo, and all I can do is find a way to be a force for good in the world. I'll find the guy's family and make amends to them. And then maybe it's going to be OK for me to be . . . happy? If I've learned from this? I don't think I've ever been happy before.'

She looks extremely pleased so I carry on quickly.

'I'm just not sure that I'm ready to see my dad, you

know? Not here, in my safe place. Maybe when I'm back in London? It's only a few more weeks.' I don't want to have to run away. I want to stay because I like it here. I like being rich. I like being hidden away.

I like being someone new.

She nods. She gets it. 'Of course,' she says. 'And that's what we'd usually say. I completely understand your feelings. But it does seem that it could be another positive development for you.'

I sigh. 'My phone?'

'You can have it the day before you leave. Not before that.'

'But can I send him an email? He's never wanted to see me before. And I'd just like to tell him that I appreciate him sending me here. But I'm not ready to see him right now. We'll arrange something for London.'

So I find myself sitting at a laptop computer that is not connected to the internet (much as I hate it, I also get it – this is massively saving me from myself). I have Tabbi's dad's email address, and I'm looking at a blank message.

The account is one they've set up for me: TCourtenay@ZenLodge.ch.

Hey dad,

I stop. I try to access Gmail, just in case, but the computer really isn't connected. I try to take it online by going deep into the settings, but of course that doesn't work. After ten minutes, I give up, sit back and stare at the screen. All I've written is *Hey dad*. Now what? I'm in the little study, a wood-panelled room that smells of old books, because there's a reed diffuser on the mantelpiece that has a label saying 'Old Books' on it. They are pumping the smell of books into the room to make it authentic. It's actually nice.

All I need to do is hold him off until his real daughter is back. I take a deep breath and try to write as Tabbi.

How would she address the man who's paid for everything she's ever done while declining to be in her life? As I don't actually know whether or not they've emailed each other over the years, I have to tread carefully. She might have an email tone that is the opposite of mine. Without any pointers, I'm going to have to work on something that feels like it captures the spirit of Tabbi, but nice-Tabbi. Grateful Tabbi. A girl who has never existed.

I write and delete, write and delete, and half an hour later I have this:

Hey dad,

Thanks for sending me here. I literally mean that. It's been amazing and I'm different now.

I have a lot to come to terms with. The accident. Also some other things I did. But mainly the accident. I'll never forgive myself and I know I have to do everything I can to make amends.

I can't see you next week. That's too much as it's still really intense here. We could meet in London when I'm back if you'd like to see me.

Tabitha xxx

I send it, and it goes to an outbox. I wonder whether I could write other messages while I'm here, whether they might slip through if they switch the internet on before anyone checks what I've done.

Worth a try. I write a quick one to the2traingirls@gmail.com.

> Tabbi! Urgent. Your dad wants to come here. I've told him he can't. Also wtf with you KILLING SOMOENE?

I send it to the outbox, typo and all. I'm too angry to go back and write it properly. Fuck you, Tabitha.

The tech guy comes back in and walks over to the laptop without looking at me. I hold my breath. He tuts, and says, 'You can send the approved one.' I hear the click as he deletes the other message. It was worth a try.

Half an hour later, I'm back in front of the computer looking at Tabbi's dad's reply.

> Dear Tabitha,
>
> First of all, thank you for messaging me. I think it's the first time you've ever contacted me of your own accord!
> Secondly, I'm delighted that the ZL has done what it said on the tin. I'd very much hoped their approach would work for you and am mightily relieved to hear you sounding so different. The reports I've had from the team there have borne that out.
> I'm going to be at meetings in Zurich on Monday. I'll call in and see you on Monday evening. Don't worry – no pressure and nothing heavy. I just want to start to fix things between us and we don't have to do more than

say hello. I've paid a lot of money to them to work their magic on you and I want to have a look at it close up. I'll be there at six. Let me know if you need anything.

Dad
xxx

No. No no no no no no.
Let me know if you need anything.
Could I ask him to pay back Maria? Then I would have nothing tying me to Ruby Robinson. I'd be free.
Could I demand that he forgets what his daughter looks like?
Let me know if you need anything.
I think about the rest of the group. What would they do? I go back over conversations I've had with them, in my head. I think very hard.
Twenty minutes later, I send another message. It's worth a try.

I'll see you on Monday under one condition.

25

As the general anaesthetic kicks in, I wonder what the hell I think I'm doing. It's too late now but what? I feel the gas seeping through me and wonder what the fuck has become of my life. Then it stops because I stop thinking. This is so trippy. The little anaesthetic molecules stride in through the drip and switch me right off. I have a moment to appreciate the lovely sleepiness, and then I'm gone.

After no time at all, and the whole of eternity, I'm awake. In a single room that I'm sure must smell clean and lovely, but I can't really smell anything. I feel trippy, but I'm used to that now.

I look down. Lying in bed. Hospital gown. I close my eyes again, woozy.

Next time everything is clearer. I bring a hand to my face. I can't touch my cheeks because they're bandaged. This is the maddest thing I've ever done, and that is saying something. It's as stupid as scamming people. Worse than leaving a note and running away. Even more ridiculous than swapping lives with a stranger on the train. I make an effort to breathe. It only really works through my mouth.

There's a woman in the room. She walks over to me. I look at her face. I don't know her. For a second, I think she's Maria O'Neill, come to demand her money. But no – she's in a medical uniform of some kind. Her features fall into place. She's much younger than Maria. She's from the hospital. I don't know her. I didn't know you could get an operation on a Sunday, but I guess you can do anything if you pay for it. She's probably being paid loads. That's why she's smiling.

'Hello, Tabitha,' she says. Her voice is soothing. 'Well, that all seemed to go well.'

When Albert picks me up a few hours later, I ask if I can sit in the front.

'By all means,' he says, but he still presses a button by the steering wheel that means I can't open my door. Not that I wanted to, but I have to check. He sees me trying the handle. We exchange a glance that is amused on his side and also, I hope, amused on mine, but I'm under so many bandages that he won't be able to tell. Now the anaesthetic is wearing off, my face is very, very sore.

'How long have you worked at Zen Lodge?' I am sick of being in my head. I want to talk about someone else.

'Six years,' he says.

'Before that?'

'I was in the military.'

'Stacks up,' I tell him. 'If I'd known that, I might not have run away.'

'Oh, I think you would.'

I take myself back there. I was shitting myself at heading into the unknown. For sure I was going to try something.

'Yeah,' I say. 'Maybe. So do you live in the lodge?'

By the time we arrive back, I know that Albert lives in Grindelwald, down the mountain from the lodge, and that he is married to the security guy Pierre. I know that he grew up in Basel, which turns out to be another city in Switzerland. He fakes being offended that I didn't know that.

'Where did you think it was?'

I shrug. 'Wouldn't have been sure it was a real place. It sounds like it's from a movie.'

Every time he tries to ask me a question, I deflect. He asks if I have any siblings and I find out that he has four. He asks what I want to do for a career and I find out that he used to want to be a pilot, then changed his mind after a bumpy flight. I'm sorry when the Zen Lodge gates swing open for us, because now I have to go back to dreading tomorrow.

The rest of the group, though, are waiting, sitting on the steps by the front door in the golden evening sunshine, breathing the crystal air. The sight of them, a reception committee, makes my heart leap. Of course they think I'm ridiculous for dashing off for surgery I don't need, but it's not a million miles away from normality for them. I got the idea, after all, from Jamie. She literally suggested it to me on our first night here.

Cosmo jumps up. I wish we could keep in touch once we're out of here, but if I'm not about to be busted by Tabbi's dad, I'll be melting away with some of his money. Still, I'm happy to see him. They're all wearing grey tracksuits, and they look like cult members. Even now, I'm still wearing my Zen Lodge prison uniform.

Albert opens the car door for me and ushers me out.

'It's been a delight, Miss Courtenay,' he says.

I hesitate. I have two black eyes, lots of bruising, bandaging like someone who's been in a fire and, somewhere under all that, a new nose that I never even wanted. The old nose was my favourite feature.

'You look fine,' says Albert, and I know I can hardly stay in the car forever so, self-conscious, I step out. Deep breath. In through the mouth, out through the mouth.

I stand up and turn my face towards the group. There is a little gasp, but it's more for show than anything. Jamie comes straight over and looks at me with a critical eye. She gives a sharp nod. 'Looks good. This'll go down fast.' She indicates my face with a sweep of her hand. 'Can't wait to see what's under there.'

Cosmo is next. 'Was it OK? Do you feel all right?'

I give him the best smile you can when your face is all bruised and bandaged. I mean, what sort of idiot has surgery under a general anaesthetic when they don't even need it?

This sort.

'I feel fine. Bit woozy.'

'Come in.'

I really hope Cosmo isn't misunderstanding our friendship. When I say something in group that no one else gets, Cosmo gets it. He laughs. He understands. I love him as a friend. I do not want anyone as a boyfriend.

I guess I've just had facial surgery: I've done something that means no one will want to make a move on me for quite some time.

My dad – Tabbi's dad, Beth's dad – will be here tomorrow afternoon. My bandaged face is the only disguise I could think of. You'd have to be a shit parent to not recognize your own child no matter what.

Luckily, the one thing I know about this man is that he's a shit parent.

26

George Courtenay is standing in the entrance hall. He's wearing a pale blue shirt and a pair of navy shorts. My face is still bandaged and swollen, to the point where I don't recognize myself. I still don't know what they've done to my nose under all that: I said I wanted it to be cuter and that did, in fact, seem to be a thing that they were up for doing. I'm a bit miffed that they just rolled their sleeves up and did it. They could have at least tried to say, 'It's cute already.'

Rich people are weird. No wonder we've destroyed our ecosystem. This guy, the man I'm looking at from the top of the stairs, the one who hasn't noticed me yet, just paid over ten grand for his own child to have unnecessary surgery.

I remember life in Sprowston. What it was like, having just enough money, but absolutely nothing for luxuries. What it was like for Frank, having much less than that. The way we brainstormed every single possible get-rich-quick scheme. When you're locked out of this system, it's impossible to break into it, though I guess I've done it in a temporary way.

Fuck that. I've done it. I'm here now and I'm never going back.

I think again of the money we scammed. If I carry on down this path, I'll be able to get it back easily. If I can make this man believe I'm his daughter, I'll probably be able to ask for thirty k. Though that's quite the *if*.

I can see from up here that he has a thick head of hair. I wonder if it's a transplant. Rich people are very fake. It's weird that when humans have infinity money they use it not to, say, ensure everyone has basic food and a home like you'd think, but to pay someone to make them look as if they've been on the planet just a little bit less time than they have. So futile. So pathetic. So intoxicating.

Deep breath. I feel like a kid in my grey PJs, running down the grand staircase to seek my dad's approval like he's Captain von Trapp or something (and he does look a bit like that – it's not just the setting). It's weirdly easy to convince myself that I'm Tabbi. *He hasn't seen you since you were three. Your face is hidden. You can do this if you believe in it.*

I don't know if he's spoken to her recently. He probably has. I lower my voice, make it as plummy as I can. I know I'm good at her voice now.

'Dad!' Wow. That's a weird word to send down a staircase.

He looks up. This is it. This is the moment.

Our eyes meet. He looks a bit shocked, but that's because I have two black eyes and a bandaged face. Then he smiles and I realize that, like a spider, he's more scared of me than I am of him.

Like a spider, I am coming to entrap him. If I can make this man believe I'm his daughter, we are ON.

'Tabitha!' His voice is warm. He has a much nicer voice, actually, than I expected. Half English, half American. He opens his arms and I walk into them. 'Oh, look at you,' he says. He pulls me back and looks into my eyes. I tense. This is the moment. But he just says: 'Look at those beautiful eyes.' He pulls me close.

I remember my eyebrows. Tabbi butchered them on the train. They look great now that they've been properly shaped. They're good camouflage.

Will I smell wrong? No. Because last time he smelled me I was three, so I would have smelled of little kid. Also, I've sprayed on a lot of Tabbi's body spray and I'm pretty sure he won't be picking up pheromones or whatever might lead him to push me away and say, 'Not mine.'

I hug him back. It feels nice. He feels like a parent. I push my face into his shirt even though it hurts. I try to push away the feelings, but they won't stop. There is nothing I could do to stop this. I feel it building and building inside me, hot behind my eyes. No! This was not the plan. What's going on? I cry and cry and cry. It hurts like hell, and I was not supposed to be doing that. This is no place for real emotion, but here it is. My facial landscape isn't ready for this, but I can't do anything about it. *Ouch*.

He holds me tight, being a parent, and even though he's a crap one who hasn't seen his girl since she was tiny, who's just spent his life ignoring her and paying for things from afar, I feel him starting to shake too.

I'm making my bandages, and his shirt, all snotty. Whatever: I can't help it. All my life I've needed a parent, and since my grandparents died I've never had one. Claire and Matthew should never have taken me on. I've always been on my own, and here is a man who's come up a mountain to see me, and I don't care if he's my real dad or not. I've missed him all my life.

Hands are on my shoulder, moving me. I am steered into a little room I've never been to before. The hands sit me down on a squashy sofa. I look up and it's Emma. She hands me a box of tissues and pats my shoulder.

My dad is next to me. He shifts up and puts an arm round my shoulders.

'I'm so sorry, darling girl,' he says. 'I'm so sorry. I should have waited – you were right.' I don't say anything because I don't trust myself to speak, so he carries on. 'I've been doing a lot of reflecting. I just – well, I broke up with someone because I realized I just didn't have the energy to do it all again. Marriage. You know: I don't know who said it but there's a quote. Maybe Groucho Marx? "I'm not going to get married again. I'm just going to find a woman I don't like and give her a house." And that popped into my head. And I felt: yes. Let's not get married again. No need. It'll only end badly. It always does.'

I find I'm smiling a bit, through my tears. My bruised nose really, really hurts. The snotty, ugly crying thing is awful for it. It throbs so much that it's probably pulsating, looking weird, as if it's about to burst open, and because I'm scared of that happening I make a huge effort not to cry any more.

I'm glad there's no mirror in here. I bet I really need fresh bandages.

'Are you going to do that instead?' I say. It comes out too high so I drop my voice to Tabbi's. 'Find a woman you don't like? Give her a house?'

He squeezes my shoulder. 'Thought I might skip that part too.'

I nod. I snuggle in under his arm. This is my dad. As far as he's concerned, I'm his daughter. This is everything I never knew I wanted. It hasn't occurred to him for one second that I might be an imposter.

Someone brings us a tray of tea, with a teapot and a milk jug and a plate of biscuits. Dad pours it and hands me a cup. I have to put the saucer back on the tray because I'm shaking so much that it keeps clattering. I just hold the cup, keeping it still by using both hands, treating it like a tiny mug of comfort.

'So,' I say.

'So.' He inhales deeply. 'Tabitha. As you know, I've been a terrible father to you.'

I start to say something, but he holds up a hand to stop me.

'And,' he carries on, 'I want that to change. Honestly, I can't believe so much time has passed. I wouldn't even have recognized you.'

I indicate my face with a hand. 'You get a pass on that one.'

'It went well?'

'Apparently.'

'I'm sure you didn't need it. But if it's going to make life feel easier. And – it's good to see that you've put on a bit of weight. If it's OK to say that.'

'Oh, cheers!' This genuinely makes me laugh. Tabbi was very skinny. So he must have seen a recent photo. 'I'd have recognized *you*,' I add. Obviously not, but it feels like the right thing to say. I'm right: he loves it. He puts his cup down and leans in.

'Can we make this better, Tabbi? What you did – the thing with the homeless man – it was a huge wake-up call to me. I feel responsible. I'd like to have you back in my life properly. I've – I mean, stop me if this sounds crap, right?'

'I will. But also –' Shall I do this? If I do it, then I'm going all in. I wasn't planning to, but it feels like the way to go. I breathe in, out, in. I do it. 'Also, can you call me Beth now? New start?'

If he's calling me Beth, then I'm taking Tabbi's life. I'm not switching back. I'm not even melting away. I'm doing this.

'Beth?'

'It's the only other way I could think of to shorten Tabitha. I don't . . . I don't think I want to be Tabbi any more.'

He nods. 'Of course. OK. We can do that. Beth. It's pretty. Yes. Beth – I've had to do some reflection. I guess a lot of things caught up with me. And you . . .'

He stops.

'What about me?'

'I guess. I'm sorry, Tabitha. Beth. Things went very wrong between me and your mother, and I'm afraid you were caught up in it. When I left, she said if I walked away

I'd never see you again, and she stuck to it. And I'm afraid I didn't try as hard as I could. And so you went off the rails, and I have to hold myself accountable.'

'You've paid for everything, though,' I say. 'Over the years. I bet you didn't have to.' I realize I have no idea what my rich dad does for a living. I wonder whether I could get away with asking.

'Throwing money at things,' he says. 'Sure. Easy. It's always been my default. I suspect it did you more harm than good. I mean, to take an immediate example, you were *not* in need of a new nose.'

I shrug. 'To take a less immediate example,' I say, 'you sorted out a terrible, terrible thing that I did. And it would have fucked my whole life – it should have done, really. I did the worst thing in the world, Dad. I went out drunk in a car and . . . killed someone. Actually killed a human being. I should be in prison. We both know that. But everything you did for me after that . . . even then, I was ungrateful. I really, really didn't want to come here. I know you sent me that Jana woman to escort me here. I'd have done anything to escape from her. I did my best.'

I feel him shaking as he laughs. 'She did mention that you didn't make it easy.'

'She hated me, and she was right to. But also *you* were right. Whoever picked this place out for me – it was the right thing. It was exactly what I needed. I'd got so messed up, Dad.'

I'm trying really hard not to cry again. Even though the story I'm telling is Tabbi's, I'm talking about myself too. And

I'm with this man who seems to love me, and I'm calling him Dad. I haven't called anyone *Dad* since the accident. I love the way it sounds, coming out of my mouth. Three little letters. One sharp spike of a word. I want to say it over and over again, to send little *Dads* out of my mouth to march around the room, looking comforting and friendly.

'I hold myself responsible for that too. Hands up: it's monstrously bad parenting. And – I know this is a huge thing for you to come to terms with. I'm full of admiration that you've done it. There's nothing we can do, sadly, to bring the gentleman in question back, but you can make sure you don't do anything like it – ever again. Make this a turning point. And you're doing that. I can see you are.'

I jump in. 'Yes! I'm going to do everything I can. I've been talking to Emma about it. I can work with charities, do voluntary work with homeless charities, whatever it takes.'

He squeezes my hand.

'Good girl. Well, let me support you. I've had some therapy after breaking off my engagement to Janelle. And I've got a lot of sorting out to do. Top of the list, of course: my daughter.'

I decide to take a risk: 'Er . . . do you have any more kids?'

'Just you.' Thank God for that. 'After I lost you, I never wanted to do it again. My little girl.' He pauses. 'Had you been imagining an army of half-siblings out there?'

'I hadn't been *not* imagining them.' He nods as if that makes any kind of sense. Then I say, 'There might be some you don't know about, though, right?'

He pauses. 'I guess there could be. Really, though, I doubt it. They'd have come to me for child support.'

It hangs there a bit. Just how much of a shit is this man? A lot of one. I know that. But he seems to want to fix it, with me at least. With his daughter. Who is, right now, me.

I don't care about the genetics. George Courtenay and I need each other. Whatever the DNA might say, I want this man to be my dad.

We talk about Switzerland. I ask if he's really here on business, and he admits that he's not.

'I just said I was in Zurich to make it feel less weird if I came to visit,' he says. 'I couldn't wait any longer to see you.' He's looking out of the window. Not meeting my eye. Either this man really is having a reckoning of the soul, or he's as good an actor as I am.

I'm not acting any more. All this emotion is real. I like this man. I'm keeping him.

'You could have just said you wanted to see me,' I say.

'You'd have hated that. Wouldn't you?'

I don't reply. Yes, I would. I feel the room closing in on me. Am I doing this? This isn't something I can undo. This will totally screw over the real Tabbi.

She is a drunk-driver. She killed someone. Fuck her.

I stand up. 'Shall we go for a walk?'

As he gets to his feet, he hands me a banknote. Some random pocket money. I guess that's what he does. I shove it into my pocket without looking at it.

*

We are out on the mountain. No one comes this way unless it's to visit the lodge so I'm not self-conscious about basically presenting myself to the outside world wearing a prison tracksuit and with a face so bandaged that I am, quite clearly, unrecognizable even to a parent. We only walk a little way: it's my first time out since I got back yesterday and the fresh air stings my lungs. I've lost all my fitness: I have spent way too much time lying around and no time actually doing anything. It's been lovely.

We stop and look at the mountains. I point at one.

'That's the Eiger,' I say. I only found this out relatively recently. 'The north face.'

He looks at it for a long time. 'How about that?' he says. The north face is basically flat and vertical. A slab of rock. No wonder it's famous for being hard to climb. 'It couldn't be done, and they did it anyway.'

Under the bandages, I'm smiling. Clichéd though it may be, I take inspiration from that mountain. I love looking at it. I love the way the green on the lower slopes turns to dark rock, to black and grey and brown, with dots of white at the top. I love the wisps of white cloud in the deep blue sky above.

'So – what would you like to do,' he says, 'after this?'

I take a deep breath. This is it. I'm going to go with it. Scale the north face. Attempt the impossible.

'I'd like to go home with you,' I say. 'Please.'

He says yes.

Yes.

He says it straight away. He says it smiling. He says he'll

collect me and take me back to his place. I don't know where his place is, and I'm pretty sure other Tabbi never told me. I haven't seen him since I was three: why would I care where he lives?

'I can't even remember where you live,' I say.

The words hang there. I worry that I've totally fucked up, but then he says, 'Based in Paris, currently.'

I nod. I can manage Paris. I mean, rich-girl Paris is not going to be shabby. Cosmo lives there, so I'll even have a friend. My French is worse than Tabbi's, for sure, so I'll have to work on that, but whatever. I'm just glad it's not London, because Tabbi's mum lives in London, and so do all her friends, whoever they are, and this is only going to work for as long as I can stay away from all of that.

I do know I can't make it work forever. I know it's not actually my life. But I think I can pay off the O'Neills this way. I think I can get myself a bit of time feeling like I have a parent. I think I can fuck Tabbi over in the way she deserves.

And I want it.

I love rich-person life. Of course I want to hang on to it. Of course I want to steal everything from that girl. And I can't disappoint George: we have bonded now. It would destroy him to find out that the girl who's finally forgiven him is an imposter.

So how about if I don't tell him?

How about if I steal her life completely?

We walk side by side. He keeps giving me little glances. The grass up here is luscious and the tiny flowers are gorgeous. They poke up through the stony soil, looking as if someone has painted them in. They're pale pink, yellow, deep purple. The air is sweet and soft. The cowbells ding away all around us.

What do I have to go back to? Nothing. I look at the flowers coming out between the rocks and I want to be like them. Flourishing, where I shouldn't be able to grow. Finding a way.

27

'Can I leave early?' I say. 'Just a few days. I could come home with you now!'

He looks at me for a long time. I almost suspect that he's busted me and I start to try to strategize. I'm opening my mouth to back-pedal when he speaks in a gentle tone.

'Probably not the best idea,' he says. 'You're doing so well. It's everything I hoped for, and more, and I don't want to risk it by whisking you away before the treatment is finished. See it out, Beth. It's not long. I'll come back and collect you myself if you like.'

Right. I cannot risk the real Tabbi coming face to face with her actual father. I don't know how long it'll take her to come and find me when I don't turn up at the station, but it might only be a matter of hours. That's too risky. I take a deep breath. That mountain air never gets old. Cold, but not old.

'If I have to see it out –' I touch my face and hope I'll be able to say this in a way that makes sense – 'could I stay a couple of days longer?' I can see from his expression that this has come out sounding nonsensical, and I scrabble around for a way to make it seem even a tiny bit logical.

'If I'm moving to Paris, can I wait until I can show my face properly? Let it heal a little bit more?'

'You want to leave early and, if you can't do that, you want to leave late?'

I try to style it out. 'Yep.' Time ticks on. The mountains probably do a tiny bit more eroding. In the end, he shrugs.

'That actually suits me. How about if I come on the twenty-sixth? I'll check with the guys at the lodge. I was meant to be in New York on the twenty-third, so this way I could go, sort out my stuff there and be back here for you on the Monday. Is that OK?'

I grin. It makes my face hurt. 'Yeah,' I say. 'Monday is perfect.'

We sit outside before he leaves. The sun is out. The air is madly fresh, and all my doubts have blown away. I'm Beth Courtenay and I'm staying that way. I'm doing this. I'm scamming Tabbi and stealing her whole life, and the best thing is that, unlike Maria O'Neill, she deserves it.

'The thing with spelling Tabbi with an i,' I say. 'It was a bit stupid, really, wasn't it?'

He gives me a 'you can say that but I can't' look.

'It probably suited you for a while,' he says. 'But you've grown out of it, and I'm glad. I always thought Tabitha was a classy name, but Tabbi sounds a bit feline, doesn't it? Your mother wanted to call you Xanthia, you know. I felt that a name beginning with an X was a bit much. Who has a name beginning with X?'

I think for a moment. 'Xavier?' I say. I pronounce it the French way. *Zavvy-ay.*

'Who's Xavier?'

I shrug. 'I don't actually know anyone called that. It was just an example.'

'Fair enough. Xavier and Xanthia. No one else, though, really.'

I nod. 'Yeah. Thanks for not letting me be Xanthia. That would have driven me crazy.'

His chauffeur appears from around the side of the building, and George starts to stand up. He stops, hesitates and then says: 'I want to say something before I go. Two things, actually.'

I smile though my heartbeat speeds up. I hope this isn't going to be a thing that brings everything crashing down. 'Go on.'

His car is parked at the side of the lodge. We walk towards it slowly as we talk.

'First – I hope this doesn't sound weird, or put too much pressure on you or anything, but – this has been one of the best days of my life.'

My heart does something very bizarre. Don't cry. Don't endanger the nose again. 'Mine too,' I manage to say, and I'm not lying or pretending at all. I have a parent. It's momentous. There's absolutely no way that I'm letting go of this. 'I've actually wanted this for ages. I guess I was pushing you away.'

'Pushing quite hard.' His voice is dry. God knows what she's said to him.

'Sorry. Not any more. What's the second thing?'

His chauffeur, who is literally wearing a uniform, opens

the car's back door and waits next to it, because of course rich people can't close the door after they get in.

Dad is about to get into the car and drive away. But he'll be back: he'll be back here to pick me up in fourteen days and then I'm going to make this work for as long as I possibly can. I'll make it work until Tabbi's mum shows up, or –

'Leo,' he says. 'Your sister.'

I frown at him. Leo isn't his daughter, so why is he talking about her?

'She messaged me. We obviously haven't been in touch for a while, but actually it was Leo who prompted me to visit you. She contacted me out of the blue to say that she'd been in Cannes with her husband and child, a week or two earlier, and she was certain she'd run into you there. That you were a waitress in a restaurant. She said she tried to talk to you, but that the waitress had no idea what she was talking about. She was adamant, though. She knew your mother wasn't the appropriate conduit, all things considered, so she tracked me down and messaged me.'

He pauses. My breathing is going crazy. Maybe it was just someone who looked like Tabbi. I bet it wasn't, though. I bet it was her.

Because I don't say anything, he carries on talking. 'And that made me see that she's worried about you too. It made me want to come here and check on you, because honestly, Beth? If anyone could have slipped away unnoticed and become a waitress in Cannes, it would have been you.'

She ran out of money and got a job. Of course she did.

My mind is whirring. I'm going to have to do something about that sister: I'm going to have to do it without her ever laying eyes on me. *Shit*.

He's looking at me. I take a deep, deep breath.

'Well, of course it wasn't me,' I say. Is my voice wobbling? It had better not be.

'I know! So just get in touch and reassure her. It's good to have family, right? And Leo was always a great kid. You know she has a daughter now? A little girl. Annabelle or something like that.'

I feel myself sinking into the immaculate driveway. I need bravado. I summon it from somewhere. I have no idea if I'm meant to know about Leo's kid so I ignore that and do my best to laugh.

'Leo hasn't seen me for a long time either,' I say. Then it feels like the right time to go on the attack. I frown, though he can't see it under the bandages. I look away from him. 'So that's why you're really here. All that stuff you said about wanting to reconnect, about not getting married again and making amends? Was that bullshit? Were you just checking up on me because you thought I might have run away?'

He sighs. 'No, Ta– Beth. It wasn't bullshit. It was the truth. Honestly – Leo's email gave me the kick I needed because it made me realize that I wasn't sure I'd have recognized you. I mean, if I was out to dinner in Cannes and the waitress was your doppelgänger or whatever, would I have known? No. I wouldn't. And that was chilling. A kick up the arse.'

I need to find out. We're standing next to the car and he's about to leave.

'Can I see the message?' I say. 'Leo's?' He stops. Thinks. Then shrugs.

'If you like.'

He gets his phone out, taps on the screen and scrolls a bit (phones! They're suddenly like something from a different universe). Then he hands it to me. The weight of it is instantly familiar in my hand. An email from Leonora Fairfax. I scan it for the word and it's right there.

Hi George. Been ages! I hope you don't mind . . .

Blah blah blah. I skip to the right place.

I was so sure it was her. I went back to talk to her and she insisted her name was Ruby and you know, maybe it was. It was just chilling to see someone who was so much like Tabbi, and so I think you should check whether she really is in the rehab place because we both know she needs to be there for her own good and everyone else's.

She insisted her name was Ruby.
Of course she did.
I hand the phone back.
'Weird,' I say. 'Well, if I was renaming myself I wouldn't go for *Ruby*.'
He smiles. 'You can let her know you're here.'
'Yes,' I say. 'Here I am!'
He looks at me with a little smile.
'Here you are,' he agrees.

28

'I'm staying a few days longer.' I say it to Cosmo. We're playing table football in the games room.

'I guessed it,' he says. He gives a little nod that I know is at my face. 'Don't wanna scare the outside world?'

'You know it.' I swing a striker round and only manage to nudge the ball a tiny bit forward. Cosmo hits it with one of his guys, and it goes past all the rest of my players and straight into the goal.

'Yay! Champion!' He pulls his T-shirt up and runs round the room, misjudging it and crashing into the door. God, I love this place. I run over to him.

'You OK?'

He laughs and pulls the T-shirt back down. 'I think I'll survive.'

We are very close. We look at each other. He takes my hand and I step away. If my face wasn't covered in bandages, I think he might have tried to kiss me just then. I step back and back and back. I don't want this.

'Bethie,' he says.

'Cosmo.'

'I wish I could . . .'

It hangs there in the air.

'You don't,' I say. 'I'm a mess.'

I feel a bit sick. I do like Cosmo, but I don't fancy him enough to risk it, and also my face really, really hurts. I feel all the little footballers cringing along with me. The chess pieces, in their box, are bent double in mortification.

Cosmo's voice is soft. 'Very gently?'

'No, Cosmo.'

He responds by leaning in and kissing my lips, so gently that it's a ghost of a kiss, a butterfly. I step away.

'Cosmo,' I say, and I'm annoyed now. 'I don't want to kiss you, OK?'

He slumps. I turn away.

'I'm sorry.' It's a whisper. 'Sorry, Bethie. Can we forget this ever happened?'

I am breathing hard. 'We can, but only if you promise not to do it again. Ever.'

The silence stretches on.

'Sure,' he says. 'I guess – I mean, I guess it's no secret that I have a massive crush on you. Have done since day one.'

We look at each other.

'I really love you as a friend,' I say. 'I'm not in any place for a relationship. But I really, really need a best friend. I think I'm moving to Paris. The thing is, I –'

'Paris! No way! Are you serious?'

I pull back. I came so close to telling him my truth. Thank God he interrupted. If I'm going through with this – if I'm fully stealing Tabbi's life – then I can never, ever tell.

On the day the others leave, I can't stay still. I try to imagine what Tabbi will do. First she'll wait in Zurich, at the station, under the clock. Then she'll look around. That'll take a while. She'll go back to the meeting place. When she realizes I'm not coming, she'll set off to find me here. How quickly she gets to Zen Lodge depends on how much money she has: if she's been waitressing in the South of France, I guess she won't be travelling from Zurich by cab. The train pass will get her to Grindelwald, and that's probably nearly as fast. We were meeting at midday: the earliest she could possibly turn up, if she waited a couple of hours then found a fast train, is about four thirty.

I think about it as I say goodbye to the others. Cosmo and I will meet soon in Paris (if Tabbi doesn't blow it all apart before then) and I hope it won't be awkward. Meanwhile I'm going to stay here like a hotel guest, no longer going to group sessions, not particularly accountable to anyone, just hanging out, being happy. This is the thing Tabbi promised me, the beautiful time relaxing in the mountains. It is finally happening.

I even get to move bedrooms for these last three nights. Although I got fond of my cell, now I'm in a proper room, a big one on the first floor, and that's a million times better. It has huge windows and a massive bathroom with a bath with jets in it. God knows what Dad paid for this. It also has a view down the drive.

I stand on the front step and wave the others off. Laila is first to leave: a Tesla turns up to whisk her away, back to the airport and then New York. We all hug. I love Laila. She will never know that she was going to be my target, before I discovered what Tabbi had actually done, and shifted focus to stealing everything she has instead.

Viggo and Clement leave together: they eventually became friends, despite being opposites, because they were the two odd ones out, and I'm pretty sure they found some extremely common ground in the form of an unlikely romance. Cosmo gets into a cab to the airport, hugging me and apologizing again into my short hair.

'See you in Paris,' he says, and I hug him tight and tell him I can't wait to meet up.

Jamie is the last to go. Her roots are longer now and she says she's done with the pink. 'I'm gonna be Little Miss Sensible for a while,' she says. 'That'll freak them out.' I'm not sure Jamie is totally on the straight and narrow. She's the loudest, most fun person here.

'Take care, you nutter,' she says. As she hugs me goodbye, she whispers into my ear, so quietly that there's no chance anyone else will hear, 'I know you're not Tabbi Courtenay, babe. I went to prep school with her. Whatever's going on here, I'm in awe.'

She steps back to look at my face. I can't do anything but laugh.

'I don't know what you're talking about,' I say. She mimes zipped lips and jumps in the waiting car. I wave her off.

Wow. All that time, she knew. I had no idea that she'd busted me. Will she tell? It's a great story. Shit.

But she didn't tell anyone in here. She could have done and it would have been dramatic. *Shit shit shit.* I had no idea I was at Jamie's mercy the whole time. I decide to message her the moment I'm out. Keep her onside.

I'm on my own now. Just me and the mountains and the sky. I walk away from the building, towards the Eiger, right to the edge of the grounds. I'm allowed to leave the perimeter now.

I check the time. I have at least two hours before she could get here.

There's a train that goes up the mountain, and it has a request stop fifteen minutes' walk from here. I know this because Albert told me about it. I tell Pierre where I'm going, put Tabbi's bank card into my pocket with the note my dad gave me and then I just walk straight out of the Zen Lodge for the first time in six weeks, and head off to explore.

It feels strange stepping out of my world. Strange and exciting.

The little train is yellow and green, and impossibly perfect. It's wood-panelled on the inside. I sit on a slatted wooden bench by the open window and let the breeze ruffle my hair. It's nice that it's long enough to be ruffled, even a little bit. I breathe deeply and try to steel myself for what's to come.

There are tourists on this train. I keep glancing around

at them. The group of older people with walking poles. The two girls who I think are speaking Chinese, who are clearly excited. Three men in high-end outdoor gear. I feel my force field separating me from everyone. They're on holiday. A holiday Ruby Robinson could never have imagined, but a temporary thing. They're in town for a week or so, maybe less. I've been here for Beth Courtenay's entire life.

My bandages are off now and, although people look a bit surprised by my bruised face, no one approaches me. I just have a nude plaster over my nose, and the remnants of two black eyes. The bump is off my nose, and, although I miss it, I feel that I look like Beth. I'm someone who didn't exist before.

I check my watch all the time. She will be at the station now.

I get off the train when it reaches the place up the mountain, which is called Kleine Scheidegg. Lots of the other people shuffle down the platform for another train, heading further up, but I don't have time for that. I just follow the path, past a cafe and souvenir shop, and walk upwards because that's what the happy girls are doing, and they have the same amount of mountain equipment as me, i.e. none.

I walk up a gravelly path, looking at the cows on one side and the Eiger ahead. It's hotter than you'd think it would be up a mountain, and I'm soon sweating. I think of the fact that I've actually spent six whole weeks confined to an admittedly massive house and its huge garden, and that all this was nearby, but we might as well have been in a different dimension. We were a short walk from people's carefree holidays, and we were being straightened out.

If I manage to carry on being Beth, I'll be able to come to places like this, just for fun.

I'm breathing heavily, panting as the sun and the altitude and the exertion are all more than I'm used to. There are cows all over the place here, their bells soundtracking my strange outing. I open a rope barrier in the electric fence, close it carefully behind me, then walk round a corner and actually gasp.

There's a lake, right in front of me. It's bright, bright turquoise. It looks like something that cannot possibly exist, but it's there. Real. Like a jewel. I want to step into it. I want some kind of ritual, to baptize myself as Beth Courtenay for real, but there's a big sign saying you mustn't get in, and I don't want to draw attention to myself. Still, I kneel down and scoop up some water with my hand. It's freezing. So freezing there should be ice in it. I wash my face with it, and am reborn.

I walk round the lake. At the far end I stand and look up at the Eiger's north face. I inhale deeply. That fresh, magical air. Climbing that slab of rock looks impossible, but (for some reason) they did it in the end.

Stealing someone's life looks impossible too, but hey. Watch me.

I was partly Ruby when I went up the mountain. When I come down, I'm all Beth.

*

She arrives the next morning, and I am ready. I'm sitting by my bedroom window, staring at the drive, and when I see a figure on foot at the end of it I know it's her and I'm glad.

Even from this distance, I'm shocked. Her hair has grown a bit and been cut into some kind of shape, but she looks like she slept in a bin. I realize that I'm a bit disgusted by that after my weeks of luxury and reflection, though I guess I look like I've been in a fight . . .

Tabbi looks like the life that should have been mine. She's the ghost of everything I didn't do. The nights sleeping rough, the scraping, the living off your wits. She's done it.

My heart, which has been so calm lately (I know that for sure, thanks to the Apple Watch), starts going wild. She is standing at the end of the drive, wearing my old jeans done up with a ropey belt because they're way too big for her, and she's looking at me without knowing it. I step back from the window.

One thing I've learned over these six weeks is that if you already have things, it's much easier to get more. And, when you have things, you'd be mad to give them up. That was a massive misstep on Tabbi's part.

As I watch, she climbs the fence. She swings herself over it easily. I guess this isn't really a place that people ever want to break into. Why would you? They're more bothered about stopping the troubled teenagers getting out.

I can't see what happens when she gets to the door because the angle's wrong. I stand at the window and look as straight down as I can, but I can't even see the top of her head.

Time stands still. I wait for the footsteps on the stairs, the tap on the door, the 'Beth?' The 'Could you just come down and help us sort this out?'

I wait and wait.

It doesn't happen. As I watch, my nemesis is escorted back down the drive by Pierre. I stand and watch, barely breathing, as she is ejected with some force. She almost falls over. She walks away, but just goes and stands behind that big rock. I can see her clearly from up here. Her eyes are scanning the building. I take several steps back into the room.

I walk away. In a bit, I'll go out on my own, and let her talk to me. It has to happen. I'll take the cash I got from Dad and I'll do my best to pay her off with it.

I find Pierre before I go. He's sitting in the entrance hall with a coffee.

'Just off for another walk,' I say.

He makes a *please don't* face. 'Someone climbed the fence a while ago. An intruder. You should stay in for now.'

I nod. 'OK. I'll stay inside the fence. But I want a bit of air. I'll go round the perimeter.'

'Sure,' he says. 'Give me a shout if you see anyone suspicious. In fact!' He grins and gets up. A moment later, I'm holding a walkie-talkie. 'Channel two. Just press this button here and talk if you need any help. OK?'

I nod. I want to hug him. This is better than I could ever have planned it.

I walk along the side path, slightly uphill, to the boundary fence, and then I start walking beside the fence. It doesn't take long. I hear running footsteps and gasping breath, and then there she is.

I steel myself.

She yells: 'Ruby!' She does it again and again. She runs up to the fence next to me and steps back, shocked.

I'm shocked too. Here we are, face to face. She's real. I'm living her life and she's right in front of me.

'Ruby,' she says. 'What happened to your face?' She thinks I've been in a fight. It's wrong-footed her: good.

I take a deep breath and stay in character.

'I'm sorry?' I say. I convince myself that this really is some random stranger, scaring me. 'Can I . . . ?' I look back towards the lodge, checking for backup.

'Ruby,' she says. 'Look, I might have got the day wrong, or else you've stayed longer because –' She points at my face. 'Whatever has happened to you, I'm so sorry. But anyway I'm here. We did it! When will you be ready to leave? I need my bank card. I'm so completely out of cash. I'm absolutely starving.'

I channel Beth Courtenay. I look her in the eye. I pick up my walkie-talkie, ready to summon help.

'I'm sorry to hear that,' I say. 'But – why are you calling me Ruby?'

PART THREE

29

Eleven months later

Beth

I sit on the bench in the school grounds and send the last thousand euros. When Maria O'Neill sees it, she will find the reference 'frank brody has the rest', and then I am done.

I've sent her fifteen grand, which is a lot even for me, even in this life, and now we're straight. I've done it via anonymous links over the course of a year, and she's never going to be able to trace it even if she has someone who's great at this stuff, which she does. They're good, but not this good, and anyway I've paid off a lot more than I took and given them a shove to find the double-crossing bastard who's really responsible, so I don't think they need me now.

I told Dad I'd done it. He thinks Tabbi did the romance scam, and even though he knows the real thing she did, which is much worse, he was disappointed. 'Thirty thousand pounds?' he said.

'I only actually had two of it. My ex took the rest.'

'That boy.' He frowned. He already knew about the break-up with Barney. I guess because it's caught up in the events of that night – the night Tabbi killed a man. There's still something I don't know about it. It's unsettling because I have no idea what it is. Dad knows and I have to act like I do too. It's to do with Barney. The way he broke up with her.

I check the money's gone and smile. Cosmo comes running down the flagstoned path and flings himself on the bench beside me.

'You look happy,' he says.

'Yeah,' I say. 'Just sorted something.'

I jump to my feet. I am fully Beth Courtenay, and this is where I belong. Cosmo stands back up too, laughing at my energy.

'Let's walk.' I set off, knowing that he'll follow. He always does.

I walk across the grass, past groups of younger kids playing tag, past some Year Ten girls baring as much flesh as they can to sunbathe. In sixth form, we wear our own clothes, but the younger kids wear uniforms in a shade of blue that somehow manages to look expensive. It's so close to the navy of my uniform in my other life, and yet entirely different.

This school is a very expensive international one in Paris. Actually just outside Paris, and we all travel here by private school bus. The weirdest thing about it is the fact that I absolutely love it. I love school: who could have imagined that? I live in the centre of this city with George, who is, no matter what the biology says, my dad. We are happy together. I'm not Tabbi: this isn't her life. I've smoothed over the things she messed up, made sure everyone knows that I hate drink-driving and that I'm sorry, and I've invented a new person.

I am brilliant at being Beth. Beth is better than Tabbi, better than Ruby. Now that I've paid off my Ruby debt, the only thing I do that relates back to last summer, apart from working intensively on my French, is spending time atoning on Tabbi's behalf, like they told me to do at Zen. Since she's not going to do it herself.

And it's one of the best things I do. Working in the homeless shelter keeps me in touch with reality. It shows me exactly what could so easily have become of me, when I ran off from Norfolk with a couple of grand in my pocket. The kids I meet there have stories that are not so different from mine. If I hadn't met Tabbi on the train, I could have been one of them. I hate what Frank and I did, but I've sorted it as best I can. Tabbi killed someone, and that will never be sorted. My hatred for her is as strong as it's ever been.

I'm glad I stole her life. She deserves it.

The only bad thing about being Beth is the fact that I have to own a past in which I went out drink-driving, ran into a homeless guy, killed him and drove off. I didn't officially do it: the police could never prove it was me because it seems I had the presence of mind to stumble out of the car and get myself home and alibied. And my mother managed to report her car stolen, and claim it had happened a couple of hours earlier. But people know I did it: my dad knows, the people at Zen Lodge know, and clearly the gossip had buzzed around my London set. And so I'm forced to own it.

And there's the other detail, whatever it is. The thing I don't know. I've tried to track down Barney, just to look at him, but I can't find him. I've tried to find a photo of Tabbi's mum, but I can't. I asked Dad if he had a picture of their wedding, and eventually he found one, handing it to me, saying, 'I used to see the young Beatrice in your photos. It's not really there in real life.' I looked quickly into his face, but it was a totally innocent comment.

I stared at her. Beatrice. She was skinny, beautiful, with blonde hair like Tabbi, probably fake like Tabbi's. They have the same bone structure. Why has she not even tried to contact her troubled daughter? What the hell happened between them?

It takes us ages to get to the end of the field. I wish my old school had been like this. Small classes, loads of space, motivated teachers. Even the food is brilliant. I've started A levels again with new subjects – that's how I have to frame it to make sure I don't trip up. Tabbi had done a year of maths, English and French at her school in London and her grades were shit, and that school wouldn't have had her back anyway, so I've joined a class of kids a year younger than me (but who are actually my age) and restarted, taking English, history of art and history. I love them all, but my favourite is art history because I live in Paris.

I live in Paris.

Once a week, after school, art-history class goes into town to look at art. We visit the actual Louvre. We go to the Musée d'Orsay, the Orangerie, the Picasso Museum. I think anyone who doesn't want to study art history when it's an option to do it right here is crazy.

Cosmo is with me because this was already his school: it's why I asked Dad to enrol me in this place out of all the international schools in the city. Cosmo has also restarted sixth form after his own fuck-up, so we're together for history, though his other subjects are maths, French and physics. He's properly my best friend, and our shared adventure feels like it's bonded us for life.

I want so much to tell him that I didn't do it, that I hate drunk-drivers more than any other people in the world, but even though I've come close a couple of times I know, really, that I won't do it. I will never tell anyone because if I can't keep it secret, I can't expect anyone else to. Cosmo, I guess, is more forgiving than I am because he still has a crush on me in spite of everything. I've been braced for Jamie letting it slip, but we've exchanged messages and she just says she thinks it's brilliant and she is happy being the only person who knows. I love her.

I have an Insta because it would be weird not to, but I never post pictures of my face. I have a mysterious follower who I suspect might be Tabbi, so I monitor that account very closely indeed. It posts seascapes without geographical info.

The other students here are relaxed and friendly. They're from all over the world, and most of them have that rich-people thing of immediately fitting in and being charming. I think I do that one pretty well myself these days. I can hardly remember what it was like being Ruby Robinson. I speak in Tabbi's voice because the other British kids here do the same, and, after my six-week crash course at Zen Lodge, I can talk to these people without tripping up.

Some of the kids, of course, are troubled and some are arseholes, and I know that as far as the school is concerned Cosmo and I are potentially in both those categories. They know we were both at rehab, and although no one ever says anything because we're super-duper well behaved, they watch us more than they watch the others. We wouldn't get much leeway, but that's fine. I don't want leeway.

Finally we reach the trees across the field. There's a fence, and then there's the river Seine. It's murky, the opposite of that crystalline Swiss lake that, even now, doesn't feel real, and the other side is so far away that you wouldn't be able to swim there without getting seriously tired. Not that I want to.

'What was the thing you just did?' Cosmo says. 'That made you so happy?'

I give him my biggest grin. He's never tried to kiss me again. I suspect he's waiting it out in case I change my mind.

'Just sorted out one last thing from before.'

He nods. Ever since I disentangled Tabbi's *before*, I've used it to deflect when I don't want to talk about something. I've never been a drinker, but knowing what Tabbi did stops me ever wanting to touch a drop. Maybe I shouldn't be smiling this much while alluding to something so grim, but what the hell. I didn't do it. And I gave her Ruby Robinson, so now she didn't do it either.

My phone beeps in my pocket, and it's a text from Dad.

Hey Bethie – can I catch up with you after school?

Uh-oh. The downside to this perfect life is that I'm constantly on edge. Waiting for her to turn up and claim what I've made from her ashes.

She's been silent since that afternoon on the mountainside, but I know she won't let it go forever. Of course she won't. She could bring me down instantly. All she'd have to do is send a photo to her sister, for example. Or just tell the truth, and invite everyone to do a DNA test. I have a constant low-level feeling of dread because I know that if she's still alive she'll come for me. The only way for me to keep this life would be to get rid of her permanently. It's an interesting thought, but unlike her I don't think I'm a killer.

I reply to Dad.

Am I in trouble?

Guilty conscience? No, nothing like that! Just want a chat.

Sure xxx

'We've come a long way from Zen, right?' I say, looking at Cosmo. He pushes his hair back and nods.

'You're my inspiration,' he says. We both laugh at how cringe that sounds, but he carries on. 'You are, though. I mean, when I first met you, you were totally wired. *My name's Tabitha Courtenay and I'm an alcoholic.* That was the first thing I heard you say. I didn't think they'd keep you sober for half a day, but then you calmed right down. And you've done it: you've stayed off everything. And you've come right to my school to make sure I do too. You're my guardian angel, babe.'

'I guess you're mine too then.'

'Nah,' he says. 'It's you, Beth. You keep me sober. If I went on a bender, I'd have you to answer to, and that's too scary. Whereas I know for sure that if you wanted to lead me astray I'd follow you there happily. I'd go back to Zen with you next summer. If that was what you wanted. A year of mayhem, another summer in Switzerland?'

We look at each other for a long time. He's semi-inviting me, I know that. He fancies getting off his face and he's telling me that if I'm up for it he is too. I know it's true: Cosmo would basically do anything I told him to do. After that one time over table football, he's kept his infatuation unspoken, and I can deal with it that way. I don't want any romance. I don't need that stuff in my life: it never goes well for anyone.

And I'm not letting him do this to himself.

'Well –' I put an arm round his shoulders – 'I'm glad to be a good influence. No, I don't want a year of mayhem and neither do you. I don't do that stuff. I'm a different person now.'

'Yeah,' he says. 'Fair. No wonder my parents love you.'

We turn round and realize that everyone's gone back into school. We're both meant to be at afternoon registration, so we set off, together, across the field.

30

The walk back from the school bus feels normal now, but a tiny part of me will always be Ruby Robinson, and that part will never take it for granted. The sun is golden, and the streets here in the sixteenth arrondissement smell of the city that now feels like home. This whole place is a drug to me. I don't care about real drugs: I just want Paris. Paris while rich. We live on the top floor of an old apartment building. There are geraniums in the window boxes all the way up the exterior walls, and plane trees along the street outside. The pavements are always clean, and we can see the Eiffel Tower from the front windows.

The main door opens as I approach, and the uniformed concierge smiles at me. I have no idea how he always does that. How does he know I'm approaching?

'Bonjour, Beth,' he says. '*Ça va?*'

'*Ça va*, Jacques,' I say. '*Ça va?*' French became a lot easier when I realized you can get through a lot of life by saying '*Ça va*' as a question or an answer.

I swish into the entrance hall, and he calls the lift for me. It's an old-fashioned lift with a grill that you have to pull open (or someone does it for you), and it has a bench in it. It's wooden and smells of polish. Yeah, I'm not giving this up.

I find Dad on the roof terrace. He jumps up when he sees me. He's nervy. *What's going on?* I glance over at the Eiffel Tower. The actual Eiffel Tower, right there across the river. Dark and iconic against the blue sky.

The terrace is tiled with pale floor slabs, and has a wooden table, a parasol, two loungers and a little table. Plus a lot of flowers in pots that are always flourishing, no thanks to either me or Dad. People come in while I'm at school and do all the housework. It's like magic.

'Have a drink,' he says. I raise my eyebrows and he grins. '*Sirop de grenadine?*' Everyone is incredibly keen never to let me touch alcohol because I'm so very much nicer now I've been to rehab. Side note: I have no idea how Tabbi managed to be so horrible all the time, but I'm pretty much in awe of it.

Dad has a lounger in the shade with a glass of white wine and a bowl of olives beside him. I pull my seat away from the umbrella, into the bright sunshine. He throws me a bottle of sunscreen and I slather it right on.

I take a sip of the grenadine squash. It's as lovely now as it was at the Zen Lodge.

'What's up?' I say.

We live in this apartment, just the two of us. It's brilliant. Somehow, no matter the biology, he is the family I need. The one I want. He gives me that look that has stopped me confessing, again and again and again. The *I love you* smile. The *you're my daughter* one. Yeah. No way am I breaking his heart with a cold blast of truth.

'Bethie,' he says, 'I know you went through a lot, and I realize that a lot of it is my fault.'

I stare at him. 'Dad – we're not doing this again, are we?'

'No. Sorry. We're not doing it again – I'm building up to something. Bear with me.' I nod. He carries on. 'I wasn't there for you. My divorce from your mother was one of my worst.' He pauses and I take the cue.

'That's a crowded field.' It's what I know he wants me to say. I imagine a crowded field, a field full of ex-wives, pushing and jostling each other, climbing over the fence to get out.

'Indeed. I'm glad you've come back to me. It's more than I deserve.'

'It's fine,' I say. I take a deep breath. 'We're more than quits, Dad. And with Mum – she and I aren't going to speak again. So you and I have to stick together.'

'True.'

God, I'm glad I'm not Tabbi. Being Ruby was crap, but I think being Tabbi was probably worse, in its way.

I see him prepping himself to say the big thing, whatever it is.

'So, Bethie,' he says, 'there's something I wanted to talk to you about. Because you've overcome so much. You've inspired me, and I need to face something. It's going to be potentially strange for you. Or, I mean, maybe it's not. Your generation has a different attitude and perhaps . . .'

I look at him closely and see that, whatever this is, it's

something meaningful to him. And it has nothing to do with me. He's not going to tell me I've been found out.

'Spill,' I say.

He takes a deep breath, casts around for distraction.

'Is that like *spill the tea*?' he says. He holds up his glass. 'I don't get that as an expression. Why would I want to spill my tea?'

'Stop filibustering,' I say. 'That's not tea. Talk.'

He stands up. He walks all the way round the roof terrace and comes back to his seat. When he starts speaking, he addresses his words to the wide Parisian sky. To the Eiffel Tower.

'You know I have a ... chequered history with the ladies?'

'Yep.'

'Well – I've known this for a long time, but until recently I haven't managed to articulate it, even to myself. Especially, I suppose, to myself. I think the reason I've never managed to hold down a stable or happy relationship for more than five minutes is because I've never been with the right person.' I start to say something, but he holds up a hand. He's still going. He needs to get this out. 'And the reason I've never been with the right person is because I was looking in the wrong places, and the reason for *that* is ...'

I realize it as he draws to a halt. It falls into place and makes perfect sense. God, I love him.

It fits him. Suits him. Works. I can't believe he's spent so long denying it. I can't believe I didn't see it before.

I am at his side, an arm round him, in a fraction of a second.

'The reason is,' I say, 'because you were looking at the wrong people, right?'

I can feel that he's trembling. I carry on.

'And that's because you might have had better luck with a ... husband? Than with all those wives?'

He grabs me and it's like being plucked from a mountain path by a bear. I'm in his arms, gripped so tightly that I don't think I'll ever get away, and then I realize that I don't want to. Right now, at this moment, we are everything to each other. He is leaning on me for support and I'm leaning on him right back.

'Bethie,' he whispers. 'Oh, Bethie. What am I going to do?'

I squeeze him back.

'Dad.' I still love that word. I like it so much I say it again. 'Dad. Dad dad dad dad dad. It's so completely OK. I can't tell you how fine it is. You don't need to be closeted.'

He still doesn't talk so I carry on. I think I'll soon run out of ways to tell him it's fine.

'It's the twenty-first century,' I say. 'Honestly, no one's going to judge you, and anyone who does is an arsehole. How could they? You can be an out gay man and everyone'll think it's cool, plus all your ex-wives will like you a lot more. A LOT more. Even my mother, probably.'

He sniffs a bit. I look for a tissue and find a tiny napkin. I give it to him.

'Oh, Bethie,' he says. 'Would you believe you're the first person I've told?'

I push him to sit back down and pull my chair right up close to his lounger.

'When did you know it yourself?'

He takes an olive out of the bowl and throws it to me. I try to catch it in my mouth but fail. I pick it up from the seat next to me and pop it in my mouth. Who knew I'd love olives? I like the Castelvetrano ones from the Marché Président Wilson. Yeah, I now have a favourite olive and a favourite farmers' market. Dad lets out all his breath at once, then inhales deeply and starts to talk. His voice falters at first, but soon it's stronger.

'Right back when I was at school,' he says, 'I was drawn to some of the older boys, but then again it was a boys' school so it's not as if there were other options. Though of course that's not true – we had social events with the girls' school sometimes. I don't know, Bethie. My parents were dreadful homophobes and I absorbed it. Not proud of it but I became one too. I met my first wife, Jen, and we were such good friends and perhaps I mistook that for something else.'

'Or maybe you're a bit bi?'

He shrugs. 'Yeah, but I don't really feel that way now. I feel . . .'

It hangs there in the air. I wait for him to say it. I nod. I raise my eyebrows. I gesture *go on, say it* with my hands.

He does.

'I feel gay! Oh my God. I feel gay. I am gay.'

He looks at me, eyes wide. His face is suddenly suffused with joy. He says it again, louder. He's literally shouting it from the rooftops.

I grin back at him. My face is going to crack with the smile at his joy and relief.

'It's the first time you've said that, isn't it?'

'It is! Thank you. Thank you, darling girl.'

We talk and talk and talk, and the fact that I'm not the focus is amazing. One thing I know for sure, however, is that now I can never let him find out the truth. I have to find a way to carry on being Beth Courtenay forever. Only one person could stop me. God, I wish I knew what she was planning.

If he found out now, it would destroy him. I realize that I am genuinely the first person he has come out to. He has never kissed a guy, or come anywhere close to it. What he told me was just his feelings, about himself.

He trusts me.

If Tabbi turns up, I'll hold out for as long as I can. I've already decided that if her mum comes back on to the scene I'll refuse to see her. They have no relationship at all. Her sister Leo feels like more of an immediate threat, but when we came back to Paris I sent her a really careful email and that seemed to work, in that it got her off my back. However, she will want to see me one day, introduce me to my niece, and I won't be able to hold out forever.

Dad asked if I wanted to go and visit Leo in Dubai sometime, but I said no. I pretended it was because of fossil fuels at first, but that didn't feel very Tabbi, so I added that I was worried that seeing Leo would upset me and make me relapse, and that sorted it. I added that the Zen Lodge people had told me to cut all contact with my old life until I felt ready for it, and Dad bought that.

It really is because of fossil fuels, actually, as well as the other thing. Rich people are the worst for that, and if I can do my tiny bit by travelling by rail and road, I will. Dad likes it: he says it's made him think, though it hasn't made him think enough to stop flying back and forth to New York.

In fact, I have lots of thoughts about rich people. It's brilliant being rich and not having to worry about money, but it's also horrible. It changes you. When you're poor, you're desperate for enough money to keep your home, or to buy enough food, and that's when money is the thing it was meant to be. A token to exchange, to make sure you can swap the work you do for the things you need, or whatever.

Then when you have enough money to mean you never have to think about that kind of thing – when you find yourself saying things like 'which house?' – you just want more and more and more. I do it: I like private school and nice olives and the view of the Eiffel Tower, and I don't want to give any of them up.

I think it's the biggest flaw in the human race because why would that happen? Not having to worry about the basics of life is an immense privilege, but the people who have that privilege don't appreciate it for one single second. They just want more. There are kids at my school who have Burberry scarves that cost a thousand dollars: I bet I could buy a fake Burberry scarf at Norwich market for a tenner and they wouldn't be able to tell the difference.

They vaguely know they should give money to charity instead of hoarding it, but they don't do it much because they don't want to.

They go to schools that cost thirty grand a year. I go to one of those too. I like it better than the free one I used to go to. I'm a massive hypocrite, but I love this life. I'm keeping it.

I wake very early the next morning. Now that Dad has told me his secret, there's more at stake. I have to keep Tabbi away. I sit at my desk, look out across the rooftops of Paris (no Eiffel Tower from this side of the apartment, but it's still gorgeous) and open my laptop.

My bedroom is actually small because we live in an attic like old-style artists (very rich ones), but everything in it is perfect. I have a window with a tiny wrought-iron balcony. I put a geranium out there to see what would happen, and somehow it worked and it's currently going wild. Who knew I could grow things? (If the cleaner or roof-gardeners are looking after it, I don't want to know.) I have a double bed with a white duvet cover, and a wardrobe, a chest of drawers, a desk and my own tiny bathroom.

It's quarter to six. I normally sleep until 7.30, but I'm up for the day now. I can't go and get a coffee because I'd wake Dad. Now that he feels sure enough of me to come out, I can't let him know he has the wrong girl.

Why did she let me pay her off with one single banknote last summer? Is she still living as Ruby Robinson?

Is my enigmatic Insta follower, the seascape one, actually her? Probably not, but it's all I've got.

I turn my laptop to private mode.

I have stayed as far away from googling my old name as I possibly can. Every time my fingers want to do it, I put the phone away, or shut the laptop, and go and do something else. Now, though, I'm thinking about George, this man who's been closeted for decades, who got married six times before he faced his truth. He's a good-looking man, I guess, in an old sort of way. Bet he would have had loads of fun at gay clubs back in the day, if there even were gay clubs then. He's wasted so much time. I actually love him and not even in a weird way. I know him infinitely better than I knew my own dad, and infinitely better than Tabbi knows him.

My thoughts keep snapping back to her. I had her shut away in a box in my head before, and now she's burst out. I take a deep breath, double-check the door is closed and search up the words 'Ruby Robinson'. There are a few people – a jazz singer, a film from a few years ago that is actually called *Ruby Robinson*. How did that one pass me by when it was my name? Anyway, what I don't find is my alter ego, so I add 'Cannes', 'London' and even 'Norwich', though she's hardly going to have gone there. I don't find her. I scroll through pages and pages of results, and there are so many people with that name and I have no idea if any of these results is about her.

When I switch to image search, I don't find anyone who looks right. She can't have had surgery without her trust fund. Can she?

I go to news results, just in case, and I've mentally checked out and am scrolling mindlessly when I see my own face.

My real face. My old nose. And a headline:

Fears grow for missing Ruby

It's from the *Norwich Evening News,* and it has a stupid photo of me that must have come from Frank. I'm making a silly face, grinning and striking a pose.

I hold my breath and open the article. Then I exhale it, all at once.

The article is from October last year. I was settled at the international school by that point with my new face. I'm part of a spread of missing people, most of them teenagers, and almost all of them, I would guess, runaways. Under the picture and headline it just says:

> Ruby Robinson, 16, has been missing from her home in Sprowston since July. She is described as five foot six, striking-looking, with long, very dark hair and brown eyes. While her family believe she has run away, they are increasingly worried about her safety. Anyone with any information . . .

And then there's a phone number.

Increasingly worried. Yeah, sure you are. I can't believe how cheeky they are, getting a photo off Frank because they never took any themselves. Letting me go, then waiting three months before even pretending to look for me. When I try to dig down, adding 'runaway' and 'missing' and things like that to my search, there's nothing else. Absolutely nothing turns up. They stuck that thing in the paper once and now they've forgotten I exist.

Long, very dark hair. Now it's blonde, like Tabbi's was when I met her. Before she cut it off to become me. I like being blonde. It's shoulder length, though I'm working on that.

I hate thinking about my birth family. I hate them. I hate my childhood. If I ever have to stop being Beth, I'm not going back to Ruby.

I know what I need to do.

I've ignored that Gmail account because I didn't want any connection with her. I've shut it away.

She must have messaged over the past year. God knows what she must have sent to me, after I paid her off on the mountain and radioed for security.

What was the password?

I go to a Gmail login screen. It offers me my real account, but I sit still and think very hard until I've remembered the other one. It was the2traingirls – I remember that much. I try a few passwords that don't work and then I find a note buried deep on my phone.

the2traingirls@gmail.com

Password: yeahwedidit!

It's time. I need to do this now. I need to find out what's happening out there. Open a link to Tabbi, just to see what's happening.

I log in.

I start reading.

31

Tabbi

I'm on breakfasts so I wake at five. It's raining gently outside, even though it's summer, because hey, this is the edge of Europe right in the middle of the Atlantic and rain is what happens. On the plus side, it's light and I love waking in the daylight. Those days we spent in Kiruna have left me craving midnight sun, and I'd go far, far north of here if I could. I'd go up to the top of Scotland. And I could have done, but I just took the first job I could find, in the place that sounded most remote, so here I am. On the Isles of Scilly, which, it turns out, really *are* remote. You have to make a big effort to get here, which is exactly what I wanted. You have to spend nearly three hours on a bumpy boat, being sick into a bag.

And then you find yourself in the middle of the ocean, on a sandy island, in a place that really is spectacularly beautiful and remote. A place where no one would think to look for you.

I grab my phone. The hotel Wi-Fi is shonky, but it's

enough for me to check 'BethieC' on Instagram. She's posted another picture of MY DAD, all father-daughter love. So proud of this guy. Why? Proud of him for being such a shit parent he doesn't realize he's got the wrong kid? She never posts a picture of her face. When she appears on her own grid or story, it's from the back or, heavily filtered, from the side. She has blonde hair now, like I did when we met, and she's clearly working on getting it long like mine was. She's totally grifting my life. Living in Paris, never quite saying where. Never mentioning where she goes to school, but making it clear that she does. Posting pictures of art. Like, we know you've seen the *Mona Lisa*, babe. The waterlilies. And often, often, raving about the wondrousness of my shitty dad.

I watch her from my own anonymous account. It's that cherries one I set up in France, but repurposed for my new life. I, too, never show my face. I put loads of landscapes and seascapes on it, and when I write a caption I try to do it in the voice of a forty-something woman. I follow Beth openly and am pretty sure she has no idea it's me, and of course if she did know she wouldn't care. She'd laugh in my face. She laughs in my face every day that she lives my life.

I've let her do it so that one day, when I rip it all away from her, it'll be as dramatic as possible.

I pull on my dressing gown, grab a towel and run across the corridor to the bathroom. We have to be showered before a shift, which is good, but at the same time the showers never actually get warm, so you have to get yourself wet and smear yourself in shower gel, wash your hair as rarely as you can get away with and run for it. I washed my hair yesterday so today I'm in and out of that shower in less than a minute, and then I wrap myself in a threadbare towel and run back to my room.

A message has arrived from Tom. We message each other all the time anyway, but this one has a screenshot with the message:

Grandma sent this. Any idea?

The screenshot is a receipt for a payment, the ones she's been getting this year, but this one has a message attached. It just says 'frank brody has the rest'.

I log on to our Gmail account because I do it every morning. She still hasn't read anything. I send her another.

Subject: frank brody
Message: who's frank brody?

I write to her every day just to shit her up, but this is the first time in ages that I've actually had something to say. Since, as far as I can tell, she has never once logged into this account, I'm not expecting an answer.

I could, of course, slide into her DMs, but she'd block me.

My plan is: I'll finish my summer here on the island and then I'll go and confront her. I'll find her in Paris, expose her as a fraud and take back everything that's mine. I will make my dad look like an absolute twat in the process.

I've wanted to do it for ages. The only thing that's

stopping me is the fact that if I do it, I'll have to confront everything about myself.

Ruby must know about it by now. She must have fake-cried about it when she made amends with MY dad. I have dealt with her shit, in the form of Tom and his family, and she must, in some way, have dealt with mine.

As I stare at the account, something weird happens. The unread messages in the inbox start changing colour. She's looking at them.

She is opening them. Right now. We're logged into the same account at the same time. I can hardly breathe.

Then a message lands in the inbox. A reply to the one I just wrote. It says:

Re: frank brody
No idea.

That's it. Our first communication since she stole my life. A second message lands.

You killed someone and now I have to pretend it was me.

I reply: You scammed someone and left me to deal with it.

All paid off now.

Not quite. Half, I type. 'Frank Brody has the rest'.

You killed someone.

I stare at it. I do not like seeing those words written on my screen. I do not like that at all.

> Who's Frank Brody?

She doesn't reply for a moment. When she does, she writes:

> You're making me act like I'm a killer.
>
> I didn't make you do anything. Remember? You looked me in the eye and asked why I was calling you Ruby.

There's a stalemate for a while, and I really need to get to work, so I just send one last message.

> You'd better be looking over your shoulder, 'Bethie'.

I lock the phone. I'm leaving it in my room today because I can't handle dealing with this conversation as I work. Before I go, though, I unlock it again for one last check.
She has replied.

> Look over yours. I know where to find you. Nice beaches.

I look at Instagram. BethieC's account is empty. She has no follower count, and the grid says 'no posts yet'.
She has blocked me. Somehow, she knew it was me all along.

I step outside the building. The drizzle has stopped, and the salty air hits me in the face. It may not be the French Riviera, but there's something about this place that hooks me. The air is misty this morning, the sky the palest blue behind the clouds. The whole place smells of grass after rain. The hotel is on the edge of the water, and the water this morning is the very palest turquoise. Sometimes you see dolphins out there. I walk slowly along the path to the main building, my feet crunching on the pale stones.

I live and work at the Kernow Inn, which is a family hotel that's currently completely full. I had no idea so many people would bring their kids somewhere so remote, so very far from soft play and amusement arcades, for their holidays. But they do. They come with buckets and spades and board games, ready to recreate idyllic holidays from the olden days. The mums swim in the sea every morning. The dads go running along coast paths, or try to spot rare birds. The kids build sandcastles and mess around in rock pools. Teens complain about the phone reception and it often rains, but I can see what they're trying to do and I wish someone had done it for me. I know we went to the Riviera, so I can hardly complain, but watching people's Cornish seaside holidays makes me nostalgic for something I never even had.

The real Ruby Robinson is a bitch. I guess she wasn't bluffing: she *does* know who I am. How, I don't know. Before I go in through the little kitchen door, I stop and look around. I hold my breath and listen. I think I hear someone moving, but then I hear a little mewl of a baby and the mutter of a male voice trying to soothe it.

I'm wired. I want to walk into her world and smash it up. I want to look into that man's face and tell him that sorry, the pretty one is not, in fact, his daughter. It's this fuck-up instead. Check the DNA. The rest of me wants to stay here and live my life on my own terms, hiding from everything that messed me up.

No one actually comes to breakfast at six, but we have to be ready. 'Assume every guest we have will be battering on the door at five fifty-nine': that's the rule. We need to have the buffet on the sideboard and be in the kitchen prepped to do the full Englishes, or whatever anyone asks for. Generally, sod all happens until at least seven fifteen, but today a knackered-looking dad brings a baby in at 6.01, and I watch through the serving hatch as both front-of-house people dash over to him. AJ explains how breakfast works (just in case he's lost the use of his brain overnight and can't remember how it worked yesterday or indeed what the word 'breakfast' means), and I start making a coffee before he asks, because these guys always want coffee. Mike takes the baby off him and walks around the room, doing cooing baby talk. The man looks at both of them as if he thinks he might actually have died in the night and gone to heaven.

I put the cafetière on a tray with a milk jug and leave it ready for AJ to pick up. In return, she passes me an order for a full breakfast with absolutely everything we have, and I get to work. I like it when they want everything. Is there a better meal than a proper breakfast? I may be a trained(ish) chef these days, but I don't think so.

This job is my world, and I'm keeping busy every moment that I can. I work over twelve hours a day, six days a week. I live here, so when I'm not working I'm at work anyway. The people in my world are AJ, Mike, Jess and Anoushka in front of house, and Halle, Lily, Reece and Matt in the kitchen. We range in age from sixteen (Jess) to fifty-nine (Matt), though most of us are under twenty-five because this is not a job you can stay in long term. It's not a job for people with kids.

It is, though, a job for people who need to escape. We've come together from all over the place, for all kinds of reasons. None of them know my real trajectory (I don't want them to think I'm a psychotic fantasist by telling *that* story), but I've mixed my real bio with Ruby's and what comes out is, believe me, a heart-wringing tale. A shit absent father (in both cases), a mother who abandoned and then betrayed me (bit of both), and dumped me in the worst possible way (me). It adds up to someone who gets a live-in job in an inaccessible hotel in the Atlantic as a barely-qualified chef, and who never leaves the island and doesn't intend to until the season ends in October.

Sometimes, particularly when it rains every day for weeks, I wonder why I didn't stay in France. I came back to the UK with Tom. We had quite the fight about it. It was our first real fight, the first one that didn't involve him telling me I was Ruby and me telling him I wasn't. We were on the beach, sitting up on the sand.

'You should stay here,' he said. 'Are you mad? Guillaume, who you love, is training you to do the thing you most want to do, in a place where you feel at home. You have

Ruby's passport that allows you to live and work here for as long as you want.'

I looked into his face. God, I miss him.

'I know that.' I made myself calm down. I took deep, deep breaths. 'But if I stay in Cannes, sooner or later Leo will come back. This is the one place where they could find me.' I was casting around. This was not my real reason. Of course it wasn't.

He frowned. 'But sweetie – don't you want them to find you?'

This is yet another point at which I could have told Tom my whole truth. Turns out those words are really, really hard to say.

'I don't want the shit that I'll get for skipping rehab.' I picked up a handful of sand and let it run through my fingers, then did it again and again.

'Did you really think,' he said, 'that you and Ruby would switch back and no one would ever find out? Did you think that she, a proven liar and scammer, wouldn't try to hang on to everything you have? When you gave her, just as a random example, your bank card?'

I closed my eyes and tried to stay calm. 'I didn't know she was a proven liar and scammer. I thought she was just some ditsy girl on a train.'

There was a long silence. The only sound was the noise of the sea scratching at the sand. When Tom spoke, it wasn't what I was expecting.

'I wish you'd tell me the rest of it,' he said. His voice was different. 'Whatever it is. You can tell me.'

I couldn't tell him. I couldn't not tell him either.

'Yeah,' *I said. I could feel his eyes on me. I looked down at the sand. The silence went on. I felt myself starting to cry, and blinked and forced it away.* 'I mean, no. I can't talk about it. Not yet.'

'OK.' *He put an arm round my shoulder.* 'So – tell me when you're ready. I'm not going anywhere. I mean, I am. I'm going to Birmingham for uni. But emotionally I'm here no matter what.'

I leaned on him and pretended to believe him. What would he think of me, if he knew?

Since he doesn't know, Tom and I are still going well, against all the odds. He was amazing when I came back from Zurich with nothing but a Swiss banknote. It's one of those moments I remember in forensic detail. I stepped off the train in Cannes, defeated and confused. Tom was standing on the platform, scanning up and down the train for me. When he saw me, he started jogging towards me. I launched myself and he opened his arms.

He stroked my hair while I tried to fight all the emotions. He already knew, of course, what had happened. I'd called him the moment I'd got back to Grindelwald and charged my phone in the foyer of a hostel.

'It's OK,' he'd said, even though it wasn't. 'We'll sort this out. You're the real Tabitha Courtenay, and we'll get it straightened out with a photo and a DNA test when you're ready. She hasn't won.'

As time went on, though, I found myself realizing that I might not want to straighten it out. Being Tabbi Courtenay had been horrible. *I* had been horrible. Ruby would be expecting me to come at her. What if I didn't? What if I let her keep my life for a bit? What if I made 'Ruby Robinson' into a person on my own terms?

A few weeks passed and Guillaume trained me, and I liked it. I imagined real Ruby waiting for me to come and loved the idea of how on edge she must be, though when I remembered what a stone-cold bitch she'd been in Switzerland I wasn't sure I could make her jumpy just by doing nothing.

Tom and I were both putting money into Maria's savings every time we were paid, and then, just as we were getting ready to leave Cannes, we didn't need to any more. Maria, who only semi-trusts me, called Tom, and he put her on speaker.

'Was this you?' she said. 'Or is it another scam? What is this?'

I really like Maria even if it's not reciprocated. She's a fun grandma who's nothing like anyone in my family and it turns out she's really, really mortified about getting scammed, and I like her for that too.

'Was what me?' said Tom. 'What's up, Grandma?'

She forwarded him an email. It was a crypto payment. Tom and his friend Brendan got to work, and it turned out to be real. A thousand pounds, untraceable. It has been happening every so often until today, when we found out that 'frank brody has the rest'.

I mean, I hate her, obviously. But I'm glad she's used my dad's money to pay Maria back. Even though Maria was baffled, she was amazed when the crypto thing turned into real money. I'm sure Tom will have already got to work this morning looking for the Frank guy.

Most of all, the thing that makes me happy here is this: I escaped. They tried to make me go to rehab . . . I really did say no. Either they have no idea that the cuckoo in the nest is Ruby Robinson, Grifter Extraordinaire, which is funny, or they've worked it out (I just can't fully believe that Leo would have been fooled) and they have no idea where the hell I am. I really don't think they're going to find me here. And I love that.

Also, I didn't need the rehab. I was just really bad at being an unwanted rich girl with too much money and (hankies out) not enough love. As soon as I had to look after myself, something inside me woke up. I never take anything now, and although I do occasionally drink mildly on my days off, there's nothing remarkable about it.

I make the tired dad a huge breakfast with two perfectly poached eggs as well as absolutely everything else piled up, and take my turn with the baby while he eats. The baby looks bald from a distance, but it actually has a load of downy blond hair, and it doesn't care at all about being passed between strangers. I know we're all making a massive fuss because it's a dad, and everyone thinks a *dad* looking after his own kid is some sort of hero because he's 'giving Mum a break' or whatever.

I focus on these trivial things to distract myself. I manage to drink a coffee while holding the baby, contorting my arm around so there's never any chance of coffee dripping on to it. The dad leaves us a massive tip even though breakfast is included in his room rate. More people begin to arrive and my orders pile up. Outside the window the rain starts up again, crashing on to the windowpane. The sea goes wild. The ferry crossings today won't be fun, and I feel bad for the people who work on the boat, having to clean up all the vomit.

As soon as I finish my shift, I run back to my room and check the phone. Tom has found a Frank Brody of about our age who lives in Norwich.

Norwich.

He's sure to be the guy. I keep checking, but there's nothing more from Ruby. I wake in the night and check again, but there's nothing. She's gone quiet. All the same, I am absolutely certain that things are about to happen.

And then, the next day, a boy walks into the hotel and asks for Ruby Robinson.

32

I'm doing sandwiches for lunch, humming along with *The Tortured Poets Department*, when it happens. I've just made three ham-and-mustard ones and am arranging them on the plates with garnish when AJ leans across the pass.

'Rubes,' she says. 'There was some guy asking for you?'

'What?' It takes me a while to process what this might mean. 'Who?' I feel myself smiling at the idea that Tom has come from Birmingham in a rainstorm to visit me. He can't have, though. He's halfway through his exams. He's totally tied to uni until next week. Next week, I would love him to do this.

She just shrugs. 'He said he'd come back at the end of service.' She takes the bowls of chips that are lined up. All of them are straight out of the fryer, so hot they're steaming. Everyone wants a bowl of chips and everyone is going to love these ones. They think sandwiches or salad are a healthy enough option, then stick in some sneaky chips with them as if that way the calories don't count.

I imagine it being Tom. I hope it's not because he needs

to finish his degree, but also I hope against hope that it is. I picture myself running into his arms like I did on the platform at Cannes station. The way his bulk will feel. The weirdness of how we met and the rightness of how we feel. Him sitting outside my tent, listening to me vomiting. The fact that he knows me and he likes me, the real me. That he knows I have a secret and doesn't push me to tell him what it is.

At the end of service I step out into the dining room, tiptoeing in the hope that I'll see him before he sees me. It's empty apart from one table and ...

It's not him. *Shit.*

It's not an adult either. It's a boy, taller and lankier than Tom. He's sitting at a table in the corner, nursing a Coke, and I have to force myself to walk towards him.

In fact, if this is Ruby bringing more trouble to my door, I'm just going to do it right back at her. It will be time to explode her perfect little Bethie life and take the consequences. My first port of call will be Leo. If it comes to it I'm ready. I think ...

My heart pounds as I walk closer. There is a lot riding on this, but it's just a normal-looking boy. He has a nice face, with freckles and messy hair. He's wearing a washed-out green T-shirt, shorts, trainers that could either be really old and cheap or else new and really expensive like Golden Goose.

'Hi there?' I say it in a brisk voice. 'You looking for me?'

I watch his face closely. A small frown. A cloud of disappointment.

'You Ruby Robinson?' he says.

'Sorry – do we know each other?'

He's quiet for a long time. Then he says: 'I guess it's a common enough name. I really thought, though, that this was it. I thought I'd found the real Ruby.'

I pull out a chair and sit opposite him, keeping my distance.

'I mean, in my world I'm the real Ruby.'

He's looking at the table. 'Sorry. Yeah, of course. I came all the way from Norwich. It was so expensive.'

Yesterday she told me to look over my shoulder. Today this happens.

'How did you find me?'

He shrugs. 'I saw it on a Substack. One of the girls working here has one? She writes a diary of island life. It was way, way, way down the google results, but . . . She said Ruby Robinson is this absolute legend that she works with. Absolute legend. That's what she said. That's why I was sure it had to be my Ruby.'

Could Ruby have done that? Faked a Substack just to rat me out? No, because that's Lily. Everyone knows she has a blog.

'You staying at the hotel?' My voice sounds weird. *Be normal be normal be normal.*

The only ex she told me about was called Nathan. They were together in Amsterdam and then she set off to look at the mountains. That was bullshit, though.

'Nah,' he says. 'Can't afford it. I've got a tent. Put it up in a field. I mean, I'll probably get shot or something.'

'So, I'm Ruby,' I prompt. 'Though clearly not the one you're after. And you're . . . ?'

He looks at me. And then he says it.

'Sorry. I'm Frank. Frank Brody.'

I grab my necklace, my little star, and hold it for strength. I have to be just another girl with the same name. I have to. I try to keep my voice normal. 'Tell me about the other Ruby. You must really want to find her.'

'I'm not stalking her.' He says it fast. 'She's my ex. That sounds worse, right? But honestly it's not. The thing is – I've been worrying about her for a year now. She just kind of ran away. Totally ran away, in fact. Left a note for her family and did a flit. We did a missing-person's appeal last autumn, but nothing came of it. And it was . . . all my fault.'

I take a deep breath. If real Ruby has sent him, then this won't end well. If she hasn't, I want to know why he's here, the day after she gave the O'Neills his name.

'OK,' I say carefully. 'How come she ran away and it was your fault?'

He sighs.

'Long story.' He starts to get up, then changes his mind and sinks back down. 'How long have you got?'

I check the clock on the wall.

'About three hours.' I wait. We are really sussing each other out here. 'We could go for a walk? If you want?'

I would never say that to a strange guy, but this is totally different. This is a key to the Ruby puzzle, walking straight into my life. I'm not letting him go.

He shrugs. Nods.

I look down at my whites. If he genuinely thinks what happened was his fault, I would imagine that he, too, has been played. Either that or, like his girlfriend, he's a really good actor.

Frank Brody has the rest.

'Give me five minutes to change.'

We follow the path that goes behind the hotel and along the cliff edge. It's warm and the air is humid, but it's gorgeous. Below, the tide is high and bright blue water is crashing on the rocks. There's so much coastline when you live on an island, and it's so wild that even though the place is busy with tourists it can still feel like you're the only person here. Back when I was Tabbi Courtenay, I would have sneered at places like this: for me, the sea meant hot, hot sunshine and cocktails. It meant whingeing if there was a cloud. My rule used to be that I would swim in the sea only if I needed to because I was so hot. Now I run over a stony beach and plunge into the cold water most days. And it wakes me up and makes me feel alive and full of energy and hope.

'How long have you been here?' he says.

May as well stick close to the truth. There's no reason not to.

'Since April.'

We keep walking. Our feet crunch on the stony path. Since he doesn't say anything, I carry on.

'I was in London before that, doing chef training. I left the course before it ended, because I wanted to get on with things. I saw this job advertised and it just seemed like a cool thing to do.'

The truth is, I left before finishing the course because I didn't want Ruby's name to appear anywhere, on any lists of anything, just in case. And I couldn't risk photos: my whole life is spent not risking photos, a policy I set out clearly to everyone by alluding darkly to family trauma (though clearly I should have spelled out to Lily that my name couldn't go online either).

I don't want to speak to them ever again, I'd say, *and so I'm living my life offline.*

This makes me cry, which adds to its authenticity, but people mainly want to know what it's like living without social media. I obviously don't tell them that I have an Instagram account full of seascapes and a Gmail I monitor daily, waiting for a message from myself, then wishing one hadn't come.

'Sounds good,' he says.

'What about you?' *Frank Brody has the rest.* He was in the scam with her. He's looking for her. I guess she scammed him too, but I can't be sure. This whole conversation is a tightrope.

'Oh, I'm not interesting,' he says.

We keep walking. I wait for him to talk. The sun comes out from behind a grey cloud and the seascape changes. I stop to look at it and Frank stops with me.

'I can see why you live here,' he says.

I nod and take a deep breath. 'I love it.'

I can smell the salt in the air, the grass, the rain gathering in the clouds. It's so real. The grey of the rocks, the grey of the ocean. The opposite of the bright sun and beautiful-people vibe of the Riviera. Nothing at all like London. Somehow it feels like my place, a place that belongs just to me. I've only been here a couple of months: no idea why it feels that way but it does.

I start walking again. Frank does too.

'My Ruby,' he says at last. 'Well – she was my girlfriend. We were together at school for a couple of years. She had a shit home life and I don't blame her for running away. Her mum had her when she was, like, fifteen, and her grandparents took her in, but they died. That really messed her life up. They weren't even old. They were only in their fifties.'

This, surprisingly, matches up with the story Ruby told me.

'So how come they both died?' I hadn't even thought about that. I'd just thought grandparents were old.

'Drunk-driver. They were –'

He carries on talking. My brain is blasting an alert signal at me. *Emergency! Emergency!*

No wonder she's kicked me out of my own life. I bet that, in her eyes, I might as well have mown down her grandparents myself. I tricked her into going to rehab, and when she got there she had to take responsibility for that. The thing that ruined her life. She can't know what the trigger was, but it doesn't matter. The trigger is not an excuse. Not at all.

Frank is droning on about Ruby's aunt and uncle, but I

don't care about that. Her grandparents were killed by a drunk-driver. She's never going to give me anything. She's going to keep my life forever.

And maybe I could be OK with that.

I try to tune back into his outpouring of story, but I can't keep my brain still.

'She aced her GCSEs, though I guess she doesn't even know it as she'd taken off by then. I just wanna know if she's still alive, really. Fact is . . . I got a message yesterday asking for money and it can only have been because of Ruby, so that's why I finally decided to come out here and see.'

'Sorry? What?' *Just keep talking.*

'It's complicated.'

We have come to the path that goes down to the beach. I scramble down. It's a sketchy one: that's why I like this bit of beach. You can't reach it if you've got pushchairs, barbecues, bodyboards. Frank follows easily. He's fitter than he looks. My mind is all over the place. I am not thinking about personal safety. Too late, I realize this is rash behaviour.

Have I learned *anything at all* since my night in Avignon with Yannick? Frank Brody senses my fear and steps away.

'Hey,' he says. 'It's OK, I promise. We can go back inside if you like.'

I look at him for a few seconds and shrug, pretending I'm calm.

'It's OK. There's always someone around anyway.' I could grab a rock. If I needed to defend myself, I could smash him on the head.

I usually love this little bay. I sit here often, and stare out to sea. I come here to swim. There are cliffs on three sides, and the beach is stony and rocky, and unless there's a boat out there it's just me and the world, exactly as it would have been thousands of years ago. Not a massive comfort, right now, but usually it is.

I pull myself up to sit on the biggest rock. He does the same and sits beside me. For a moment, we stare out at the heaving water. I pull my knees up and hold them. He doesn't do anything weird or creepy.

'So,' I say. 'Complicated?' I want him to tell me about the scam. I need the processing time.

He inhales deeply.

'OK – first of all, I know how shit this is gonna sound, but I needed money. It was just me, my dad and my brother at home and my dad – well, he drinks. He's in hospital right now, actually. He's a shitshow. As the big brother, I thought I needed to hold it all together for me and Mick. That's my brother. He's named after Mick Jagger. I wanted to get the bailiffs off our back and I needed cash. So Ruby and I tried really, really, really hard to work out how to get, like, a load of money really fast.'

I try to keep my voice level. I watch a seagull on the water, floating away from land. I don't even remember the name of the man I killed. That thought pops into my head. I push it away so hard my body wobbles.

'And did you do it?'

He is silent for a long time. 'Let's just say we did it. We found a way to get the money and technically it wasn't theft.'

I wait. He's not saying any more. I mean, you wouldn't, I guess. To a stranger. He has no idea that I already know. I keep my voice light, interested.

'And why did that make your girlfriend run away?'

He blinks a lot of times. He wants to cry, but I'm not going to comfort him.

'She . . . made a mistake that meant we were in trouble – or she was. It was a message she sent from her Facebook. She unsent it straight afterwards, but it had her name on it and because of that they found her. Some enforcer guy started blasting her with messages, demanding the money back. It was pretty scary – it felt like it suddenly got real, having some thug threatening her – and I . . . could have helped. Didn't. We'd broken up by then, and I was seeing someone else.'

'Oh nice.'

'So she took off.'

I know what's coming. 'With the money.'

He winces. 'No. Without it. I had to dip into it a couple of times to pay a payday-loan guy, and then somehow it was gone. She only ended up with a couple of grand. And my brother went into care anyway so what was the point?'

I was not expecting this. 'She didn't get the money? You kept twenty-eight grand and gave her two?'

The wind blows in my face. I wait for him to answer.

It takes me a stupid amount of time to realize what I've done. I edge away. I don't look at him, but I feel his eyes on me. I drop down from the rock and stand on the sand.

'How did you know,' he says, landing next to me, 'that it was thirty grand? I didn't say that.'

His voice has changed. He takes a step closer, moving between me and the path. I sense that we're both sizing up the situation. I'm trying to work out how to get away. He's trying to work out how to stop me.

'Who are you, and where is my girlfriend?'

I stand very still for a moment, then bolt, aiming for the element of surprise. He runs after me, and although I scramble up the path as fast as I can, gravity is on his side and he gets me by the ankle and tugs. I pull away from him. I kick him and shake my leg. I try to stamp on him.

He pulls me down as the first drops of rain start to fall. I tumble and plummet, twisting my ankle, but not (I hope) badly. We're on a wild beach in the middle of the ocean, in the rain. The wind has blown up around us. It's blowing the hair around my face. Carrying my words out to sea. He's looking at me with fury and confusion, and he could do anything right now.

He knows that I know.

He steps towards me so I step back. In a couple of paces, I'm cornered up against the rocks. *Shit shit shit*. He sees the fear in my eyes, clearly, and exhales. He takes half a step back.

'I'm not going to hurt you,' he says. 'Just tell me what's going on? What's happened? Is she . . . is she alive, at least?'

The birds squawk, high up in the sky. The rain is still light, but my hair is wet.

'Um,' I say. I have messed up here and the only way I can find to get out of it is to channel Ruby. Real Ruby.

I pretend I'm her. I remember the haughty way she looked at me in spite of her bruised face, and I try to give that same look to Frank Brody in spite of my twisted ankle.

'I have no idea what you're talking about,' I say.

'You do,' he says. 'You knew the amount of money. I didn't say it.'

I shove my way past him. He doesn't stop me.

'You did say it,' I say over my shoulder. It's weak, but it's all I've got.

I limp off and I keep going and this time he doesn't come after me.

33

I get through the rest of the day on autopilot, waiting for whatever is coming next. I cook fish, make steaks to order, arrange food on the plates so it looks nice. We're never going to get a Michelin star here, but I often plate things up as if this is the *Brise de Mer*. I put blobs and smears of sauces on the plate, and arrange things gorgeously. Sometimes the customers appreciate it and usually they don't notice. Occasionally my handiwork pops up on Instagram. We do comfort food, hotel food, and back when I was an arsehole I would have sneered at it. The menu always contains steaks, fish, chicken and one vegan thing. Tonight it's a butternut squash and chickpea curry, and I'm pleased with it. I'd order that, and I'm not even vegan. It's hard to present in a fancy way, but I do my best, garnishing with sprigs of coriander and dots of coconut yogurt.

Service is under way and I deal with everything as it comes in. There's something soothing about it: someone can ask for what they want for dinner and ten minutes later it'll be in front of them, and there's no time to think about the fact that you don't even know the name of the man you killed. We play music loudly in the kitchen – tonight it's Daft Punk, *Random Access Memories*, while the dining room has Mozart – and I lose myself in the immediacy of the work and shove everything else aside, which takes a lot of effort.

I came so close to calling Tom this afternoon. He's the only one who can help me here, the only person who understands. He'd drop everything to make this OK.

And that's why I didn't tell him. It's the week of his final exams, and he would drop everything. I'm not going to let him mess up his degree for me. His exams finish on Tuesday and after that I'll tell him about Frank Brody. If things are still the same by Tuesday.

I keep busy while the Daft Punk album plays out and the noisy fans rumble in the background. I do everything I'm meant to do, and I do it well, and when there's nothing happening I clean the inside of the dishwasher because there's quite a lot of gunk in there and I've been meaning to do it for ages. I wipe down surfaces that don't need wiping. I'm hyper-alert for everything. There's a weight suspended over my head and it's about to fall on me, and all I can do is scurry around, trying to hold it off by doing something else.

Frank Brody seems to have gone away. But I know he hasn't really. Of course he hasn't.

I flip a steak, stick the meat thermometer in the chicken. I start plating up the order for table twelve. One steak, one chicken, one curry. All almost ready to go.

And then it happens.

*

'Ruby?'

Nothing seems amiss at first. It's just Halle poking her head round the kitchen door. Generally this means someone's on a break and is hoping for chips.

'Yeah?' I look at her. Halle is gorgeous, with long curly hair and a constant smile. I notice that she looks uncharacteristically worried. 'You OK?' I add.

'Yeah, all fine. It's just – there's someone looking for you.'

I take a deep breath. 'Who?' My voice comes out squeaky. I try to drop it to my old voice, my deep posh one. 'Who?' I say again. I know it's going to be Frank Brody.

'The . . . I mean, I hope everything's OK because she's from the police.'

Breathe. Breathe in. Breathe out.

The police. Frank Brody went to the police.

Before I can process that, a woman in uniform is standing in the kitchen. She's maybe forty, and she looks friendly enough for someone who's come to arrest me. She has huge glasses that cover most of her face and brown hair. As I make an effort even to carry on breathing, my mind starts to spiral. What crime have I committed? Apart from the obvious one, which I mustn't confess to, have I done anything illegal? I'm using a different name, but is that . . . I realize this woman is talking to me. Why would you choose glasses frames that size?

'. . . Robinson?' That's all I catch. I take a punt.

'Yeah,' I say. 'I'm Ruby Robinson.'

She looks at me a bit strangely. 'Yes. I was asking if you could show me some form of ID, and then we'll be able to reassure him that you're just another young woman named Ruby Robinson and not his missing friend.'

I nod. 'Sure. Yes. Of course.'

'I also said I'm PC Sharon Smith.'

I text Reece to come and cover me, and I walk with PC Sharon Smith, all the way to my room.

'Sorry to bother you like this,' she says as we go. 'I can see you were busy. And I'm sure it's nothing. It's just that, this isn't nice I'm afraid, but sometimes bodies wash up here. Or body parts. And when someone comes to us with a potential missing person we do see if it fits with the identification of remains we've found. It's macabre but there we go.'

I unlock the door to the staff accommodation. 'Are you saying a body has washed up? Because I haven't heard about anything like that. And surely everyone would hear?'

'Not exactly. We just need to check. There was a girl with your name reported missing last year. And a potential match with some ... material we have. Just tying up loose ends.'

'Sure.' *Ew.* That's not nice.

We take the stairs without talking. I unlock my room and open it.

'Sorry,' I say. 'I'd have tidied if I'd known.'

'Oh God,' says PC Smith, 'I've seen much worse, believe me.'

I look around the room. It's small but it's not too messy. There's a pile of clothes on the chair and the bed isn't made. The desk drawer is slightly open. There's a heap of books on the floor. I go straight to my bag, on the end of the bed, and take out my purse. I hand over Ruby's bank card and hope for the best. While the woman is looking at it, I straighten the duvet.

'Yeah, thanks,' she says. 'But have you got a passport or driving licence? Anything with a photo?'

I'm still trying to think how to handle that one when she just opens the desk drawer the rest of the way and takes out my passport.

'Here we go!' She's happy now. 'This'll do the job.'

I didn't even know there was a police station here, and it turns out it's only open sometimes. There are two cells. One seems to be full of junk and the other contains me.

None of the hotel guests or staff saw me go because we just went down the stairs and got into the car. I guess the police will have told the hotel, because I'm not turning up to finish my shift, but I have no idea if that means I'm fired. I guess everyone on the island probably knows what's happening by now as news travels instantly out here. Also, this feels like overkill. I mean, I know Ruby's alive, and I'm not sure why I need to be arrested.

I haven't said a word since she saw the picture of Ruby in my passport. I haven't said anything because I didn't know what to say. PC Smith looked at the photo, looked at me, and asked if I would come to the station 'for a chat'. I just shrugged. In the car, I looked out of the window at the beautiful, nearly midsummer landscape and couldn't think of a plan. Can't run away. Can't switch identities. Going to have to go with it and see what happens.

I've used that passport to check into hostels, and for

job ID, so many times. No one has scrutinized the photo properly. I used it to cross the border from France to Britain at the ferry port because I thought that would have less scrutiny, and, even though I thought I was going to shit myself, I got away with it. I just handed it to a person, who checked it was valid and gave it back. No one has noticed, before, that I'm the wrong girl.

I didn't bring my phone. I wish I'd picked it up before we left.

It's exactly like it is on TV. I sit in a little room with a desk between me and the two police officers on the other side, and everything is recorded. Earlier this evening, I was sticking a meat thermometer into chicken. Now I'm being interviewed by what must be a large proportion, or maybe all, of the Isles of Scilly police force.

'Who are you really, Ruby?' says PC Smith. 'Mr Brody contacted us to say he had come here searching for his missing girlfriend and found you living under her identity. He is very concerned for her safety and said you were acting unpredictably, and so we thought we'd come and find you. Also there wasn't anything else happening. And then it turns out he's right. Ruby is missing and here you are, using her passport.'

I look her in the eye. I need her to see that I'm actually telling the truth here.

'Frank Brody is a scammer,' I say. 'He tricked an old lady into giving him her savings. Then he scammed his fellow scammer. I wouldn't trust a word he says.'

They look at each other. It's hard to read their expressions.

'Why are you using Ruby Robinson's identity though?' says the man. His tone is so mild. Maybe this is going to be fine. 'Do you realize identity theft is a serious crime?'

I want to tell them what I really did, the reason they should actually be arresting me. The thing that could really send me to prison like I deserve. I nearly do it. I open my mouth to say it. The words are right there, fighting to come out. I killed someone. With my car. Then I ran away and lied about it. I got away with it, and I shouldn't have done. I'm sorry. I'm sorry I don't even know his name.

Fuck it. I'm crying now.

Some kind of self-preservation kicks in and I manage not to say the words. I don't actually want to go to prison for the rest of my life, or whatever it would be. I'll take the identity theft. I will tell them where to find Ruby and bring her perfect little world crashing down. It's time.

'I do,' I say through my stupid tears. 'I do know it's a crime. Yeah.'

Then I remember from the TV that you don't have to say anything, though no one has cautioned me so I guess I'm not under arrest anyway. Just here 'for a chat'. I decide the safest thing to do is to stop talking. They ask loads of questions – easy questions, *what is your name?* type stuff – and I just sit there, lips pressed together, silent. They say nice friendly things and pass me a box of tissues. I blow my nose in a really gross way.

I refuse to say a word. That way I can't mess it up.

'How do you know Ruby Robinson?'

Nothing.

'Why do you have her passport?'

Nothing.

'Just tell us who you are, bird?'

Nothing.

Then it takes a weird turn. 'I told you,' says PC Smith, 'that we need to check Ruby against the human remains that sadly arrive here from time to time. You asked me for more details. Well, here they are. We have a bone that was found a couple of months ago on Bryher that comes from a female of around sixteen years old. So, when we get a report from a distressed young man about his missing girlfriend with a connection to the islands, we take it seriously. He tells us you know details of her life that you shouldn't have known, and when we check your documents we find a photo of this young woman in your passport. You won't tell us anything about her or who you are. You won't engage with the fact that we have evidence of, at the very least, identity fraud. I'm sorry, bird, but we can't let you go.'

That makes me engage. 'You think that's Ruby's? The bone? It's not. Definitely not. Ruby Robinson is alive and well and living in Paris.'

I want to laugh. After all my careful silence, it just comes straight out, and I find myself telling the story from the beginning. I keep having to stop and yawn because I got up at five and this is the same day. I walked down to the beach with Frank when I would normally have gone for a nap. Anyway, I get through. Sometimes they get me to stop and go back and say it again, but basically they just let me talk.

Then, when I reach the present day, they look at each other.

'So as far as you know, the real Ruby Robinson is living under the alias Tabitha Courtenay, which is your original identity? You just switched?'

'That's right,' I say. 'She's living in Paris with my dad. He's called George Courtenay. He actually believes she's his kid because that's how bad a dad he is.' I have to stop there and regulate my breathing. 'Also, you need to talk to my sister,' I say, remembering. 'Leonora. She lives in Dubai. She's married to a guy called Graham Fairfax, and she's got a daughter called Arabella who's about three. She'll know.' I cast my mind back to the *Brise de Mer*. 'She saw me working in Cannes. She asked me . . .'

I tail off as I realize that the encounter with Leo might not help. I told her I was Ruby. All that will show is that I was using this identity last summer, after the real Ruby went missing.

'OK,' says the man, who is now looking at me with a lot more interest. 'Complex.'

'Indeed,' says the woman. 'So, to sum it up, the reason you're living under someone else's identity is because you met on a train a year ago and switched places, and she refused to switch back.' I nod my head, mainly to see if she'll say 'for the tape' like they do on TV, but she doesn't.

'We'll need you to log into this email account.'

They produce a massive clunky laptop, and the man opens Gmail and stands behind me as I log on. The2traingirls. Yeahwedidit! I'm half expecting her to have deleted the account, but she hasn't, so I guess she doesn't know that Frank Brody turned up or that I'm at the police station and her carefully constructed life is about to fall apart.

I pass it over. They look at it together. I remember our message exchange this morning.

You killed someone. That was what she wrote. I didn't argue with it. This might, I realize, not be looking great for me after all.

Shit.

'This is just one person writing to herself,' says the woman, and I'm not sure whether she's talking to me or not.

'What does this mean?' The man looks at me. '*You killed someone and now I have to pretend it was me.*'

'It's a long story.'

They look at me in a *we have time* kind of way. I decide to go silent again. In my head, I scan through the Gmail account. Of course it looks like one person sending wild and irrational messages to herself. Of course the most recent ones look like a back and forth with herself, in which she fully accepts that she killed someone. I close my eyes. *Shit.*

'Can I make a phone call?' I say. That's what they do on TV too.

They bring me a phone and I call Tom. He answers straight away, even though I'm calling from a random number. It's a landline. The Scillies have their own area code. I guess he can see it's me.

'Tom,' I say.

'Hey!' He sounds happy at first. I hear my breath hitching, and his voice changes. 'Are you OK?'

'Yeah,' I say. 'I mean, no. Not really. I'm at the police station. I'm not sure if I'm under arrest.' I look up. PC Smith shakes her head. 'Oh – I'm not. But I think I'm about to be.' I look at her again. She shrugs. 'They know I'm not Ruby. They think I . . . did something to her. Frank Brody turned up.'

'Frank Brody??'

'I know. You messaged him, right?'

'I wouldn't have if I'd known he'd do that. How did he . . .' He hesitates and, because I know him, I know that he's working out a plan.

'Fuck it. I'll skip my exams. I'm coming down.'

'You are not!' These are his finals. I can't let him miss this. 'You are *not*. Do your exams, Tom! It's OK. I've told them where to find the real Ruby.' I sound a lot more confident than I feel. 'Do the exams. Come on Wednesday.'

In the end, he agrees, subject to me updating him as often as I can. He doesn't like it, but his grandma will *really* hate me if he messes up his degree for me, and it took me long enough to get his family to trust me even a tiny bit. Other than Flossie, who loves me.

As I hand back the phone, it occurs to me that, even though I feel that I've been living in a police drama for the past couple of hours, I haven't said my most important line.

'Do I need a lawyer?'

No one says anything for a while. Then the woman says: 'You know what, bird – I'd say you do. We'll get you over to the mainland in the morning.'

And they do. They take me to the mainland on the ferry, and drive me to a much bigger police station in Camborne. At that point, they arrest me on suspicion of murdering Ruby Robinson.

34

'I did not kill her!' It feels like the only thing I've said for ages. I am starting not to believe myself. Did I kill her? Did I kill that girl? Is BethieC on Instagram a random stranger? Have I fixated on her for no reason?

'I didn't kill her.' I say it again, as much to convince myself as anyone else. 'For a start, she's not dead. She's in Paris. Like I said. The girl who used to be Ruby Robinson is living in Paris under the name Tabitha Courtenay, or "Bethie", and I didn't steal her identity. She stole mine.'

I think about that poor girl. The dead one. I look at the two officers interviewing me. A man and a woman. The woman looks exhausted. Like she might have a million other things on her mind. The man is a bit older, and I bet he's counting down until he can retire. There's also my lawyer and a woman called Sonia from social services, who is apparently the 'Appropriate Adult', because even though I'm eighteen, they are treating me as seventeen since the only ID I have is Ruby's. We all know it's fake, but it's all they've got to go on.

I thought the Appropriate Adult might be my friend, but

she's not really interested in me. She's interested in making sure the police do everything by the book.

Everyone is looking at me. They're not angry with me. The police are both being really nice. That encourages me to keep going.

'Whoever the bone belongs to? I'm really sorry for her. But it's not Ruby. I promise it's not.'

The woman, DC Thomas, leans forward. 'Great. So just explain it to us. That's all we need. Tell us the truth and we can all be on our way. Why did you write to yourself talking about killing someone?'

That bit I can't answer. However, I have to give them something. It has taken a year away from my life for me to say this next bit, but, under the pressure of the interview room, I do.

I take a deep breath. 'If you want to check my story, find my mother. She's called Beatrice Yardley, once Courtenay. Last I heard, she went off on a cruise ship.' I take a deep breath. Here it comes. 'With my ex.'

That's the thing that, even through all of this, I've never been able to confront. This is the thing that pushed me over the edge and led to the total destruction of everything. The trigger. The fact that it all began when I walked in on Barney and my mum.

I had thought Barney and I were solid. We'd been together six months, which makes it the longest relationship I had ever had. Although I was away at school, and he went to day school in London like a relatively normal person, we were in touch all the time. Barney pursued me for ages so of course I relented. I was sixteen and there was this tall, handsome head-boy type who everyone fancied, constantly asking me out.

Once I started seeing him, I loved having a boyfriend. I loved having someone who would check in with me every day. During the Easter holidays, we saw each other all the time. He came over to the house often. The first time he met my mum, we were watching TV, sitting together on the sofa, Barney's arm round my shoulder. It was just a rerun of Friends or something. I was loving the fact that someone wanted to cuddle up to me and watch random telly together.

Then my mother was standing in the doorway. She'd probably been there for ages, watching us watching TV, but she announced her presence by saying, 'Er – knock knock,' and laughing.

We looked round. She said, 'Sorry to disturb, lovebirds. Hi – I'm Tabitha's mother. Beatrice.'

Barney jumped to his feet and started being charming.

'You cannot possibly be her mother,' he said. I remember it word for word because it was so cringe. 'Her sister,' he said. 'Surely.'

My mother loved that. She tossed her hair, which was, of course, better, glossier, thicker than mine, and simpered.

'You charmer,' she said. 'Keep an eye on this one, Tabbi.'

I didn't keep an eye on him. Not closely enough.

I ran away from school one Wednesday night because I was bored, basically. I caught a train into London and then out of Waterloo, heading home. I got a cab home from the station and let myself in. I wondered whether my mother was home, because if she wasn't I hoped I might get away with it until morning.

My mother and I were, at that time, the only two people living in a much too big house, and even if she was home there was a chance I might have been able to get to bed without her realizing. Of course I knew I'd end up being carted back to school, but I was taking whatever I could get.

I closed the front door as quietly as I could and listened. There was music playing somewhere. Classical. That, I knew, meant Mum had a date over. She always stuck on some random bit of classical to make herself seem sophisticated.

I started creeping up the stairs. I could hear voices from the living room. I didn't stop to listen to the words: as long as there wasn't about to be loud sex, I reckoned I was fine. I'd just stick earbuds in once I got to my room. I got in there, closed the door, lay on my bed and wondered when school would notice I wasn't there.

Then in the middle of the night I met my own boyfriend, naked, coming out of the bathroom.

I broke down, drank everything I could find, took a few pills too and set off to drive my mum's car into a wall.

I didn't hit a wall.

We covered it up. Pretended the car was stolen. My mother and Barney gave me an alibi, my absent dad stepped in from afar and threw money at it, and no one could prove anything.

That poor man.

'They got together,' I say, through my tears, and I hear how tight my voice is. I'm looking down at the table, telling my story to a little coffee ring on there. Taking care not to tell them about the crime. About the cover-up. 'Even after I caught them, they stayed together. They went on one of those really long cruises. That sent me right over the edge.'

'That's rough.' The man is sympathetic.

'How did it send you over the edge?' The policewoman's voice is soft and interested, but I realize that the story I've just told them might not help.

'I am Tabitha Courtenay and Ruby Robinson took over my life. Find Beatrice Yardley and get her to show you a picture of her daughter. And then you'll know.'

I mean, I doubt my mum will have a picture of me, but it will be sorted out sooner or later. Maybe one day Ruby and I will laugh about it, but no, that won't happen because I hate her. I could take it before, when it meant she gave me space to make myself a secret life, but not now. Not now I'm in actual prison. Custody suite, but it feels like the same thing.

They think I *killed* her. They think I killed *her*.

'Why would I even do that?' I demand. I realize I'm saying this out of the blue, that no one asked me a question. I press my lips together and tell myself to shut up. I look at my lawyer.

For the first time in ages I wish I had access to my trust fund because my legal rep is the duty person, the free one, and he's barely older than I am. I am starting to think that unless I can fund a proper lawyer I might end up in serious trouble here. Because, although I didn't kill Ruby, I did kill someone, and I'm right on the brink of confessing.

Innocent people don't always get off. They often don't. Everyone knows that. Guilty people get off: I should know that.

For the first time in a year, I really want a proper drink. I want an oxy. I'd take a line of coke. I am desperate for anything that will blot this out. I'd do anything to escape from right here, right now.

I hope my lawyer will ask for a break. He does.

Jaz-the-lawyer and I are sitting in a tiny room that smells of farts, but it's better than my cell.

I have told him the whole story. He's made loads of notes, which I'm glad about. His eyes look panicky, which can't be good. I've called Tom again and pretended to be fine. I haven't told him I've been arrested. I haven't told him I'm not on the island any more, but in Camborne, a town that is not a part of Cornwall that I, Tabitha Courtenay, would ever have visited. It feels weird lying to my boyfriend, but I do it so he won't mess up his exams. I'll tell him everything on Wednesday.

'So,' says Jaz, 'you're saying the police just need to talk to the real Ruby in Paris and it'll all be fine. You've given us her Instagram so it'll be easy enough to follow up. That'll be the end of it.' He looks up with a little smile. 'I've seen the passport photo and it's definitely not you. There was a missing-person appeal for Ruby Robinson in a local paper last autumn, but there's not been any more publicity than that. The bone thing is clearly some other poor girl. The timings on that don't even work out, and we'll soon have the DNA back on it so they won't be able to keep you in. As long as we can find her, then obviously no one can say you killed her.' He pauses. 'The only thing, though, is the Gmail account. Your messages talking about killing someone. The fact that you refuse to explain it. Put together with the rest of it – that's what's worrying me.'

I don't answer that. I never do.

He stands up. 'However, emails prove nothing. Let me make a start.'

He looks at me. His eyes are deep brown and he seems sincere. Maybe someone just starting out is an OK person to have onside. Better than someone cynical, counting down to retirement. Maybe he wants to nail this so he looks good.

'I'll be in touch.' He gives me a little smile. 'Tell you what: every other time I've been duty lawyer, it's been drunk and disorderly. Drink-driving. All that. This is much more interesting.'

Little does he know. 'Find the smartest part of Paris and she'll be there,' I tell him. 'With my dad.'

'And your dad really doesn't know he's treating the wrong girl as his daughter?'

I nod. For some reason, I can't speak.

I normally try to keep active when I'm stressed, but in here I can't. I distract myself by attempting to work out how many places I've slept since I was last at 'home', in my luxurious, loveless bedroom. Avignon, Cannes (tent and room), Hamburg (sofa), Kiruna, various trains ... I stop counting before I reach the end. I try to do a plank for five minutes but don't even manage one. I stretch. I get bored. I miss my phone.

Someone comes round with books, and I pick a thriller that's been read a hundred million times before: it's been handled by so many other locked-up people that it's a bit greasy and the back cover has come right off. I feel a connection to all those other criminals. Here I am, where I belong, at last. The book takes me away from reality for a while, into someone else's drama.

It's evening by the time they come back. They take me into a different interview room and sit me down and everyone waits. The police talk to each other about the rain and how it always happens in the school holidays. I say nothing. After about ten minutes, Jaz comes in.

'Sorry I'm late,' he says.

No one else tells him it's fine, so I do. He flashes me a huge smile. That must mean something good has happened. Mustn't it?

'So,' says the woman, 'we've been busy today and we do have some news. First of all, Tabitha Courtenay is alive and well and living with her father in Paris, as you suggested. We've spoken to Tabitha and to her father, and local police have also visited. We have a photograph of her and, according to biometric data, she is *not* the girl in your passport photograph though there's a resemblance. She is, as far as we're concerned, a dead end.'

'She is not!' I half stand up. 'She is totally Ruby Robinson! I told you she was living with my dad and . . .'

The woman gives me a look. Jaz puts a hand on my arm. It's clearly a hand that means *shut up*. I sit back down. Then I remember her, all bandaged up.

Of course.

'She had a nose job.' My voice is quiet as everything falls into place 'Facial surgery. That's why she looks different.'

They ignore that.

'We've also spoken to Leonora Fairfax in Dubai who was, it's fair to say, surprised to be contacted by Devon and Cornwall Police. Once she got over that, she confirmed that she met a waitress she thought was her sister Tabitha, in Cannes. But that you assured her you weren't Tabitha, but Ruby, and she hadn't seen you for a few years so she was unsure. She spoke to Tabitha's father, and at his prompting Tabitha messaged her and said she had gone to Switzerland as planned. Ultimately this all coincided with Leonora's therapist telling her it was OK to cut ties with her birth family and find her own peace, so she deleted her social media.'

'Sensible girl,' says the man. There's a general nodding of agreement around the table. Yes, yes. Social media is terrible.

'We sent photographs and she picked out Tabitha as her sister, as she's seen pictures of her with her father since then.'

Leo! Why would she do this to me?

I can't believe Ruby has a relationship with my dad,

and I haven't. Even more than that, I can't believe she's somehow made everyone believe her, even the police. She's not blinking. She's dealt with the law in the same ice-queen way she dealt with me.

The police officers look at each other.

'And,' says the man, 'we think it's possible that the conversation at the restaurant in Cannes is the thing that alerted you to the fact that you looked a little like someone called Tabitha Courtenay. This is where you heard the name. She's nothing to do with you. You just seized on her identity. So, because none of us like having you here, and we all want to get this wrapped up as fast as possible, you just need to answer our questions. Then if you haven't done anything wrong, as you say, you won't be in trouble any more. Who are you really? And again – where is Ruby?'

I must not tell them. Must not.

'What about my mum?' I say. 'Beatrice?'

The two officers look at each other. 'We haven't been able to track her down.'

'But –'

'We're working on it. So the update is that your story is not standing up to scrutiny. Staff at Zen Lodge have, of course, identified Tabitha as the Tabitha Courtenay who stayed with them last summer. Her friends, the young people who were there at the same time, have confirmed it.'

'She had friends there?'

'And one member of security also recognized a photograph of you. He said you tried to enter the premises last summer, and accosted a resident. They sent us the CCTV footage.'

'I did! I *told* you that. Right at the start.'

'So – again, what really happened to Ruby Robinson? And who are you?'

'Tabitha Courtenay! We met on the train!' I remember something. 'I have a photo! We took it when we switched!'

There's a little flurry while they get my phone, which has somehow been delivered from the hotel, and charge it up enough for me to find the photo and show it to them. The moment I see it, though, I realize it's useless. It's just a picture of me with a girl in a purple wig, who's not looking at the camera.

She looked away at the last minute. Even then. I remember the other one we took, for make-up purposes. We deleted it. I look in deleted photos but it's long gone.

'We're pretty sure you've never met Tabitha Courtenay, except when you approached her in Switzerland. So who are you?'

Then, happily for me, the answer appears. I can't believe I didn't think of it before. Tired, I guess.

'Do a DNA test,' I say. I slump back in my chair. 'That's all you need to do! Test my DNA against my mum's, or my dad's, or Leo's, and you'll see. You'll see that I'm Tabitha Courtenay. Then test that girl's, and you'll see that she's Ruby Robinson of – some place near Norwich.'

I sit back and look at them. Jaz the lawyer looks a bit worried, I have to say.

The woman is annoyed, but only because I said it before she could.

'That was, of course, going to be our next move,' she says. 'We'd just hoped you'd be a little bit more forthcoming, to save us the expense. We'll need to keep you for another twenty-four hours. We're sorting it with the custody sergeant.'

Sonia gives a little huff at that. She hasn't really said anything at all.

Jaz leans forward. 'And the bone?' he says.

'Fast tracking results,' the woman says, and, even though we all know it can't have anything to do with me, she gives me an assessing look. She knows I'm hiding something. We all do.

35

They are allowed to keep me in custody for another day because they believe that I am some unknown third person who came along and did away with Ruby, stole her passport, and landed on a stranger called Tabitha to use as a backup identity. And who also emailed herself loads of mad stuff about killing someone, then argued back at herself. I can tell you, I feel very much like murdering Ruby right now. I'm careful not to say that bit out loud.

It's mad that the one thing we all agree on is the fact that I'm not Ruby Robinson, but they're calling me Ruby because they refuse to call me Tabbi. They're even more sure that I'm not Tabitha Courtenay. It makes my head spin so much that sometimes I believe I actually am a mystery third person. After this, I think I'm going to need to be.

So I make myself at home in the little cell. It's not comfy, but it's not that different from my tiny room at the hotel either, and it's comfier than the tent in Cannes. A man comes in, chaperoned by Sonia, and scrapes some cells from my cheek, and I know that this is the thing that is going to save me. It will prove to everyone that the person they believe is Tabitha Courtenay is an imposter, and that what I've been saying is true, and then, surely, everything will get better.

I wait for something to happen. I ask for notebooks and write it all down because I need to anchor myself in reality. I write it down again and again and again: my life before I met Ruby.

They could go to my old school and everyone would know who I was because I was a total nightmare. Any number of teachers would have been ready to tell them what I was like. The girl who climbed down fire escapes and went clubbing all night, twice a week, until she got caught coming back at 6 a.m., drunk. The girl who never bothered. Who didn't have anyone or anything to make her want to do well. The girl who everyone picked on, and that made her a hundred times worse.

Who ran away from school and found her boyfriend naked with her mum.

I read and write and wait. Nothing much happens. I'm not in prison: I just live in a locked room at the police station now. It's weird but I guess at least it should be safe. Jaz tells me that Halle from my job on the island has asked to visit, but when you're in custody rather than actual prison you're not allowed social visits. Which doesn't seem fair.

Even though I'm not allowed to see Halle, I feel myself warming up from the inside out, just at the fact that she wanted to come. I've come to realize, over the past year, that I'm absolutely terrible at people. I've never been able to have friends. I've always pushed them away. The one time I did let someone close, he went off with my mum. I can only have a long-term boyfriend if I'm living away from him on a remote island. One of the things I love about kitchens is the fact that you instantly have a gang of friends and an enforced closeness, but I know that's through circumstance, and not through any skills at friendship or anything like that. I'm too messed-up.

So the fact that Halle has found out where I am and come to see me really does undo me.

'Tell her I love her,' I say to Jaz.

That's the good part of that day. The bad part is in the afternoon when I get called into another interview room with Jaz. DC Thomas looks a bit triumphant. Before the tape is turned on, she tells me that I'm 'a massive pain in the arse', but she looks so happy about it that I know something bad is coming my way.

'We've fast tracked the DNA results,' she says. 'So first up, that bone is not a match with Ruby. No huge surprises there because of the time frames, though we had to check. More interestingly, though, it turns out that George Courtenay is not your father. Definitively not. It's over. Time to tell the truth. Who are you? Who did you kill, and where is Ruby Robinson?'

36

I would do anything for a drink. I want to break out and go to the nearest pub and drink everything they've got.

So that man is not my dad. Does he know? I'm guessing he doesn't, or he wouldn't have thrown so much money at me over the years.

I swear a lot. Jaz and Sonia both tell me to stop.

I wonder who my real dad is. Weird to think there's some guy out there I've never met who's my actual parent. I wonder again whether I really am this mysterious other person. Maybe I'm not Tabitha Courtenay. Maybe I have imagined the whole thing.

I mean, I'm not delusional. I know who I am. But how did I get to a point where I have no one in the world to vouch for me? The only people who would walk in here and say: 'I know her. She's my friend,' are the people from the hotel, or Tom, and that's no use to me because they never knew me in my Tabitha life.

'Go to my old school!' I tell them where it is. 'The head's called Mrs Paul. She'll remember me. Definitely. I was a nightmare.'

'Surely not,' says DC Thomas. Her voice is amused. 'We've looked into Tabitha Courtenay and you're not her. We've spoken to her. We've tested your DNA against her only available parent. We showed Tabitha your photograph and, as I said before, she remembers you from your encounter outside Zen Lodge.'

'Talk to Jana!' I know they won't, but I have to say it anyway. I just get a huffy sigh and a change of subject.

'So,' she says. 'Here we are again. What has happened to Ruby Robinson, who are you and why are you travelling on her passport? The truth this time, and then we'll be able to move on with this.'

I look at Jaz.

'I need a word with my client,' he says.

We go into a separate room. As soon as the door closes he turns to me. He's happy, enjoying this, the bastard.

'So?'

'So that guy isn't my bio dad,' I say. 'Stacks up, I guess. They need to find my mum.'

'I believe you, you know,' he says. He leans back in his chair and puts his feet up on the table. I mirror him and do the same. 'But they don't. They think you're messing with them. They're going to try to keep you in for another twenty-four hours. They probably won't get it because the bone DNA means they don't have any evidence. I actually think you're telling the truth.'

'Thank you!'

He gives me a little *you're welcome* nod.

'What happens if they let me out? Can I go back to the island?'

'No. You'll be bailed. Social services will step in.'

I have no idea what that would involve, but I don't fancy it.

He sees my face. 'Don't worry, Tabbi. This isn't going to court. Now that they know that poor girl from the bone, whoever she is, is nothing to do with you, their only "evidence" that you killed someone is those rambling emails, plus the fact that you have her passport. Which is all weird, particularly since you won't explain, but it doesn't stand up. If you're telling the truth, and like I said I think you are, plus my job is to represent my client, then we're about to make them look very stupid indeed.'

'This,' I say, 'is a plan I can get on board with.'

I give him a list of names to start with. My old schools. My old 'friends', such as they were. My cousins and uncles on my mum's side. Pericles and Ptolemy with the silly names. Everything I can think of that will make this house of cards collapse. Ideally we would prove that George Courtenay isn't Ruby's dad either, but I guess she'll resist that.

When we go back into the interview room, I am feeling much better. We're going to take their case down.

And he does it. Before they've even released me to social services, Jaz comes in with a bundle of witness statements. He and his colleague have got on the phone to everyone I mentioned, and in the space of a couple of hours they've got me an enormous amount of backup.

'We were careful,' he says. 'We didn't say your name, ever. We sent people your photo and asked who it was.' He gives me a little smirky grin. 'Fair to say, you left quite the impression behind you.'

'Told you!'

'You did tell me. I believed you before, but now I know your story is the truth. We're going to get you out of here, Tabbi. Not bailed, but free. Today. Also – it's Wednesday today. And there's a young man out there in Camborne who is very much looking forward to seeing you.'

'It's Wednesday?'

'It is. I called him last night, as you'd asked. He's just arrived.'

I've got so used to my life in the custody suite over the past few days that I don't think I'll know what to do with myself out there. A part of me knows that I belong here, locked away in a little room. A tiny part of me doesn't want to leave.

'Where do I go, though?' I say. 'I've got no money. Pretty sure I don't have a job.'

Jaz looks at me for a long time. Then he says: 'Tabbi – you have Tom, for one thing. But also you have a home, right? I mean, your real home. Your mum's somewhere in the Pacific on a boat with . . . Well, we've covered that. So why can't you go to her house? That's what I'd do. It's your house too?'

I remember myself storming out of there. Shouting that I was never coming back, that I was done with her forever, that they were never going to see me again. I slammed the door behind me, though it was a posh door with some mechanism in it that meant it didn't slam: it just closed itself politely. I swore at it, kicked it, cried a lot and I got in the car.

Simon MacDonald.

I know his name really. I always have done. I had pushed it away. He was sixty.

He was called Simon MacDonald.

The evidence is reviewed and the custody sergeant lets me go. There's loads of admin to do before that, but I get there in the end, and finally they accept that I'm Tabitha Courtenay after all.

'Go after the fake Tabitha,' I advise.

'Bird, we're the Devon and Cornwall Police.' DC Thomas looks exhausted. 'Do I look like I'm going to go to Paris to carry on untangling your mess?'

I look at her. Her hair needs sorting out and she should get a different lipstick, but there's something cool about her. I can admit that, now that she's not my enemy.

'Not really,' I say.

'Well, there you go then. I mean, Paris. I would, but there's no budget.'

Jaz brings me my stuff from the island, which I'm glad about because I was wearing chef's whites when they brought me in. They give me my phone again so I sit on an uncomfortable chair and try to switch it on. It's out of charge because no one turned it off after I showed them that photo.

When I step outside the police station into the pounding rain, there's the person I most want to see.

Tom is standing under a red umbrella, and when he sees me his face lights up, and you can't fake that level of relief and happiness. I step into his arms and lean on him. He holds the umbrella up so it covers both of us.

'How were your exams?' I say into his shoulder.

'I wouldn't have done them if I'd known,' he says, 'but basically fine. Now, what are we going to do with you, Ruby Robinson? Can I keep calling you Ruby?'

'Yeah,' I say. I don't feel like reclaiming Tabitha any more. I'll just keep Ruby.

Tom, Jaz and I walk up the road and there's a Wetherspoons so we go in there. It's weird to be free. It's strange to be believed.

I want to get drunk. I want to get properly, properly drunk. We find a table near a socket, and I borrow Tom's charger and plug my phone in. It lights up the moment it can with messages and missed calls. Loads are from Tom, but others are from Halle and my other friends on the island. It warms my heart that people actually noticed I was gone. Friends.

My finger hovers over the Gmail icon, but I don't do it. Let her wonder. I delete it instead.

Jaz is at the bar: now that we've established that I'm eighteen, he's buying me a drink, and I feel pretty sure I can have *one* to celebrate without drinking myself into oblivion. I sit back and try to take it all in.

This is a comfy chair. The place smells like all of these

kinds of pubs – old beer, carpet, people. It's a regular pub, but no one in here is accusing me of murder. No one seems to think there's anything very interesting about me at all. I watch a table of women cheersing with Prosecco and try to take deep breaths. To be calm. I have got away. I killed someone, and I was arrested for killing someone, and I got out because they had the wrong victim. Jaz got me out of custody, and Tom is here because he likes me better than anyone. Maybe Tom and I really will go back to my old home, find someone to let us in (there's a housekeeper: that should be fine) and then ... then I'll work it all out. It's weird. So many things left hanging.

I take his hand. He squeezes mine. That's all that matters.

I'm thinking about my dad when Jaz puts the drinks on the table. I've asked for a brandy because that's what people do. Tom has a bottle of lager. Jaz has a soft drink because he has to drive home.

'Cheers,' I say.

We all clink glasses. I take a sip of brandy. It warms me all the way through. Is it a bit too nice? Maybe.

'So,' says Jaz, 'I got an email forwarded from the office. Thought you might want to see it. Or maybe not.'

He passes his phone to me. As I stare at the screen, I realize how much time I used to spend doing this, and how long it's been. I have to zoom in to read it properly. Maybe I need an eye test. It's sent from the traingirls account. The first time, as far as I know, that that account has messaged anyone other than itself.

Dear Sir or Madam,

I'm attaching a message for the girl you may know as Ruby Robinson, or Tabitha Courtenay, or maybe something else. Could you pass it on?

Many thanks
Train Girl

There's an attachment. I open it, but it's only three words long.

Call me, bitch.

And there's a French mobile phone number.

Epilogue
A month later

Even though I'm meant to be meeting her, I almost walk past because she looks so different. I'm heading down the train in search of my nemesis, the girl who got me arrested and held in a cell for two long nights. The girl they genuinely thought I'd killed, as if I would ever be able to outwit a criminal mastermind like that. I'm looking for a girl whose life I led for a year, a girl who found my dad and made him be an actual parent to her. That's fair enough since he does ultimately turn out to be the same degree of biological parent to both of us, i.e. none.

Anyway, I'm looking for the girl who messed up my whole life. She summoned me and, in spite of everything, I found I had to come. As I sway from side to side, walking down this train that is speeding towards Madrid, I walk right past because she looks absolutely nothing like OG Ruby Robinson. I only stop because she gives a little cough and, when I look over, those huge eyes are assessing me. I see them flick, up and down. Taking it all in.

She has a jaw-length black bob, and, yep, a different nose. She looks about five years older than she did on that first train, just over a year ago. She's obviously rinsed George Courtenay for everything he's got, because she's wearing a dress that I think is vintage Prada. Her make-up is subtle and impeccable, very different from the thick eyeliner of that first train. Rich life suits her: she's like a movie star. I hate her but am in awe.

I have questions.

I sit opposite, fully aware that she outmanoeuvred me at every turn. I don't know why I had to get on this train, but she emailed a ticket for it and here I am. We're going through the French countryside again, heading for Spain this time.

'Hey,' she says.

I look at her. She holds my gaze. A lot of things pass between us.

'Bonn. Jour,' I say, deliberately mimicking the first thing she ever said to me.

'*Enchantée*.' She says my line back to me in a perfect French accent.

Then silence. It stretches on. I can't believe we're here, together. Right back where we started, but different people from the ones we were back then. Literally different people. I don't know what to say. I wait.

'So,' she says. 'You sent the police after me, in the end.'

'Wouldn't you?'

She gives an unamused smile. 'I thought you'd stay away from those guys, all things considered.'

She's talking in my voice now. She's kept it.

'Your ex got me arrested for murdering you,' I counter. 'So, ultimately, it was out of my fucking hands.'

She nods, her face serious. 'Frank's in a lot of shit.'
'I know.'
'We can make sure they get him.'

For a fraction of a second, we share a smile. Then I remember, and make my face go grumpy again. Still, there's something about her. She has a star quality these days. I guess she always did, but when we met before she was showing me what she wanted me to see. And I do want to do everything I can to get back at Frank. He may only have been doing the 'right thing', but it sure as hell wasn't the right thing for me.

'I was doing OK, you know,' I say. 'I was actually fine.'

She gives me a hard look. 'I had all your money. Don't bullshit me.'

'I mean, fuck you for looking me in the eye and telling me you were me.' I can't say it without laughing a bit, even though it still hurts. She laughs too, and makes a *sorry* face. 'But in the end I actually was OK. I was hiding on an island in the Atlantic, working as a chef, and I liked it. I liked it that no one knew I was there. Almost no one. I mean, I was totally gonna rock up in Paris at some point and make you pay. You know I was. But not yet.'

She looks at me for a long time, then nods.

'I mean,' she says, 'your life is pretty messed up. So yeah, I can see why you'd stay away.' Then she smiles, her wide smile, and she looks like the first Ruby again. The one I met last summer. 'It was fun, right?'

I try not to smile back at her. In spite of everything, though, I know what she means.

'Can you believe,' I say, 'that we got away with it for a year?'

'Sorry you got arrested for murdering me. I hope they find out whose body that was.'

'Bone. It was a leg bone. It had been there much too long to be yours.'

She taps her leg. 'Present and correct. Poor girl.'

'We'll never know.'

She opens her bag and gets out a bag of Haribos. Our eyes meet.

'Lucky for me I had a good free lawyer,' I say.

'Oh, sorry about that O'Neill stalker guy coming after you. I did pay him off in the end. I paid back much more than I ever took.'

'With my money!'

She shrugs.

'And I volunteer for you, you know. In Paris. Atoning.'

I look away. I don't want to talk about this yet. It's going to take a while.

'I don't mind that stalker guy,' I tell her. 'He's my boyfriend. So actually, thanks.'

She laughs so loudly that the person at the next table looks over. She lowers her voice.

'Seriously? You hooked up with Tom O'Neill?'

I nod.

'What's he like? In my head, he was like . . .' She pauses, reaching for the right words. 'Like a kind of Nazi or something. A monster. A nemesis. Hunting me down. Just thinking about him made me hyperventilate.'

That makes me laugh. I'm unreasonably proud of myself for surprising her. I tell her who Tom really is – what a sweet, lovely, genuine guy. I tell her about Flossie, who's doing brilliantly, and she has the grace to wince. I tell her that he followed me to Kiruna. That we shared a bedsit in Cannes. That he came to Camborne for me. She nods.

'Curveball. I'm glad something good came of it then.'

I take a deep breath.

'Ruby – I'm never going to forgive myself for what I did. The man was called Simon MacDonald. He was just there, on the street. And I drove into him. I know what happened to your grandparents. And I'm just – really sorry. I'm working on myself. I know I can never make it better, but I'm going to do what I can. I stopped drinking in Cannes, and I hardly drink at all now. I'm never getting drunk again. And I'm never going to drive either. I'm looking at working with homeless charities too. I'm doing what I can.'

She's looking at the table. After a while, she nods.

'I guess I just needed to hear you say that. To hear you owning it. Thanks.'

'I was terrified of having to face up to it. That's why I wanted to switch with you. You looked like your life was so straightforward. I wanted to be you instead.'

There's a moment between us, a moment of moving on. Then she speaks.

'Your dad's great, you know. He really is.'

'Well, he's not actually my dad ... But even now? You and he are still ... ?'

She smiles. 'Yeah. Even now. I mean, we had a lot to

untangle. He threw me out when he discovered I wasn't you. Just threw me straight out on to the street.'

'Where did you go?'

'Moved in with my friend Cosmo. His parents love me, and they have a massive apartment so they just gave me a room.'

I can't help laughing at that. 'Ruby Robinson the First lands on her feet once again.'

I look out of the window. We're coming into a city, but I have no idea where it is.

'Right? And then Dad thought about it for a bit, decided he didn't have enough family to be able to disown me, particularly since you're no more his daughter than I am. So he came to get me and I moved back in.'

'You're living together in domestic bliss?'

'Do you hate that?'

I think about it. 'Yeah. I really hate it. Do you think I could message him?'

She considers it. 'Yeah. You could. So tell me what happened with Frank.'

I launch into the story of his arrival, and how close I came to convincing him I was just another Ruby Robinson. This is the first time I've laughed about my spell in police custody.

I hear it from her side.

'When the Devon and Cornwall Police emailed my dad, he only told me because he thought it was so weird. A mistaken-identity thing. He thought it was funny. But I knew. Course I did. I knew it would fall apart then.'

'Is he married at the moment?' I lean forward.

She shrugs. 'Nah. He's a bit over getting married. He has . . . stuff going on. We bonded. A lot.' She takes a fried-egg sweet and chews it. 'These are actually gross, aren't they?'

I shrug and take three.

'As you know, I go by Beth now. Are you still Ruby Robinson?' she says.

I nod. 'I like it. You have a nice name. And Ruby can do things Tabbi couldn't. I mean, I also hate you and I have no cash. And travelling on the wrong passport is scary.'

'It's kinda limiting.'

'Right.'

She takes her passport out of her bag and puts it on the table. I do the same. We push them towards each other.

I realize that the train hasn't moved for ages. When I look out of the window, I see that we're in Perpignan. Random. As it's getting ready to go, there's a flurry at the end of the carriage. Then two girls come down the train. They are white, about our age. Maybe a year or so older. Twentyish. Both blonde, both incredibly healthy-looking. Glowing. Rich.

They're deep in conversation.

'But we're not gonna know anyone,' says one of them. 'Maybe we could just go home. I mean, I never wanted to in the first place.'

Ruby looks at me. I look at her. She raises her eyebrows. I realize that she might have planned this. She is always one step ahead.

'It'll be fine,' says the other. They both have American accents, I think. Maybe Canadian. 'At least the food's going to be good.'

Ruby motions with her head, offering it to me.

I have no idea where they're going, but they won't know anyone and the food's going to be good. What the hell – it's worth a try. And if we're actually targeting them – if Ruby has actually got me on to this train specifically because of these girls, which her facial expression suggests she has – then I guess she's done her research.

What's the worst that could happen?

I lean across.

'Hi there,' I say. They both turn to me. They have big wide smiles. I don't look enough like either of them to use their passports, but we're in the Schengen Area now. There are options. Ruby looks a little bit like the shorter one.

'Hey!' says the tall one. I study her. I mean, I'd never fool anyone who'd met either of us, but maybe I won't need to.

'Where are you two off to?' I say.

Ruby shifts across in her seat. 'Do you fancy an adventure?'

Acknowledgements

This book has been a blast to write. First of all, massive thanks to my wonderful editor Ruth Knowles, as always. From the moment I mentioned the premise you were as into the idea of a train-based identity switch as I was. Thanks to everyone at Penguin – Shreeta Shah, Jane Tait, Lily Ross, Debs Warner, and to Katy Finch and Sophie Donaj, who designed this wonderful cover. Thanks to the brilliant Steph Thwaites and team at Curtis Brown.

This book involved train travel across Europe: I found myself Interrailing on my own, swimming in the Med, taking a train up the mountain from Grindelwald, sleeping in a dormitory in a hostel and generally stepping outside my comfort zone. Thanks to the people I met along the way, and particularly to Rose from Texas, who immediately made me feel happy about sharing a dormitory for the first time in many years. And thanks to Theo Merz and Amy Worrall for extra train info.

A huge thank you to everyone who talked me through the way police interviews work, and particularly to Elizabeth

Haynes, Kate Barden and Steve Rome. All the mistakes are completely my own.

Thank you to my brother Adam Barr for early reading and all kinds of other support. Mercy Brewer: thanks for reading with a young person's eye and for your advice on Scillies life. Thanks to Gabe, Seb, Charlie, Lottie and Alfie, for always being there, in real life or at the end of a phone. To friends: Silvia Salib, Tansy Evans, Natalie Hart, Lisa Thompson, Clare and Keith Sparrow and everyone else – I appreciate you all very much indeed.

Finally, heartfelt thanks as always to Craig for the endless support, love, cups of coffee / fizzy water / wine, and for keeping the household working in a million different ways while I write. You're wonderful and I love you.

MORE FROM
EMILY BARR

Intriguing mysteries, thrills, and a dash of romance . . .

MORE FROM
EMILY BARR

intriguing mysteries, thrills, and a dash of romance